"You have to marry her."

Cooper couldn't imagine why his daughter had gotten all worked up over being without a stepmother. Her mother had been gone a long time, nearly half Katie's life. They'd adjusted, moved on, tried to make a family with just the three of them.

"Why?"

"Because I wrote a letter and asked Mrs. Bauer to come here."

Cooper deposited Katie on the floor and bolted from the chair. "Let me get this straight. You wrote a letter to a perfect stranger and asked her to come here?"

"To marry us."

"How did you find Mrs. Bauer in the first place?"

"I bought a newspaper advertisement."

"You placed a request for a mother in a newspaper?"

Katie's eyes still brimmed with tears. "No. I pretended to be you...."

Dear Reader,

Welcome to Harlequin Historicals—stories that will capture your heart with unforgettable characters and the timeless fantasy of falling in love!

Jillian Hart, who made her publishing debut in our 1998 March Madness Promotion with her enormously popular *Last Chance Bride,* returns this month with another heartwarming Western, *Cooper's Wife.* The local sheriff saves a widow and her little girl when their stagecoach is robbed and learns that the woman is a mail-order bride for *him*—thanks to his meddling daughter. He responsibly proposes a marriage of convenience, and unexpectedly finds a lasting love.

In *The Dreammaker* by Judith Stacy, also a Western, two people who are swindled by the same man go into business together to recoup their losses and realize their dreams—when love, the dream of a lifetime, is right in front of them! Award-winning author Gayle Wilson returns with *Lady Sarah's Son,* an emotional Regency-style tale of sweethearts, torn apart by tragedy, who come together again in a marriage of convenience and can no longer deny their enduring love.... And don't miss *The Hidden Heart,* a terrific medieval novel by Sharon Schulze. Here, a beautiful noblewoman must guard her heart from the only man she has ever loved—the Earl of Wynfield, who has returned to her keep on a dangerous secret mission.

Enjoy! And come back again next month for four more choices of the best in historical romance.

Sincerely,

Tracy Farrell, Senior Editor

P.S. We'd love to hear what you think about Harlequin Historicals! Drop us a line at:

Harlequin Historicals
300 E. 42nd Street, 6th Floor
New York, NY 10017

JILLIAN HART

COOPER'S WIFE

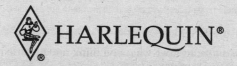

HARLEQUIN®

TORONTO • NEW YORK • LONDON
AMSTERDAM • PARIS • SYDNEY • HAMBURG
STOCKHOLM • ATHENS • TOKYO • MILAN • MADRID
PRAGUE • WARSAW • BUDAPEST • AUCKLAND

ISBN 0-373-29085-3

COOPER'S WIFE

Copyright © 1999 by Jill Strickler

This edition published by arrangement with Harlequin Books S.A.

Visit us at www.romance.net

Printed in U.S.A.

Books by Jillian Hart

Harlequin Historicals

Last Chance Bride #404
Cooper's Wife #485

JILLIAN HART

grew up in rural Washington State, where she learned how to climb trees, build tree houses and ride ponies. A perfect childhood for a historical romance author. She left home and went to college and has lived in cities ever since. But the warm memories from her childhood still linger in her heart, memories she incorporates into her stories. When Jillian is not hard at work on her next novel, she enjoys reading, flower gardening, hiking with her husband and trying to train her wiggly cocker spaniel puppy to sit. And failing.

To Henry, my husband and best friend,
who is all of my heart

Prologue

Montana 1864

"Candy, Mama?"

"In a minute, pumpkin." The bank was busy and the line behind her long, but Anna Bauer smoothed the gold curls from her tiny daughter's forehead.

"One hundred twenty-five dollars and thirty-seven cents." The clerk counted out Anna's life savings with crisp flicks of twenty-dollar bills.

So much money. Anna's heart flickered as she counted to make sure of the amount. She would need nearly all of it to buy stage passages across the Ruby Range and up into the rugged Montana Rockies. What kind of man awaited her there? What kind of life?

"We'll be sorry to see you go." Kind and genuine, Tom Brickman had always treated her with respect, despite her illegitimate daughter. "I've heard you are to be married."

"Yes, I am." Anna's stomach quivered with a mix of excitement and trepidation.

"Then I wish you and your daughter a safe journey

and a happy future." Tom pushed the last of the coins across the counter.

A door opened; she felt the breeze sweep through the bank. A murmur rose through those standing in line behind her. Anna folded the six twenty-dollar bills in half, then in half again. She saw Tom's smile fade and fear shadow his eyes.

Bootsteps knelled in the silence. "Hands up where I can see them. Now."

So dangerous and lethal, that voice. Prickles skidded down her spine. Anna tucked the folded twenties into the top of her glove. Her sleeve fell forward to hide the money from sight.

"Mama." Mandy's whisper came quietly, and the girl held tight to Anna's skirts.

"Just stay with me, pumpkin." Anna tucked her little girl behind her. Those footsteps knelled closer, ringing in the tensed silence. She could see one of the robbers. He held two gleaming revolvers, one in each unflinching hand. A hat was pulled low over his forehead and a handkerchief masked most of his face from view.

Anna swallowed, fighting fear. Sometimes innocent people waiting in line were killed in bank robberies. She heard Tom's quick intakes of breath, saw the tensed line of his jaw. He was afraid, too. The second outlaw stepped out of sight, gun on the bank owner. The vault was in the next room and the two men disappeared.

"I'll just take that from you." Deep, that voice. Somehow familiar. He dropped a canvas sack on the counter. "Put your money in there, little lady."

"Yes, sir." She didn't want to anger him. She thought of her daughter with her little fists wrapped in her skirts. Anna's fingers felt wooden and clumsy, but she took a deep breath and forced herself to drop the remaining $5.37 into the empty canvas bag.

"That's right." The robber's guns gleamed in the lamplight as he waved them at Tom. "Fill the sack, boy. Do it and I'll let you live."

Anna took a tiny step back. She felt Mandy's tight hold on her skirts, felt the child pressing hard against the backs of her knees. She needed to get her daughter as far away from that gun as she could.

"Not so fast." Almost laughing, that voice.

She studied the broad brim of the sweat-stained hat, the dust marks on the bandanna, the fine cloth of the robber's shirt and trousers. Blue eyes met hers.

For one brief moment she thought she was looking into the eyes of a man she'd almost married. It hadn't worked out between them. Could never work out. He wasn't fond of children, and she wanted a large family. She wanted to give Mandy brothers and sisters to play with.

"I want the reticule, too."

Oh, her nicest one. Anna's heart sank. She unwound the string handle from her left wrist. Nothing of value was inside, just a small comb, a few hairpins and Mandy's favorite hair ribbon. Not much to lose, considering.

Tom reached into his drawer and piled crisp bills on the counter. Anna dropped her reticule into the robber's sack. Mandy stumbled, clutching Anna's skirts. She laid a hand to steady the child. She did not like that this armed outlaw was only a few inches away from her daughter.

He watched her, watched all of them. She heard the tick of the clock on the wall, the rattle of old Mr.

Fletcher's watch chain as he stood in line, the squeak of the outlaw's left boot when he shifted his weight.

"Hurry up," he threatened Tom, waving his guns. He moved and again his boot squeaked.

Anna felt a prickle along the back of her neck, felt the cold knowledge low in her stomach. She cast her gaze downward and saw the shiny leather boots, brown and highly polished, scuffed along the left toe where he'd caught it on her sister's loose porch step.

The man behind the mask, the man with the guns and the familiar blue eyes and voice was none other than Dalton Jennings. Her breath caught. She had to be wrong. Dalton was the sheriff, a leader of the town.

A clatter of metal against the counter broke through her thoughts. The robber—no, Dalton Jennings—snatched up the half-full sack. He held it out, walking down the aisle, accepting watches, wallets and reticules, scaring one old widow woman out of her ruby wedding ring.

Anna had never felt so afraid. It was Dalton. She recognized his walk, a slight limp in his left leg from a once badly injured knee.

"Count to one hundred before anyone steps outside." The second robber joined him, two huge money bags in hand. Together they pushed out the door. "I have an armed man hidden across the street to make sure you all know how to count."

Anna tried to think what to do. Then the robber's gaze latched on to hers. Her heart fell. Sweat broke out beneath the brim of her bonnet. Recognition thudded in the air, heavy like thunder. Dalton Jennings' eyes narrowed, his gaze sharp on hers. A sensation passed between them.

Did he know that she recognized him? Fear tasted

coppery in her mouth. Like a deer caught in a rifle's sight, she waited.

Then Jennings strode away with his money. The door snapped closed. The bank owner and Tom rushed around making sure their patrons were safe. Mandy cried and Anna held her, debating what to do. No doubt the town sheriff would show up soon, dressed in his black trousers and black vest, sporting his tin badge, wearing those boots with the scuff mark on the left toe.

How could she face Dalton when he returned as the sheriff? Anna rocked Mandy, cradled the girl tight in her arms. Thank heavens she still had her money, tucked out of sight against her wrist.

The men robbing banks and stagecoaches in the Ruby Range area had killed before. People who could identify them, be they men, women or children. What would Dalton do to her when he returned?

She would go home and think of what to do.

Chapter One

"Bumpy, Mama."

"I know, pumpkin." Anna ached at the sight of exhaustion pinching Mandy's button face, bruising the skin beneath her big blue eyes. "The stagecoach driver said we'll be in Flint Creek before suppertime."

The three-year-old sighed. Suppertime was so far away. Knowing just how she felt, Anna took the child on her lap and hugged her tight until she smiled.

Anna hadn't dared to relax since their desperate flight from home. Was Dalton already on her trail?

But with each passing mile, Anna breathed easier. This was the third day of travel and no sign of trouble. Did she dare to hope that Jennings wasn't following? Maybe, just maybe, she and Mandy were safe after all.

But despite her hopes, the worry tight in her stomach didn't ease. Dalton wasn't a man to forget.

"Too tight, Mama," Mandy complained.

Anna loosened her hold on the child. What would happen to the little girl should Jennings find them?

The first sound of trouble came as a gunshot from outside the stage. The second was the scream of a horse. Was it Dalton? Fear pumped through her veins.

The stage rocked fiercely to the right side, then limped to a stop.

What should she do? How could she protect Mandy? She glanced at the other travelers seated beside her and across the aisle. Would they help her? The banker who boarded the stage at Dillon mopped sweat from his brow with a monogrammed handkerchief. He didn't look armed. But the ruffian seated beside him, who smelled of stale cigarette smoke and whiskey, hauled out a highly polished revolver.

"Don't you worry, ma'am," he said through gritted teeth. "I won't let those no-good bandits do you harm."

"Thank you, sir." The gun looked deadly. Thank heavens he was on her side.

The stage door burst open. Anna choked, unable to scream. A masked man fired a gun. The passenger fired, then slumped over. Burly arms tossed the brave man and his gun on the dusty road.

They'd killed him. Shock washed through her. Anna couldn't breathe. What was to become of them? She heard voices outside the stalled stage. They were laughing.

Laughing. How dare they? No one had the right to take joy in an innocent man's death. Hot rage tore through her midsection. She'd seen just about enough of men's violent ways.

"Get out," a gruff voice ordered from the doorway.

Anna swung her reticule. It smacked the aimed revolver from the outlaw's hand to the floor at her feet. "Stop this killing right now."

Shock rounded his eyes. "Lady—"

"I said, enough." She pushed at the scruffy brute's

chest. No one should be hurt because Dalton wanted her. "Where is he?"

A brutish laugh. "What kind of woman do we have here? I like a lady with some fight."

Why was he laughing? Anna took one look at the cold glitter in the outlaw's eyes, and her courage wavered.

Three other robbers stood on the road behind him, armed and mean-looking. They weren't Jennings' men. And now she'd made them angry. What would they do?

"This is the first thing I intend to take from you." Cruel blue eyes laughed at her over the edge of a dirty red bandanna.

She gasped as the masked man tore the cloth bag from her wrist. A snap of pain bit her skin. Her money! This time it wasn't tucked away in her sleeve. What was left of her life's saving was dug out of the now ragged reticule.

A twisted gleam sparked in the villain's eyes. "I'll be back for more from you."

He gave her a shove. Anna's knees buckled and she lost her balance. Her shoulder slammed into the side of the coach. She hit the ground hard, tasting dust. Already the outlaw was reaching into the coach, sunlight glinting off the nose of his revolver. Mandy was in there, defenseless.

"No!" Anna launched forward, stumbled, then found her feet. She grabbed at the outlaw, pulling at his shirt. "Leave her alone. She's my child. She—"

A gunshot split the air. Then another. She felt a fiery pain. Blood fell across her sleeve. Was she shot?

"Come here, little girl," the blue-eyed outlaw cooed. "I won't hurt ya."

"No!" Anna hit him hard with her shoulder, trying to knock him aside. "Don't you touch her."

The outlaw spun from the coach and raised his hand. She saw the blow coming. He struck her face hard enough to make her ears ring. The pain seemed distant. It was nothing compared to her fear for Mandy. She dropped to her knees. Dizziness spun through her head. Tears stung her eyes as she pulled herself to her feet. She would stop that villain. She would protect her child.

Then voices filled the air. She looked up, confused. She heard shouts of "It's the law!" and "Jed, where's my mare?" and "the gold, it's getting away!" and then "Run!" Gunfire popped as she jumped to her feet. Already the outlaw had run from the stage, leaving Mandy untouched inside.

"Looks like the law's here." The banker climbed out, his voice low, sweat beading on his forehead. "She's scared but all right. You'd better take cover, ma'am."

"After I get my daughter." She had to shout over the gunfire. "Don't wait for us. Those rocks over there should shelter you."

Horses thundered past. Guns fired so close, it hurt her ears. A stray bullet lodged into the side of the coach. She had to hurry. She reached through the doorway. "Come, grab my hand."

She saw a peaked face, eyes wide with fright. Mandy crawled off the seat. "That's right." Anna leaned forward and caught the child's hand.

Then the stage rocked hard. Small fingers clutched hers and held tight, then were wrenched from her grip. The stage shot forward. The frame slammed into her jaw and cheek, then her shoulder, knocking her to the ground.

"Mandy!" She held the child's glove in her hand. Cold horror washed over her as the driverless stage rattled up the road. In a flash she saw the danger, all that could happen. She leaped to her feet, already running hard. "Mandy. Jump!"

Gunfire, bullets and mounted riders swirled around her. She kept running. She had to get to Mandy before something happened. Before the stage crashed or tumbled over the narrow edge of the trail and down the mountain.

Air wheezed out of her lungs. Pain slashed through her side. She was almost there. Almost gaining. Every step brought her closer to catching hold of the boot and climbing aboard. Every step brought her closer to saving her daughter. She reached out and just missed the heavy leather strap holding the luggage to the rear of the coach. She reached again.

One back wheel hit a boulder. The vehicle careened to one side and skidded sideways. She watched in horror as the front right wheel struck another boulder. The stage rolled over and landed on its top, hesitating at the edge of the road. It tottered, then tumbled forward.

"No!" Anna skidded down the embankment, flew down the edge of the mountain. Rocks cascaded beneath her feet. She slid, went down. Pain skidded up her leg when she crashed into a low scrubby pine.

Breathing hard, she broke free and kept running. All she could see was the stage, rolling end over end, falling apart each time it struck the ground. An axle broke with a crash. Two wheels flew through the air and hit the ground rolling. A door came off. The vehicle hit the earth so hard, the sound of the impact cracked like thunder across the face of the mountainside.

And Mandy was inside. Anna had to get to her. She tasted the grit of dust and dirt in her mouth, felt them in her eyes. Her feet gave out beneath her, and she skidded on loose rock and earth. Time stood still as she watched, her heartbeat frozen. The stage rolled over the edge of a cliff and out of sight.

No sound of impact, just the eerie silence of falling. *No. It couldn't be.* She couldn't lose her daughter, her whole heart. Anna fought for balance, but the earth beneath her feet gave way. Rocks and gravel and bits of stubby grass tumbled ahead of her. She saw the bright sheen of the sun flash in her eyes.

She scrambled, struggling for any purchase, any solid tree root or boulder that would stop her fall. She had to save Mandy. She would not let her daughter die.

"Sheriff, Corinthos is getting away."

Cooper spun his palomino and headed toward the snowy ridge. His deputies could take care of the robbers, but he wanted Corinthos, the leader of the gang. He was sick of the killing and carnage in this part of the county. It was his job and his responsibility to end it.

The outlaw swung his gelding around and fired.

Cooper shot back. A direct hit. Corinthos' gloved left hand covered his shoulder, blood seeping between his fingers. Shock lined his dirt-smudged face as he slipped from the saddle.

Got him. Cooper felt grim satisfaction as he cocked the Colt, ready in case the outlaw drew on him again. He drove his mount closer to the fallen man. A woman's cry of distress and then a crack of wood breaking spun him around. A woman?

Before he could contemplate that, he caught sight of the six runaway horses, still harnessed, dragging the dangerously tipping stage around the bend in the road. Cooper kicked his stallion into a gallop just as the harness broke apart. The coach tumbled over the edge.

The woman, blond hair flying, screaming as she ran, jumped feet first down the dangerous mountainside and out of sight. Crazy woman. Whatever she had in the stage wasn't more valuable than her life. Flint Creek Mountain was a place of cliffs and sheer edges.

Gunfire drew his attention, reminded him of why he was here in the first place—to bring in Corinthos and put an end to his gang's violence. But the sight of the desperate woman tugged at him. He was responsible for her life, too, responsible to help her if he could.

Resigned to fighting Corinthos another time, Cooper galloped after her. "Hey, lady."

She didn't answer. Gunfire popped behind him as he loped his mount along the road's edge. His stomach fell at the sight of a woman tumbling down toward the edge of a cliff, a sheer drop of a hundred feet, maybe more. It was hard to tell from where he sat.

She was in trouble. There was no doubt about that. He reached for his rope, trying to judge how best to save her. Then he spotted a little pink bonnet crushed and torn, lying amid the splintered fragments from the stage. Was a child was in that stage? No wonder the woman was frantic.

Cooper drove his stallion off the road and down the mountainside. The great palomino struggled to stay afoot, crashing through the low brush and along unstable earth. Cooper stood in his stirrups, leaned back and loosened the noose with one hand. He couldn't see the stagecoach, lost somewhere over the edge of the cliff. But he could see the woman sliding feet first to a stop. Thank God. He could catch her in time. He swung the rope, once, twice. But before he could throw, the ground broke apart beneath the woman and she fell straight down the cliff.

The earth could very well give out beneath him, too, but Cooper drove his mount harder. He tasted dust and the sharp scent of pine. He saw the danger ahead, heard the crash of the stage as it came to rest somewhere out of sight. Heard the woman's voice shriek her child's name with such agony, it tore at his heart.

Cooper drew his stallion to a halt. He could see the wrecked stage a good fifty feet below, hung up on an outcropping of pines, and the woman, holding tight to a root. The earth beneath them was sheer granite. So barren and hard not even weeds grew there. To fall would mean death.

"Hold on, lady." He slung the lariat over his neck and knelt down. He caught her by the wrist, holding her tight. "Let's get you safe."

"But my daughter—"

He lifted the woman onto the cliff's edge beside him. "Don't worry. I'm going to go down and get her."

"Her name is Mandy." Blood streaked the woman's torn dress, scrapes from her fall, no doubt. Panic rang in her voice. "She's only three years old. She has to be hurt. I want to go down with you."

He secured the rope to the closest tree, a sturdy pine. "This rope can't hold both of our weights. I only have the one rope."

"But she's my little girl."

Her blue gaze met his, and he saw her fear, felt the

determination as strong as this mountain. He knew what love felt like, the all-encompassing affection for a child. He had to admire her for that.

Fine, he had a soft spot for caring mothers. "You just stay here, ma'am. I promise I'll take real good care of your girl."

"I think I can hear her crying. Surely that means she's not hurt too badly, if she can cry."

"I sure hope so." He eased himself over the cliff, hand over hand. Sweat broke out on his forehead, on his back. He wasn't afraid of outlaws and gun battles, but heights terrified him.

He stared hard at the craggy granite in front of him and didn't look down. Hand over hand. Just a few more feet. He reached what was left of the stage, a smashed wooden cage missing more parts than he could count. He spotted a scrap of pink. He reached inside and brought up a small child, sputtering and bloody. She was the tiniest thing, all gold hair and pink ruffles.

Reed-thin arms wrapped about his neck. She held on with all her might. Her little body was rigid against his chest. "Don't worry, little girl. I won't let you fall."

"Mama!" The little girl's voice came weak. Her breath against his throat felt choppy and irregular. She wheezed, and he held her tighter. It was as he feared; the child was badly injured. Town and medical help was so far away.

He secured the girl to his chest, using the lariat he carried. Then he began the arduous work of climbing hand over hand up the rope. The wind gusted, knocking them against the granite wall. He turned to take the blow with his shoulder, to protect the fragile child he carried. The rope swung them out away from the rock, and he caught sight of a dizzying glimpse of brown-gray rock below. His stomach lurched. Yep, it was best not to look down.

He kept climbing hand over hand, listening to the rattle of little Mandy's breathing. Another blast of wind knocked him against the cliff side, sent him swinging.

"Mama." The little girl sniffled. So small, she was hardly any weight at all against his chest. Her blood stained his shirt and he felt her shiver, even in the bright sunshine. Not a good sign.

"I'm right here, Mandy." The woman's voice rang like bells, sweet and clear. She peered over the edge of the cliff.

It wasn't much farther.

"Is that you, Coop?" His brother's voice.

"Where the heck have you been?" The muscles in Cooper's arms and back burned with fatigue. He kept climbing, but tipped his head back just enough to see the worry lining his younger brother's face. "Don't just stand there being useless. Help me up."

"Useless. That's me." Tucker could grin even in a crisis. He curled both gloved hands around the rope and pulled.

Cooper handed the child up into her mother's arms. Tucker helped him over the lip of the cliff.

"She's hurt." Sorrow rang in the woman's voice.

The tiny girl looked blue and wasn't breathing right. He couldn't help but fear the worst. The woman, white-faced with fear, cradled her daughter tight in her arms. She kissed the girl's forehead, the love for her child as unmistakable as the sun. It was a priceless emotion his wife had never managed to feel for their girls. He liked knowing some mothers did.

"Sheriff." One of his deputies crested the bank. "Corinthos got away."

Turning away from the mother and child, he began coiling the rope. "I shot him myself. He must have mounted and rode off." Cooper mopped his brow with his forearm. "We've got wounded. We see to the girl first."

The woman knelt beside her daughter on a bed of clover, checking her wounds. "Is there a doctor close?"

"No, ma'am." Cooper untied his stallion. "We're just lawmen. We feared there might be problems with the stage today. This pass is notorious for trouble."

She took a breath. Worry crinkled the corners of eyes as deep as a summer sky. "But Mandy needs a doctor. I think she may have broken her arm, maybe her ribs. She isn't breathing well."

"I can see." Cooper left the stallion standing and took a look. "Are you hurt, little lady?"

The child looked up with teary eyes and nodded. No sniffle, no whimper. Her lips were slightly bluish. Her breath came rapid and shallow.

"You're a brave girl, too." He knelt down on one knee, broad shoulders braced. He was all strength, but tenderness, too. "You must get that from your mama."

Anna's heart ached. So many cuts and bruises on the girl. She tore a strip of petticoat and covered a nasty gash on the child's forearm. "How far away are we from a town?"

"Quite a ways." The sheriff's low, rumbling voice sounded warm as sunshine. He pulled a clean and folded handkerchief from his shirt pocket and tore it into strips. Those big blunt-shaped hands deftly tied a neat bandage at Mandy's wrist.

"You're good at this, Sheriff."

"I have little girls of my own who are always getting one scrape or another."

Oh, that smile. As scared as she was for Mandy, Anna couldn't help noticing the sheriff's handsome smile. And on a closer look, he had a handsome everything. From the strong straight blade of his nose—not too sharp, not too big—to the chiseled cut of his high cheekbones, to the square jaw sporting a day's dark growth, he was quite a man.

"Owie." Mandy bit her lip, trying to hold back her tears like a big girl.

"Let me see, pumpkin." Anna gently pulled Mandy's bandaged arm away from her chest. When she loosened a few buttons on the now ragged dress, she saw a horrible bruise marking her skin. But it was the sight of the left side of her little chest rising when her right side did not that terrified Anna. Something was dreadfully wrong.

"Tucker." Calling to one of the deputies, the mighty sheriff strode away.

Would Mandy die? Fear condensed into a tight, hard ball in her stomach. Her hands trembled as she used a thin stick from the ground as a splint. She wrapped the last strips from her petticoat around Mandy's broken arm, trying to keep hold of hope.

"I'm going to ride her into town." Cooper squinted against the midday sun. "With the trouble she has breathing, I don't figure we have a lot of time. My mount is the fastest."

"I'll go with you. Just give me a minute—"

"You'll only slow me down." Apology rang low in his voice.

"No, I'm not leaving her." Anna held her daughter tight.

"You have to, ma'am. I can get her to a doctor faster than anyone can."

"But Mandy needs me."

"She needs medical care."

It was as if she were on that cliff again, knowing there was nothing she could do to stop the coach from breaking apart. She could not let a stranger care for her daughter. Yet Mandy needed a doctor. Immediately. And this man could provide it.

He said he was a father. And it was true that he'd braved the cliff to rescue Mandy. Judging by the breadth of those strong shoulders and the honor shining like a promise in his eyes, Anna decided she had to trust him. Mandy would die without help.

Her decision was already made, even though it was hard to let go. "This little girl is my entire life."

"I know." He produced a warm blanket to wrap around Mandy. "Flint Creek is the first town on the other side of this pass. The doc's clinic is the third building on your left past the hotel. Tucker will take you there."

Anna's knees wobbled with the worst kind of fear. But the badge pinned to the sheriff's vest glinted in the sunlight. When he mounted his powerful horse, he looked heroic enough to topple any foe, right any wrong.

Anna wiped the wet hair from her eyes. She prayed he would make it to town in time.

Chapter Two

"How's the little girl?" Tucker strode through the jailhouse door, trail dust thick on his hat brim and boots, and everything else in between.

"She's still alive. I hope the doc can keep her that way." Cooper closed his eyes, unable to block out the remembered image of tiny Mandy so blue and struggling hard to breathe. "How's the mother?"

Tucker swept off his hat. "She's a widow. Imagine that. She told me so herself on the ride down here. Yep, Mrs. Bauer sure is pretty, don't you think?"

"I don't need anyone to play matchmaker, especially not you." Cooper thumped his brother on the shoulder. "I take it the rest of my deputies are on their way?"

"Yep." Tucker followed him out onto the late-day street. "It took a while to find the gold shipment. We thought it had gone over the cliff, too. The men will be bringing it to town soon and they'll need help. I was just going to head back. Are you coming?"

"Yes. I hope we've seen enough trouble from the Corinthos gang for one day." Evening scented the air. The sun was fast sinking toward the horizon. Cooper's gaze focused on the doc's clinic down the street. He thought of the woman and child inside. He thought about how lucky they were, how lucky all of them were.

Anna brushed back gossamer curls from her sleeping daughter's forehead. The dim light of the room in the back of the doctor's clinic cast just enough glow to see by. But not enough to ward off the many fears that increased as each hour passed.

"My wife made you a supper tray." The door whispered open on its leather hinges. The faint rattling of dishes filled the quiet room, then footsteps as the doctor strode across the floor. He set the meal on a low table. "I hope you like beef stew."

"I'm sure it's very good." Anna straightened in her chair, careful of her hurting arm. Her stomach grumbled, but she wasn't in the mood to eat. Not until she knew Mandy would be all right. "Thank your wife for me."

"You need to keep up your energy if you're going to care for your girl. So you eat, and let me check on my littlest patient."

His kindness touched her, made her ache deep inside. When she had explained she couldn't pay the bill because her savings had been stolen, the doctor told her not to worry. Now he was treating Mandy with care and skill.

She watched him listen to Mandy's breathing, saw for herself the uneven rise and fall of her chest. He'd said a punctured lung could be fatal, but there was some hope.

Hope. It was what had brought her here in the first place. A new start for Mandy, a home of her own. She worried about what kind of man Mr. Cooper Braddock would be—kind or strict, stern or forgiving. But now her big plans felt false and foolish with her daughter so injured.

Anna stood and somehow made it to the table. Her own body ached, especially her arm, but she hadn't said anything. Would not detract the doctor's attention from Mandy, even for herself.

Steam rose from the fragrant stew. Her stomach turned, but she knew she had to eat. At least had to try. She sat on the rickety chair, one leg shorter than the other three. It bumped against the floor when she shifted her weight. The warm scent of gravy, the hearty scent of beef tickled her nose. She lifted the spoon and filled it. But how was she going to get any food to stay in her twisted-up-with-worry stomach?

"Mrs. Bauer?" A low rumbling voice called to her. She turned around to see the sheriff, his broad-shouldered form filling the threshold, his dark hat shading his eyes. "How's your little girl?"

Just looking at him made her feel better, the same way she'd felt when he climbed hand over hand down that rope to rescue Mandy. "She's doing better. Thanks to you. You got her to the doctor in good time."

"I was just doing my job. Serve and protect." He swept off his gray hat, looking uncomfortable with her praise. "Daughters are priceless."

"Yes, they are." She couldn't picture this enormous and powerful man as a father to little girls. Yet his presence comforted her, just as she imagined it would a small child. Goodness shone in his eyes, the strength that came from tenderness. He was not the kind of man who harmed others. Not like the cowards who'd caused this injury to her daughter and the passenger on the stage. "How is the wounded man?"

"He took a shot to his chest, but he will live." The sheriff stepped back into the hallway, his hat clutched in his big capable hands. The silver badge pinned to his wide chest glinted in the lamplight. "The driver's not as lucky. He may never walk again."

"Those horrible outlaws." Anna shivered, wrapping her arms around her middle. "If you hadn't come along, we might all be dead by now."

His smile broadened, etching dimples into his cheeks and softening the hard, tough lawman look of him. "We've been having trouble at that pass. There are few towns and fewer lawmen to keep the peace, and too damn many renegades who think they can take whatever they want from innocent people. It's my job to teach them differently."

"So, you were waiting to protect the stage at the pass. That's how you were there to save us?"

"Yes." His face shadowed. He studied her for a moment. "It's getting late. I can recommend the hotel just down the street. Janet, the innkeeper, will look after you. I'll ask her to warm up a room for you."

"I can't leave Mandy." Especially not now that she'd almost lost her.

"I understand." His half smile dazzled. If she were in another place in her life, another time without worries and secrets and promises to marry, she would have found him attractive. Yes, very attractive.

"Is there anything I can do?" He was a good man, just wanting to help.

"Did your men find a child's book amid the wreckage? Mandy likes to be read to. She's still—" *In danger.* Anna couldn't say the words. It hurt even to think them. "I have to believe she'll be all right."

"I believe it." The sheriff towered over her, radiating strength and kindness mixed with a hard male toughness. A dizzying combination. "You take care of your daughter. I'll check on that book for you."

"I know it's getting late, Sheriff."

"I don't mind." Twin dimples edged that calming grin. "And stop calling me sheriff. The name's Cooper."

"Cooper?" The word froze on her lips. Anna watched in amazement as he strolled from sight down the hallway, those shoulders wide, that gait confident.

The man she'd come to marry was named Cooper. Surely he couldn't be—

No. A man like that didn't need to write away for a bride. He just had to smile and every woman within a half-mile radius probably fell at his feet.

"Mrs. Bauer?" The doctor gestured her back into the room. "Your daughter is doing better, but her condition is still very serious. I can make no guarantees. The only thing we can do is keep a close watch on her and see what the night brings."

Cold fear curled around her insides. Anna forced back tears, more afraid and angry than she'd been in her life, and she'd been plenty of both before this.

Damn those men who'd done this to her defenseless, tiny daughter.

Anna settled down in the wooden chair at Mandy's bedside. The little one slept still, as if death already claimed her. Even her hand felt cold to the touch.

All her troubles faded. Why she'd come to Flint Creek and what she'd left behind no longer mattered. Not now. Only Mandy mattered.

Please, she prayed. Don't take my daughter.

* * *

"Did you get a good look at that lovely widow?" Tucker asked as he poured a fresh cup of coffee.

"I saw." Cooper hung his hat on a wall peg and gave the door a good slam against the cool night wind. "No ideas, brother. I'm not interested in the woman."

"Well, that's just not natural, big brother. Not natural at all." Tucker shook his head, feigning deep concern. "After saving her daughter the way you did, she's not going to look twice at the rest of us poor saps. Oh no, she'll only have eyes for you."

"So you say. Let's face it, Tucker, every single woman who has come to town has been charmed by *your* dimples, not mine."

"True." He took a sip of coffee. "What are you doing? I thought you were going to head home."

"I'm on my way. Did you find a child's storybook in the wreckage?"

"Nope." Grim lines frowned across Tucker's face. "Most things fell to the bottom of the cliff. How's that injured girl?"

"Not good." Cooper rubbed his brow. "How many outlaws did we bring in?"

"Just one. I shot him myself. He broke his jaw when he fell off his horse. The doc said he's pretty hurt, but I'm not letting him in the clinic with innocent women and children. I locked him up. Wanna see?"

"I'll wait until morning." Cooper regretted they hadn't caught more of the gang, as he'd planned. But circumstances had intervened. Rescuing Mrs. Bauer and her child was more important than nabbing a few outlaws.

"It's a damn lucky thing you're good with a rope." Tucker's gaze fastened on his, serious as a hanging judge. "Or the child would be dead. There's no way she could have survived that fall."

"I know." Cooper grabbed his hat.

"Where you goin'?"

"To find a storybook." He gestured toward the messy desk in the corner, hiding a grin. "And you straighten up around here. Some innocent taxpayer is going to walk into this office and regret how much they pay slobs like you to protect their town."

"Hey, watch who you're calling a slob!"

Tucker's laughing protest followed Cooper out the door and into the crisp spring night. Cold sliced through his coat. Mountain snow still clung to the ground in places, even though it was spring. He saw the light in the window and once again thought of the woman and her child. Took comfort that some mothers stayed. Some mothers loved their children more than themselves.

His house was dark except for the twin lamps lit in the parlor and the merry glow of the fire. Laura looked up from her embroidery. "I heard about the excitement."

"Yeah, it's been a tough day." He felt tired. He felt drained. "How are my girls?"

"In bed asleep. I think." Laura's grin was mischievous. "I'm only an aunt, not a miracle worker."

Cooper didn't bother to shrug off his coat. "Would you mind staying longer? I've got an errand to do."

"Sure. I have nowhere to go." Laura poked her threaded needle through the stretched-tight fabric. "But we need to discuss the situation with the housekeeper."

"Again?" There was a conversation he wanted to avoid.

"Mrs. Potts found a salamander in the empty soup kettle."

"Just a salamander this time?" If only his oldest girl could be as sweet and obedient as the youngest he wouldn't have to worry about the housekeeper quitting every day of the week.

"We can be happy it wasn't a skunk."

"Don't give the child any ideas." As he climbed the stairs to the dark second story, Cooper thought of little Mandy Bauer and how he'd cradled her close on the long hard ride down the mountainside. She was frail and tiny like his own littlest girl.

He nudged open the door to the girls' room. The moon played through the window, casting enough of a silvered glow to see their sweet faces, relaxed and content in sleep, each in her own twin bed.

Careful not to wake them, Cooper found a book by feel on the bookshelf, the nursery rhymes his Maisie treasured.

"Papa?"

So one of them wasn't asleep. "What is it, Katie?"

"Laura said there was a lady come today on the wrecked stage."

"There was." He knelt down beside his oldest daughter's bedside. "Tucker's already told me how nice and pretty she is. I hope you aren't going to try to match me up with this poor woman."

"Oh Papa, Laura says cuz you're a man, you don't know what's best for you."

"She does?" He laughed at that. "No more talk. You lie back down and go to sleep. You're going to need your rest if you want to have enough strength to try to marry me off tomorrow."

"Go ahead and joke." Katie shook her head, scattering dark curls against her thin shoulders. "I don't think it's one bit funny."

"I know." He pressed a kiss to her forehead.

Katie had been trying to marry him to every available woman she came across for years now. She didn't understand. As a child she never could. How did he explain to her that a stepmother was not a mother? A woman could love her own children, but love for a stepchild could only run so deep.

He'd learned that painful lesson as a young boy, and it was one he vowed to protect his daughters from. He would protect them from any harm, any hurt, any heartache. If he could.

Besides, he loved his girls. And one loving parent was more than a lot of children had. He'd seen that in his work, too.

Katie laid down with a rustle of flannel sheets and down comforter. He stood in the threshold, watching them both, grateful for their health and their presence in his life. Maisie with her gold curls tangling on the pillow and her stuffed bunny clutched in reed-thin arms. And Katie too old and tough, or so she said, for such things.

What would he do if harm came their way? Cooper thought of Mrs. Bauer sitting vigil beside her tiny daughter's bedside. He knew how he would feel if one of his girls were in that bed, clinging to life.

He strode out the back door, headfirst into the cold night wind.

Anna fought the dream and swam to the surface of consciousness. Night spun around her. The sepia glow of the kerosene lamp turned low brushed the bed, shadowing the defenseless child so still beneath the blankets.

She had to stay awake. Mandy might need her. Anna sat up straight in the hard-backed chair, willing her gaze not to leave her daughter's face.

Her own chin bobbed. Exhaustion curled around her like a blinding fog, but she fought it. She stood, ambled to the window. A late quarter moon lit the night sky, brushing the white curtains and the world outside with a soft veil of silver. The town looked peaceful, windows dark, tucked in for the night. She hadn't even taken a look around the town when she'd arrived, she'd been so afraid for Mandy.

Now, she could see the striped awning of a bakery, the big false front of a general store. She had come to Flint Creek to make a home, a marriage and a family. A new life for her and Mandy. But shadows moved along the dark street, kicking up the beat of her heart. She thought of Dalton, remembered how his gaze had met hers across the length of the bank.

He knew she'd recognized him. She knew in that way of friends well acquainted with each other. She'd grown up in Ruby Bluff, went to school with Dalton. They had been in the same class all the way through graduation. And when he'd started courting her last year, she'd been flattered, but nothing more.

For Mandy's sake, she'd thought that maybe she could make it work. But no real affection other than friendship had grown in her heart. And she began to see traits and tempers in Dalton that gave her pause. He didn't like children, had no patience for them. She turned down his proposal, and she knew it had hurt him. But they could never be happy together.

That's why she had chosen Mr. Braddock's letter,

agreed to his proposal. He seemed to truly care for his daughters. In fact, his letters had been full of written details about the girls and little else. She could overlook a lot of faults as long as he was kind to children, both those that were his and those not his own.

Anna had told her sister about her decision the evening of the robbery, when she'd hurried home, shaking. If the stage left that day, she would have been on it. But Ruby Bluff was a small town with stage service just once a week. Meg had agreed with her. She should leave town, just as planned.

Remembering, she could hear her sister's voice. How she missed Meg. She needed her hug, would have liked to have her here to share her fears with. But that night, Meg had made tea, listened, and counted out all of her butter and egg money. Fifty dollars.

"Take it," Meg had said. "If Dalton is the robber that's been troubling this area, then he's dangerous. He's killed innocent people."

"I know." But Anna could not take her sister's hard-earned money. "I have enough."

"Not enough if you leave tonight."

"There is no stage tonight." Anna rubbed her brow. Her head ached from worry and fear. She wished she'd never looked down at the robber's shoes.

"You take my horse and wagon."

"No. You need them for the farm work."

Meg's smile was soft like her voice, warm with a lifelong love some lucky sisters shared. "Listen to me. Take the morning stage from Rubydale. Ben will drive you there tonight."

Would Dalton come after her? Even with that fear, it was hard to leave. When she'd shown up pregnant without a husband, Meg had welcomed her in. She loved her sister. She would miss her.

Meg's Ben had reported that Sheriff Dalton Jennings was taking a late supper at Mary's Diner. Anna could leave while he and his men were eating. Rubydale was only a few hours away. She and Ben could make the trip safely.

With promises to write and Mandy wrapped well against the coolish spring night, Anna had stepped out of her sister's farmhouse and into the darkness.

"Take me to the moon, Mama." Mandy pointed up at the canopy of broadleaf maples hiding the sky.

Anna's heart twisted. "All right. But we have to be very, very quiet."

"I'm very quiet."

Anna followed Ben out into the driveway.

"Silly Betsy," Mandy giggled as the mare grabbed the little girl's hem with her wide long tongue.

"Betsy, are you going to let us by?" Anna patted the animal warmly. The sweet horse rubbed against her hand, then waited patiently as they passed by.

Ben helped her up into the wagon seat, and she thanked him. Anna cradled Mandy on her lap and drew Meg's best fur around them. "Look up. Can you see the man in the moon?"

Mandy nodded. "He's watchin' over us."

"And he chases all those night monsters away and keeps us all safe." Anna pressed a kiss to her daughter's forehead, wishing on the moon. Ben released the brake and the wagon moved away in the darkness, leaving the warm, lit windows of Meg's house behind until there was only black forest and night.

"So far, so good," Ben whispered.

But then a horrible noise shattered the peace of the

night, the stillness of the mountain valley. The sound of horses galloping down the road behind them, voices low and loud. Five, maybe six, riders.

"Meg." Fear snaked down her spine. She twisted around, straining to see through the impossible dark. "We can't leave her."

"Don't worry." Ben pulled the wagon off the road and set the brake. "If there's any trouble, you go on without me."

Ben jumped down, took out his revolver, and ran. Anna sat in the wagon for what felt like hours, fearing the worst. Dalton wouldn't hurt Meg, would he?

Finally Ben returned. Meg had feigned innocence and told Dalton and his men that Anna had headed south toward Wyoming. They had believed her, believed Anna had said nothing about Dalton's dual identity. Meg's lie would buy them enough time to reach Rubydale and the morning's stage. If their luck held.

"Mrs. Bauer?"

His voice came low and gentle, but Anna bolted away from the window. A man towered in the threshold, nothing but shadows and powerful male steel and strength.

"I couldn't find your daughter's storybook." The sheriff lifted one shoulder in an apologetic shrug.

"Thank you for looking."

"It was no problem." He strolled closer, his boots resounding on the floorboards. "But I didn't want to come here empty-handed, so I brought my daughter's book. It will have to be a loan, I'm afraid. But you keep it as long as your little one needs to hear stories."

Anna's throat tightened. "I can't tell you how—" Tears stung her eyes. "This means a lot."

"Is there anything I can get you?" He offered her

the book gripped by big, blunt-tipped fingers. Very male. Very capable.

"You've done so much already." Anna took the well-worn volume that looked lovingly opened and read across many years. "It's late. You should be home with your family, and yet you're here."

"I'm on my way home. I just felt sorry for your little one. I'm partly responsible. If my men and I had arrived earlier, we might have prevented this." He knuckled back his hat, and she could see the shine of sincerity, of strength. "Good night, Mrs. Bauer. I'll check back with you tomorrow morning. If your daughter is improving, I'll need to ask you some questions."

"Questions? What kind of questions?"

"About the outlaws." His voice was calm. "You saw the men up close. I would like to write up a report on what happened. I keep in contact with other lawmen in the county. We need to work together to catch those outlaws, and you can help."

"I see." She thought about that. This sheriff was in contact with other lawmen in the area. Dalton Jennings was also a lawman just a few counties away. "I didn't get a very good look at the robbers. They wore bandannas."

"Think on it. I'll check back tomorrow." His voice soothed. Or maybe it was his strength, his competence that radiated like heat from a summer sun.

"The book will make a difference, Sheriff," she called him back, unable to let him go, still touched by his generosity. "I will return it as soon as I can."

"Cooper, remember?" His smile was warm, and then he was gone.

She wasn't used to calling men by their given names. But the warmth in her chest put there by his smile and thoughtfulness didn't fade with his departure. He'd brought his own daughter's book. She couldn't believe it. Couldn't believe a perfect stranger would be so kind.

Mandy still slept, her breathing shallow and uneven. Anna turned up the wick and smoothed open the book.

On the inside cover was a mark, a child's handwritten scrawl. Anna peered close to look at it, to make out the careful, badly formed and somehow familiar letters. Katie Braddock, it said.

The sheriff's daughter. Cooper's daughter.

The book fell from her fingers, clattered to the floor. The sound reverberated through the room, but it wasn't as loud as the pounding of her heart.

That handsome, wonderful man who'd rescued her daughter, who'd taken care of them both. Was he truly Cooper Braddock? The man she'd come to marry?

Chapter Three

"Katie, don't slurp your oatmeal." Cooper reached for the sugar jar. "It's not ladylike."

"I'm in a hurry. Davy and me are ridin' ponies."

"Did I say you could do something so foolish?" He spooned sugar into his steaming cup of coffee and struggled to keep a straight face.

"Ridin' ponies ain't foolish, Papa. It's fun."

He clinked the lid down on the jar. "It's not something a polite little girl does with her time."

"Papa," little Maisie chimed in, "Katie ain't never polite."

"True." He laughed at his littlest, wishing he could spend more time with his daughters this morning. Thinking of the Bauer girl who may not survive, he knew he ought to carve out the time. But his work—and his sworn duty—called. "Katie, I want you to obey Mrs. Potts today."

"You know I try real hard, Papa." Katie wiped off her milk mustache with a practiced swipe of her sleeve.

"Try harder." Making a little lady out of his first-born could prove impossible. "I heard all about the trouble you caused yesterday from Laura. I'm none too pleased with you."

"I know. I'm sorry." Katie bowed her chin.

"But I didn't cause no trouble, Papa." Maisie was all golden curls and big blue eyes. "I was a good girl."

"I already knew that." He kissed both girls on the forehead and took the coffee cup with him. "Katie, I want you to do something for me."

"I don't gotta embroider, do I?"

Shouldn't a little girl want to embroider? "Gather up a few of Maisie's dresses and nighties she's outgrown, bundle them up, and take them over to the doc's. There's a little girl who was hurt in the stage accident yesterday, and she lost nearly all of her belongings."

Maisie gasped. "Even her bunny?"

He saw the stuffed animal on the floor beneath his littlest one's chair. "Yes, even her bunny."

"How does she sleep?"

"Only babies need a bunny." Katie dropped her spoon with a clatter. "Papa, you want me to do it now?"

"Yes, before you go play with Davy. Promise me."

Katie thought about it, obviously torn at the sad idea of a hurt little girl and tempted by a wild morning racing ponies. "I promise, Papa. I'll do it right away."

"That's my girl." Despite her spiritedness, she was a good child. "Take the clothes over to the clinic and ask for Mrs. Bauer."

"Mrs. Bauer?" Katie froze stiff as an icicle.

"That's what I said. She's a real nice lady, so don't scare her with any matchmaking schemes. She has enough worries on her mind."

"Uh, what does she look like, Papa?"

"Don't worry, you'll find her." His daughter wasn't shy with strangers, especially pretty women. Cooper didn't know how else to interpret Katie's behavior. "If you have any problems, just ask the doc. He'll help you."

Leaving his daughter to nod in answer, Cooper stopped in the kitchen to praise Mrs. Potts for showing up this morning and for providing a good breakfast, despite yesterday's salamander incident.

Too wise, the plump woman managed a sour comment and asked about a raise. He had no choice but to agree.

Not a good way to start the day. As long as the militant housekeeper didn't quit. Troubled, he stepped out into the morning. Pine and fresh mountain rain scented the air. He headed down the street toward work, hoping for a quiet day. Just one quiet day. It wasn't too much to ask, was it?

"You must eat," the doc said as he stepped into the sick room. "You haven't touched your tray."

"I know. And after your wife went to the trouble of fixing me a meal." Anna rubbed her brow. In truth, she wasn't just exhausted. She felt sick and dizzy. Her arm hurt something terrible from a wound she'd sustained. She could barely move her hand this morning.

Yet every time she thought about showing the doctor the ragged tear through flesh and muscle, he was hovering over Mandy. With his stethoscope to the girl's chest, he listened to her punctured lung. And as always, concern lined his face. There were other people also seriously wounded from the stage robbery. She could not take the doctor's attention from any of them, not for something as small as her tiny little injury.

He frowned. "You're terribly flushed. How you are feeling?"

"I'm fine." She said it, hoping to make it true.

A cool hand touched her brow. "You're burning up."

"No. I'm just tired."

Understanding warmed those eyes. "I know you're concerned about your daughter. You have every right. But don't forget Mandy needs a healthy mother to depend on."

"She needs me now. Right here." Anna patted the open book in her lap.

"I'm not going to argue with you. For now." The doc stood. "Anna, if you feel worse, you must tell me."

"Agreed." Her eyes filled, and she looked away. The doctor left to check on the other patients. She rubbed her forehead. She really wasn't feeling very well at all.

"Are you Anna? Anna Bauer?"

"Yes, I am." Anna turned, surprised to see a spindly brown-haired girl, maybe nine, maybe ten years old, leaning against the threshold, hugging a bundle in her skinny arms. Mud spattered the hem of her dress, crooked above scabbed knees.

The girl dragged her feet forward nearly lost behind the ball of what looked like an old sheet. "Papa said to bring this. On account of your little girl gettin' hurt."

Anna's heart twisted. She accepted the offered bundle. "Who is your papa?"

"The sheriff."

"I met him just yesterday." Anna began working

the knot in the sheet. "He brought me your storybook so I could read to Mandy."

Katie's dark gaze slid to the bed then flicked back nervously. "Did you know it's all my fault?"

"What is?" The knot came loose. "The book really helped. Thank you for loaning it to me."

"It's my fault she's hurt." Big tears began pooling, but they didn't fall. That stubborn chin jutted upward. "I didn't think anyone would get hurt."

"The stage accident isn't your fault."

What a thoughtful, sensitive child. This was the sheriff's daughter. Cooper's daughter. The Katie mentioned in those wonderful letters. Letters that fed her hopes and dreams for Mandy's future. How Anna wished she could reach out and comfort the girl with a touch, maybe a hug. Heaven knows she looked as if she could use a woman's care. Maybe a mother's love.

"Why, you brought Mandy some clothes." Anna unfolded an adorable pink gingham frock with a little sunbonnet to match. Starched clean drawers, a pretty flowered nightgown and cap, a little sweater with embroidered strawberries to go with a strawberry print dress.

"We don't want your little hurt girl to go naked when she wakes up." That lower lip trembled. "Is she gonna die?"

"Don't you worry. Mandy is going to be just fine." Anna carefully folded the beautiful clothes, throat aching. It was hard not to reach out and comfort Katie, who looked as if she needed it so desperately. "Tell your papa thank you for the clothes."

"I will." The girl kicked the toe of her shoe against the floor. "My name's Katie. Maybe you know me."

"I sure do." Anna set the clothes and sheet aside. "Your father wrote all about you and Maisie."

"That's why you're here, right?" Katie tilted her head, scattering dark wisps that had escaped her twin braids. "Can I ask you somethin'?"

Anna took one look into those curious dark eyes just like Cooper's, carefully hiding so many emotions. The idea of a new stepmother must be worrisome for a child. That she could understand. Anna rose, held out her hand. "I'll answer any questions you want. Let's go out into the hallway so we don't wake Mandy."

"I know you already met Papa." The girl hurried out of the room. "Do you think he's handsome?"

"Who wouldn't?" Anna took one look at the girl and shook her head. And that made her a little dizzy, so she leaned against the wall to rest a bit.

"Maisie needs a new mother, you know, because she ain't rugged like me."

"Maisie is your little sister," Anna remembered.

"Yep. Papa hasn't married anyone since our mama left. So that's why I did it. I used my own money I earned looking for gold dust with Davy Muldune for the advertisement—"

"Advertisement?" Her brain felt a little fuzzy. Really, she needed to sit down before the doctor caught her swaying in the corridor.

"You're awful pretty," Katie added in a rush. "And you got a little girl, too. I seen her in that bed. She sorta matches us."

"Katie, I—"

"That's why I had you come, and not just for Maisie. My poor lonely papa needs a wife."

"Poor lonely papa?" a man's voice boomed.

Head spinning, Anna looked up into a lean, handsome face. His gaze, dark as midnight, sparkled with what could only be humor. Her pulse thudded in her ears. She felt hot, then cold all over.

He must have known since last night who she was, that she was the woman he'd proposed to just last month. And yet he'd waited to talk to her about it. Maybe out of respect for Mandy's condition.

Her head spun. Her knees wobbled. Cooper's iron hard arms encircled her, held her tight against his chest. She tried to tell him she was fine.

But the world faded, and all went black.

She opened her eyes and saw him, Cooper, sitting at her bedside, a dark shank of hair falling over his forehead. His dark gaze brushed hers, bold as a touch.

"You gave us a scare for a minute there."

Anna tried to sit up, but the blood rushed from her head. She landed back on the pillow.

"Don't worry. The doc's with your girl. I made him promise to stay with her until you were awake." Cooper unfolded his hard-muscled body from the chair and crossed the room. Anna heard the scrape of porcelain and the tinkle and splash of pouring water. "I also made Katie stay and read aloud to your daughter, since at first I thought she was the cause of all this."

"The cause?"

He handed her a tin mug with a half grin, lopsided and attractive. "I thought she'd shocked you with her outrageous propositions and that's why you fainted."

"Propositions?" She nearly spilled the water.

Cooper's bigger fingers wrapped around hers. His skin's heat scorched her and sent sparkling little frissons dancing up her arm.

"She does this to every woman she comes across.

Tries to charm them first into going out to dinner with me. And then into marrying me, that little scamp.''

The rim of the cup brushed her bottom lip. His hand still guided hers. The cool water washed into her mouth, but she hardly noticed it. Cooper—he seemed to fill her senses—the whiskered days' growth along his jaw, the scent of leather and pine, the rumbling richness of his voice. He was all she saw, all she felt rushing through her heated body.

''Katie?'' The cool water hadn't washed away the confused fog in her mind.

''Then the doc discovered the gunshot wound in your upper arm. You should have told someone before this. You're going to be all right, but the doc had to give you a few stitches.''

She closed her eyes. ''I didn't mean to faint.''

''You were thinking of your daughter, not yourself.'' When she looked up at him, she saw approval lining his face, and he nodded once.

''Mandy—''

''Lie back. She's fine.'' Cooper stepped away, but his warmth, his presence remained. She thought of all the trouble she was in and knew it was wrong to lean on him.

''Katie just wants a mother, but she shouldn't have bothered you with your daughter hurt.'' Cooper's dark eyes shone with sadness. ''I just hope you can find a way to forgive her.''

Confusion rang in Anna's mind. What did she need to forgive? Katie only wanted to meet the woman her father planned to marry.

Or did he? Cooper Braddock was not acting as if he'd proposed to her. Polite, helpful, concerned. But not personal. It was as if he didn't know who she was.

He hadn't even mentioned their future. And now he was walking away, as if they were perfect strangers.

"Maybe we could talk about the letters now." Anna struggled to sit up. She'd been wrong to postpone discussing it.

Cooper turned, framed in the threshold, a powerful and handsome larger-than-life man any woman would want. "My deputies didn't find letters in the wreckage, ma'am. I hope it wasn't anything important."

He quirked one dark brow, a silent question offering help. But nothing else. No recognition. No comment. And no evasion.

Anna didn't understand. Surely, Cooper Braddock knew her full name. Surely, by mentioning the letters he would say something about their correspondence. Then Anna remembered Katie's look of horror and jumbled words when her father walked in.

Realization hit her like a falling brick. Her too-many hopes fell. She'd made this perilous journey for nothing. She still had to worry if Dalton Jennings would somehow figure out where she was and follow her. Now there was no husband waiting, no man to marry, no one to help raise her daughter.

It was Katie who sent the letters. Katie who'd written of the need for a mother able to ride ponies and bake cookies for little Maisie. Katie who wrote with the unpracticed scrawl Anna had mistaken for an uneducated man's handwriting. So many men in the area just didn't have much schooling.

Tears burned in her eyes. She'd never felt at such a loss. She'd never felt so foolish.

"Lie still for a few hours more." Cooper's voice rumbled like thunder, but was gentle like spring sunshine. "Give yourself a chance to heal first. Then go to your daughter. She's doing better."

Better. Anna clung to those words.

Cooper sat down at the kitchen table and listened to the stillness of the house, of the night. He'd had a hell of a long day. Too damn long. And he was no closer to bringing down Corinthos.

He reached for the sugar jar to sweeten the cup of coffee he'd just poured when he heard the pad of little bare feet. "Katie, is that you?"

"Yes, Papa." So sad.

"Wanna come keep me company?" He pulled out the chair next to him.

"I guess." She dragged her feet.

"I'm a pretty good listener if you want to tell me what's wrong."

She plopped down on the chair, her hair disheveled, her nightgown wrinkled, her feet bare. A heavy sigh. "What about Mrs. Bauer?"

"She hurt her arm."

"Does it hurt?"

"Probably." He remembered the look on Katie's face when Anna Bauer had fainted. "See what you get for trying to marry me off? It scares some women so bad they lose consciousness."

"Oh, Papa." Almost a smile. "It's all my fault."

"What is?" He tugged his chair around to face her. Something weighed mighty heavily on her conscience. "What did you do, Katie?"

"It's my fault they're hurt." Another sniffle.

"Mrs. Bauer and her daughter? Why Katie, you didn't rob the stage, did you?"

"No."

"And you didn't scare the horses that ran off with the coach, did you?"

"Papa, that's not what I mean." Exasperation blended with that sadness. "They're all hurt because of me, and I can't sleep."

"Mrs. Potts said you didn't eat anything for supper."

"I w-wasn't hungry." Sobs broke apart her words. "Oh, Papa, this is the baddest thing I've ever done."

She flew into his arms before he could react, and he held her good and tight, relishing the rare moment. Katie never cried like this, always declaring herself too tough. Yet she felt frail, all bird-thin bones and heartbreak.

"You're always in trouble, Katie," he said lightly, his chest tight. He didn't like his daughter hurting. "I bet it's not so awful."

"It is." Her arms tightened around his neck. "You have to make it right, Papa."

More soul-deep sobs rocked her body. "You gotta tell me what to do so it don't hurt no more."

His chest tightened. So many childhood troubles. He dug a handkerchief from his shirt pocket. "All this crying isn't going to solve a thing."

"Oh, Papa." Katie blew, wiped, then refolded the hanky. "There's only one thing to do."

"Just one thing to fix the baddest thing you've ever done?" He tried to coax a smile from that serious mouth. And failed.

"You have to marry her."

"Not that again."

"But it's the right thing!"

Cooper couldn't imagine why she'd gotten all worked up over being without a stepmother. Katherine had been gone a long time, nearly half Katie's life. They'd adjusted, moved on, tried to make a family with just the three of them. Katie knew he was never going to remarry. As a boy, he'd managed to endure being a stepchild, but his daughters would not be exposed to such a situation.

He swiped at two of Katie's tears with his thumb. "How many times have we talked about this?"

"Probaby a million." Another sob. "B-but Papa. It's different now."

"Why?" He brushed tear-wet curls from her brow.

"Because I wrote a letter and asked Mrs. Bauer to come here."

"You *what?*"

"Maisie needs a mama. She needs one real bad."

Cooper deposited Katie on the floor and bolted up from the chair. He hit the ground pacing. Anger flared. "Let me get this straight. You wrote a letter to a perfect stranger and asked her to come here?"

"To marry us."

White-hot anger speared through him. "Katie, you're right. This is the baddest thing you have ever done."

Cooper spun at the back door and crossed the length of the room, fists jammed at his sides, his jaw clenched so tight his teeth ached. Nice little girls didn't do the things Katie did. They didn't climb trees and play in mud and race ponies. Or propose to innocent strangers.

Maybe it was because those other little girls had mothers.

Katie burst into tears again. "They got hurt and Maisie still doesn't have a m-mama!"

Frustration, rage, defeat. It all melded together in his midsection and churned. He wanted to punish her. He wanted to comfort her. He wished to hell and back Katie would learn to embroider or something ladylike and stop with the wild harebrained schemes.

"It is your fault that Mrs. Bauer and her daughter were on that stage." He managed to keep his voice calm.

Harder tears.

"But you couldn't have known they would come to harm."

"I d-didn't." True sorrow shone in those eyes, the same color as his.

Cooper stared at his reflection in the dark window. "How did you find Mrs. Bauer in the first place?"

"I bought a newspaper advertisement."

"You did what?" Renewed fury roared through him. He would never understand his daughter. She was too flighty, too headstrong, too— He didn't know what, but it wasn't a good thing. Little girls were supposed to be demure and polite, cute and neat—not muddy and outrageous. "You placed a request for a mother in a newspaper?"

Katie's eyes still brimmed with tears. "No. I pretended to be you."

"Anna Bauer thinks that I—" His knees buckled. Speechless, he simply stared at his daughter. The pony rides, the trousers, the mud, the disobedience and now this. Katie didn't need a mother, she needed a warden and steel bars on the window.

Cooper held out his hand. "There's no need to cry."

She tipped up her tear-wet face. "You'll fix everything, Papa?"

"Of course I will. I'm the sheriff. That's my job."

A smile nudged away the sadness and Katie's fingers wrapped tightly around his. "I knew you would."

All the trust in the world shone in those eyes. Cooper's chest filled. How he loved his little girl. "Come, let's get you back in bed."

It was a sweet task, tucking the covers up to her chin, wishing her good dreams, waiting as she drifted off. His two little daughters, safe and snug.

A noise downstairs spun him around. With his five shooter strapped tight to his thigh, he started down the stairs. This part of Montana was isolated but saw its share of trouble. That's why the good people of Flint Creek had hired him. He had promised to keep their families and their businesses safe from crime. It was a tall order, but Cooper Braddock was a man of his word.

"I saw your light on," Laura's voice called out to him before he strode into the kitchen.

"More problems with Katie." He unbuckled his gun belt, the day's work done.

"That's nothing new. What is it this time?"

He studied his young sister's pretty face, the concern so bright in her eyes. He knew Laura loved his daughters, but the emerald flashing on her left ring finger left no room for doubt. Laura would soon be married, starting a new life, making her own family. It was time to stop depending on her so heavily.

He laid the gun belt on the table with a soft clink. "She can't sleep. Nothing to worry about."

"With Katie, there's a lot to worry about." Those caring eyes twinkled. "Will you share your coffee?"

"With pleasure. If you can stand my bitter brew."

"Let's just say I'm used to your cooking, big brother." She lifted the enamel pot from the stove, just as she'd done hundreds, maybe thousands of times. "What are you going to do when I marry?"

"About the girls?" He sat down at the table. Sighed.

"I've tried not to think about it. I don't think Mrs. Potts is going to stay without you here."

"I think Mrs. Potts is ready to run screaming to Canada if Katie brings one more slimy creature into this kitchen, whether on purpose or not." Laura's fondness rang in her voice. She set her steaming cup on the table and sat across from him. Her gaze met his. "Cooper, those girls of yours need a mother."

"They have me." He lifted his chin.

"A father's love is important, but you're a man. You're busy providing for your family, protecting the town and doing your job. A man has to do that, I know. You need to provide for your girls and that takes you away from them. I'm not faulting you."

He rubbed his brow, tired. "Whatever my daughters need, they have my love. Not every man stands by his family."

"You've made a fine home for them."

Those tender words, brimming with understanding, hurt more than Cooper could admit. He'd worked hard to do right by his girls after Katherine walked away. To love them, provide for them. "I couldn't have done so much without your help, Laura."

"I've been glad to do it, Cooper." Her lower lip wobbled. "I'm proud of you for taking a risk and doing what's right for yourself and my two beautiful nieces."

Love filled him up. "That means a lot to me, Laura. Life would be damn empty without my daughters."

He thought of Anna Bauer and how she'd come so close to losing her child. His family was safe, healthy and happy. Yes, he was a lucky man indeed.

Laura's hand covered his, an act of comfort from sister to brother. "I haven't taken the time to meet your

Anna yet, out of respect for her injured girl, but from what Tucker says, she's wonderful.''

Cooper's hand shook, the cup slipped. Hot coffee scorched his thigh. ''What has Tucker been saying, that no-good brother of ours?''

''Only that he found certain letters in the stage wreckage and because they were so personal, he's keeping them away from the other deputies' prying eyes.'' Laura's face beamed with happiness. ''Oh, Cooper. Why didn't you tell us? I'm so happy you've found a wife.''

Chapter Four

Lee Corinthos held the revolver in a white-knuckled grip. He hated the way the gun shook. Hated weakness of any kind, no matter how hurt he was. "Are you sure you ain't causin' more harm?"

Fear glittered in the doc's watery eyes. "No, sir. I'm doing the best job I can. Your man is hurt real bad."

Excuses. Corinthos was tired of those, too. "If my man dies, you die too, Doc."

More fear in those eyes. Educated men didn't know how to fight, Corinthos knew. The doctor brought up from Rocky Gulch would prove no threat. Men like him didn't have the guts.

"I'll do all I can." The doc swallowed hard, as if realizing the importance of his surgery, and returned to digging the bullet out of Jeffrey's thigh.

"Those lawmen were waitin' for us." Dusty wiped his brow, winced in pain, then lowered his bandaged hand. "It's that sheriff Flint Creek hired to replace old Joe."

"Old Joe made things easy for us."

"With a little bit of bribery and just the right pressure," Dusty cackled.

"I wish to hell he'd stayed. We've got problems."

"We'll find a way to deal with Braddock. Every man has his pressure points." Dusty stopped. "Want me to keep a gun on the doc?"

"I can do it," Corinthos growled. He was the toughest son of a gun in all of Montana Territory. He refused to show weakness in front of his men, even if he was hurt bad enough to pass out. "Yep, that damn new sheriff is a problem."

"Braddock's his name. Cooper Braddock."

"He's gotta cooperate or we'll take him out of our way. I plan on keeping my business profitable." With the amount of gold traveling from the mines on this side of the Rockies, he'd be rich before long. "First, I'll have to pay that Braddock back for plowing a bullet into me."

"I wanna be there to see it." Dusty chuckled, as always relishing even the thought of violence.

"Doc, are you done yet?" Corinthos nosed the revolver against the scrawny doc's neck. The room was starting to spin and the outlaw couldn't keep standing much longer without a flask of whiskey, but he wouldn't say it. Wouldn't let his men know it.

"I'm just closing up now."

"Then I'm next." Corinthos gritted his teeth against the pain. He would get his damn wound stitched and then he'd be heading right back to Flint Creek. He had a witness to silence and a score to settle.

And settle it he would. Lee Corinthos always got what he wanted—at any cost. It didn't pay for a man to be honest and polite. No, it was a ruthless man who won every time. Corinthos had learned that bitter lesson the hard way, for it was the way of the West.

* * *

As the hours passed watching Mandy sleep, Anna had to struggle to tamp down her fears. She could stand any amount of grief and hardship, but not the death of her daughter.

Anna reached for the borrowed storybook, smoothed open the rich paper pages to a favored tale. Over the rasp of Mandy's breathing, she began to read. The story was familiar, often read in quiet hours back home, and Anna's mind drifted. She thought of Dalton. Thought of her sister, who'd sent him in the wrong direction. She hoped Meg was safe. Anna thought of the stage robbers. Hoped that they, like Dalton, didn't favor silencing every last witness.

Fear coiled through her, squeezing tight. What could she do? Where could she go? She had no money, no belongings, no help. Mandy was too critically injured to move. And Cooper Braddock hadn't proposed to her. There was no husband, no home, no family waiting for her.

"Anna?"

A jolt of awareness skittled along the back of her neck. She knew by the commanding feel of him that it was Cooper. Did he know why she'd come to town? What should she do now? Troubled, she rubbed her tired eyes.

"You've been crying." His voice rumbled with concern. "Is it your daughter?"

"Mandy's doing much better. She's sat up and taken some chicken broth. The doctor has high hopes." Thank heavens for that.

"May I come in?"

"You? Always." What should she say to him? He still stood in the threshold, one wide shoulder propped against the door frame. He was a big man; he filled the small dark room with his powerful presence. Dizzy, Anna caught her breath as he pulled up a chair. "You don't need to keep checking up on me."

"It's the least I can do, being the sheriff and all." He winked, and the kindness, the strength of him shone in his dark eyes. "I take it you're a rather independent woman."

Was he commenting or criticizing? She couldn't tell for sure, but he looked to be holding back a smile. "And you're a rather overbearing man. Maybe because you take your badge a little too seriously."

A broad, lopsided grin stretched his mouth and reached all the way to his laughing eyes. "Smart mouthed, too. I must warn you, I have a lot of experience dealing with your type of female."

"Because you're a sheriff?"

"No, because I'm a father."

They laughed together. There was no mistaking the affection in his eyes, the great love he had for his daughters. Anna wrung her hands, truly awestruck by such a man. Such a wonderful man.

"I was hoping since your child is out of danger, that we can talk." His eyes darkened.

"Talk?" she squeaked.

"It's important." He gestured toward the door.

Anna hesitated. She wasn't up to discussing the letters. Had he figured out why she was here?

Embarrassed, afraid that her feelings showed, she stepped out into the hall.

"I've got a real serious situation." Cooper gestured toward a chair in the doc's parlor.

Anna sat, her pulse beating like a drum in her ears. Had he found out about Dalton? It was possible. After all, both men were sheriffs in the same county, even if nearly a hundred miles separated their towns.

"This is the first time anyone has survived a stage robbery by Corinthos' gang. You stood the closest to him. He spoke to you. Could you identify him if you saw him again? If this goes to trial, we will need all the witnesses we can get."

"You want to know about the robbery?" Relief shivered through her veins. At least she still had some secrets.

A noisy clatter pounded outside the window, and then the door swung open. "Papa! Papa!"

Two little girls tumbled into the clinic, Katie wearing trousers and a big flannel shirt, and a smaller child in a pink calico dress.

"What are my two favorite girls doing here?" Cooper turned toward the little intruders, a smile tugging away at the stern set of his mouth.

"Mrs. Potts is shopping, so she said we gotta come on over and see Anna." Katie ground to a stop in the middle of the parlor, braids bobbing. She rubbed several strands of escaped hair out of her eyes. "Papa, Mrs. Potts is really, really mad at you again. Hi, Anna."

A little blond sprite of a girl stared out at her from between Cooper's knees.

Anna's entire heart warmed. "Hello."

He cleared his throat. "You mean Mrs. Potts is really mad at you. What did you do this time?"

"Nothing. A snake got into the pantry, that's all." Katie's eyes twinkled with barely restrained mischief. "She's awfully scared of things like that."

"You and I will discuss this later." He didn't look pleased, but he wasn't angry, wasn't punishing.

A good father, Anna decided. Just the sort of man she'd hoped to find. "Katie, I haven't forgotten about returning your storybook. I'm still reading to Mandy from it."

"Only Maisie likes those stories now." The girl turned serious, obviously concentrating on more important matters. "Do you like my papa enough to marry him yet?"

Anna couldn't hold back her chuckle. She looked up and caught the surprise in Cooper's eyes, laughed at the astonishment slackening his unshaven jaw. "No, Katie. I don't like your father *that* much."

"Pretty women always say that." Katie affected a troubled sigh, her heart-deep need for a mother's love dark like lost hope in her eyes.

"Katie. Maisie. Let's go outside." Cooper wouldn't meet Anna's gaze as he headed for the door. Apparently he did know about the letters, about her embarrassing situation. Why hadn't he said anything? Was he afraid she'd demand marriage whether he wanted her or not?

"Anna, come see Bob," Katie called as she bolted toward the door, braids flying.

"Yeah. Come see Bob," Maisie chimed.

Cooper's gaze snared hers, intense and unflinching. The air stalled in her chest. She saw the warmth of this family and couldn't help wanting to be a part of it, just in a small way, for this one moment. "Who's Bob?"

Katie hopped out onto the sunlit boardwalk. "Bob is my pony."

"A very bad pony." Big blue eyes met Anna's. Maisie blushed shyly, then dashed outside in a pink blur.

"She's precious." Delight transformed Anna's heart-shaped face.

"You see what I'm up against. Two adorable girls who have me wrapped around their little fingers."

"I'll say." She smiled, but it was warm, without censure. Not judgmental, not disapproving. When it came to Katie, he got the latter reaction most of the time.

He could only stare at Anna, liking her for liking his girls. He couldn't help it, even if he was looking disaster in the face. Not only did Anna know he knew about the letters, but now both his girls thought a marriage between them was possible.

That matchmaking Katie had gone too far this time! Cooper gave Anna one more look, for he was too angry to speak, then stepped outside.

He had to remember Anna wasn't all that different from Katherine. Needing his help. Seeking his protection. Looking up at him with doe-soft eyes so that he would lay down his life—or his honor—to protect her, no matter the cost. He would not make that mistake again.

"Anna, come on!" Katie's voice lifted in the spring-scented wind, loud enough to make people turn on the other side of the street and look.

"Katie," he admonished, grabbing her arm and pulling her close. "This is going too far and you know it. You can't go against my wishes like this."

"What?" Innocent eyes. Yes, they really were innocent. With Katie, he had to be certain.

"You know very well Mrs. Bauer is not going to be your mother. I thought we agreed no more—"

"But you promised!" Dismayed, she stepped back. Then remembering, lowered her voice. "Papa, you promised. You said you would fix everything. Make it all right.''

He closed his eyes. Counted to ten. ''Yes, that's what I said. But I never said I would marry the woman.''

''Nor should he,'' Anna's voice, firm but gentle, interrupted. Thank goodness she was on his side. ''I know you wrote the letters, Katie.''

''You do?'' Eyes so filled with surprise.

He turned and looked down at her exhaustion-lined face. His skin buzzed with her nearness. He breathed in the scent of the dust-filled air and Anna, soft as roses, intoxicating as fine whiskey.

''I appreciate this, Anna.'' He caught her gaze, as soft as a featherlight touch to his face. ''I didn't know how to bring up the subject.''

''I understand.'' And she did. It shone clear and honest in her eyes. She didn't blame him. She didn't blame Katie.

The guilt and his burden doubled. A harridan or a manipulator he could send out of town on the next stage without a thought. But Anna… She posed a real problem.

Yep, she was as appealing as the lemony shafts of sunshine burnishing her gold curls. She breezed by him, and the hair stood up on his arms. She smiled at him and his heart stopped beating.

Maisie hid behind his legs, her grip on his knees keeping him from stepping forward. Bob's mouth opened, those beady intelligent eyes focused on Anna's dress.

''Come pet her,'' Katie coaxed. ''She don't bite.''

''She bites,'' Maisie whispered.

Anna offered her slender hand to the defiant pony.

Big teeth closed around Anna's ruffled hem and tugged.

"Watch out." He dove forward, breaking away from Maisie to rescue Anna.

But already she'd waved away the concern with a flick of her slender hand. "No harm done." Her smile shone as true as the North Star. "Bob looks like a great pony."

Approval shone in Katie's eyes. That mischievous, certain-to-be-punished Katie. "My Bob's the fastest pony in town. Everyone says so. And she jumps really high, too."

"Jumps?" he boomed. When did she start jumping that pony? She was under express orders not to—

"She?" Anna interrupted his thoughts and then laughed with such honest gentleness he forgot to be angry. "You named a girl pony, Bob?"

"She's tough like me. I didn't want her to have no frilly name." Katie patted Bob's brown side with pride before springing up onto the pony's back.

"Being tough must be pretty important."

The breeze lifted through Anna's hair, shivering around her shoulders. So delicious, so inviting, he had to fist his hands. What would it feel like to wind his fingers through those gold locks, to feel that rich silk against his skin? The touch of a woman, her gentleness in his life—he hadn't realized he'd missed such things.

Until now.

Maisie stepped out and tugged at Anna's skirt. "Katie said you are gonna be my mama. That's fine by me."

Anna's face crumpled, charmed and touched. Cooper rushed forward to grab his littlest girl, but Anna was already kneeling before her, laying a hand to that child-soft face. "Dear heart, what a sweet wish."

"Ain't no wish." Maisie set her chin, a world of adoration lighting her berry-blue eyes.

Cooper scooped the child up into his arms as anger tore through his chest. He hadn't realized how much his daughters might need a woman's love in their lives. He hadn't wanted to see it, but he'd only lied to himself.

Dreading the talk to come, Cooper set his Maisie up on Bob's back, snug behind Katie. As Maisie wrapped her slim arms around her sister's waist, he warned his eldest to ride slowly, no racing and no jumping with Maisie astride. Katie's earnest promise reassured him.

"No need to worry, Cooper." Her gaze didn't move from the sight of the little girls astride Bob, trotting down the street, Maisie bouncing off-rhythm to the pony's stride. "I won't hold you to your daughter's proposal."

His throat went dry. He couldn't look at her. "That's mighty generous of you. Considering all you risked and almost lost in coming here."

"Not generous. Practical." Her voice lowered, soft as a setting sun. "I need to check on my daughter."

"Wait." He caught her hand and looked down into eyes so sad it hurt him. "For what it's worth, I'm sorry for this confusion. Katie just wants a mother so badly. I'm not excusing her behavior, but I want to make things right. Let me help you."

"No help is necessary." Her eyes shone. "You're a good man for offering."

A good man? No, he was just trying to find his way, like anyone else.

She strode away, light and simple, without accusation or guilt.

But he felt guilty enough. He took off after her. "I fully intend to help you. Considering my daughter brought you here, I could do no less."

"Put that billfold away." Anna's blue eyes rounded.

"I ought to compensate you for your passage here." He thumbed through the bills.

"*No.*"

"But Anna, you lost all your money in the robbery."

"That doesn't mean—" Her eyes sparkled, as if she were holding back tears. Pride lifted her chin, kept her spine straight. "I'm not the kind of woman you can pay off."

"I didn't mean—"

"I don't need your money." She spun, skirts swishing, marching quickly back into the doctor's clinic.

He bolted through the door after her. "If you won't take my money, then let me pay for a room in the hotel."

She turned and lifted her gaze to his. "I can't let you do that. I don't belong here, not really. And I won't accept your help."

"Not even for your daughter?"

"I can take care of her." Pride. It had been a long time since he'd seen much to admire in a woman. He had to admire Anna Bauer, had to admit she was a different sort of woman than Katherine, even if she now needed help. "I don't need your pity, Cooper. Or charity."

"Soon she'll be able to leave the clinic. She'll need a place to stay."

Anna wrung her hands, slender fingers that were red and rough, callused-looking, hands that had known hard work. "Let me worry about providing for my daughter. She isn't your responsibility, Cooper."

"I pulled her from the wreckage. I held her in my arms throughout that ride back to town. I handed her over to the doctor. I feel a duty. I want to know she's going to be well, that men like Corinthos can't destroy every life they touch."

She lifted her face. Tears glistened there, clear as morning dew. "We're alive today because of your bravery, your strength. You're a wonderful man."

"Aw, you don't know the real me." He blushed, uncomfortable with the admiration clear like morning in her eyes. "Cantankerous. Bossy. No woman will have me."

"So Katie said." A single tear slid down her pale cheek. "Don't you worry about me, Cooper. I can take care of myself."

"Against a man like Corinthos?"

"Against any man." That stubborn chin hiked higher.

He stepped forward and watched the pupils in her eyes darken, watched her take in a steady breath, lifting the curve of her small, firm bosom. Real fear shadowed her face, and he wondered why. Maybe she was remembering the stage robbery, he reasoned. She had a right to be afraid. Corinthos wasn't known for leaving his witnesses alive.

Or maybe she was as wary of entanglements as he was.

A clatter and a horse's squealing whinny erupted on the street outside. Cooper pulled back the drapes at the front window. He saw the tanner's unruly horse shying at a dust devil, nothing more. Still, he had to be on guard with Corinthos alive and gunning for him.

"I gotta go." He knuckled back his hat, avoiding Anna's compelling gaze, wishing he could do more for her. Wishing he could lift her burdens from those slim shoulders.

"You don't have to do this on your own, Anna. You're here because of my daughter, and I'll make sure you have a hotel room, money, a ticket out of here. Whatever you want."

She looked away and said nothing.

He didn't know what to think about this woman, so determined to stand on her own. He'd never met anyone like her before. So independent, so proud for a woman. And while he didn't understand, he did admire her for it.

As he strode out onto the street, Anna's rose scent lingered sweet in his mind.

"Mrs. Bauer is one pretty woman," Tucker commented from across the room.

Cooper looked up from his paperwork. Judging by the tone of his brother's voice, he was up to something. "Are you thinking of courting her?"

"Heck, no. I'm not ready to settle down."

"You're twenty-five."

"Far too young to be chained down by wedding vows." Tucker winked. "But you, on the other hand big brother, are a prime candidate for marriage. Yep, Anna Bauer is just about right for you. Got that cute little daughter. Would fit right in with your girls. Even survived an introduction with Bob, or so I heard."

"Enough." Cooper uncrossed his ankles and put both feet firmly on the floor. "Has Katie been confiding in you? Or conspiring with you?"

"Now don't go blaming everything on that wildcat

girl of yours.'' Tucker laughed, clearly amused. ''I know what's going on here. And I have to say I'm proud of you, realizing how much your girls need a mother and going about finding one. If I knew a woman that nice and pretty would answer a newspaper advertisement, I would have placed one myself years ago.''

''I thought you didn't want to settle down.''

''I don't. I meant I'd look for a wife for you, big brother.'' Tucker laughed. ''It's just what you need.''

''That's the very last thing I need.'' Something had to be done about the misimpression of those darn letters. Cooper stopped at Tucker's desk. ''Hand them over.''

''I thought I'd save them for their rightful owner. Mrs. Bauer's letters are personal.''

''They are also none of your business.'' Cooper waited while Tucker dug them out of his bottom drawer, damaged and torn, but clearly Katie's undisciplined scrawl marked those envelopes. How the girl engineered something like this was beyond him.

''There you go.'' Tucker leaned back in his chair, the devil laughing in his eyes. ''I trust you'll see your betrothed gets them.''

Betrothed? Cooper swallowed his anger. He'd taken just about enough teasing from both siblings. He stuffed the letters in his shirt pocket. ''This is a matter between me and the lady, Tucker. I don't want you breathing a word of this to anyone.''

''You can count on me.'' Tucker tried not to laugh. ''So, are you going to marry her?''

''You know the answer to that question.'' He didn't believe in love. He'd made that mistake before and he'd lost more than his wife, more than his heart. She'd destroyed his honor, the very code by which he lived.

No one was going to do that to him again. Especially now that he had children. He felt badly for Anna Bauer, soft as morning light and good-humored to match. She'd risked so much because she needed a husband. Now, she would not accept his help. Anna, so kind and caring, deserved more than a few broken promises. What should he do? Cooper stared out the window, at a loss.

A pop of distant gunfire brought him to attention. He saw no trouble on the street, but he sensed it. Corinthos was back to break his gang member out of jail.

The deputies were all headed home, their day's work done. "Tucker, alert the men. We've got trouble."

"Mama?"

"Yes, pumpkin." She turned, her mounting troubles momentarily forgotten. All that mattered was the tiny little girl hardly more than a wrinkle beneath the thick blankets, her button face so pale.

"Thirsty."

"Let me get you some water." Her hand shook as she grabbed hold of the pitcher's porcelain handle. Splashes plopped in the basin, kerplunked on the table. But she held the tin cup steady so her child could drink. Just three small sips, then Mandy sank back into the pillows, already asleep.

Anna hated seeing her daughter injured, in so much pain. Far too weak to enjoy the captivating stories in Katie's book. Or to play in the sunshine. Or sing songs. Frustration knotted in her throat. No one had the right to hurt a child like this. No one. She well knew the world wasn't fair, but a child should know compassion and safety, not fear and injury at the hands of a ruthless stranger.

The door flew open with a bang. Anna spun around. Fear lodged in her throat when she recognized the cold-eyed man standing in the threshold, revolvers aimed straight at her chest.

Chapter Five

Cooper's blood quickened at the sight of the familiar horse and rider sneaking into the alley behind the doctor's clinic. Corinthos. He'd spotted the outlaw creeping along the back streets, trying to stay hidden while the rest of his gang attacked the jail. Cooper could guess what the outlaw was up to. It was said the bandit never left a man behind. Or a witness.

The back door clicked open and Cooper caught sight of a second man, a cohort of Corinthos, running from the direction of the jail. Cooper ducked a split second before gunfire popped and two bullets thunked into the board not a foot away. With revolvers in hand, loaded and cocked, he fired. The outlaw fell, hand to his side. Looked like another patient for the doc.

Cooper threw open the back door, checking the corridor. Empty.

"Sheriff." The doc's voice rang out from the closest patient room. "What—"

"There's an injured man out in the street."

"I'll get right to him." The doc reached for his black bag sitting on a low table. "I didn't hear anyone come in. Is something wrong?"

"Just stay out of the line of fire." Cooper waited, listened. He heard the tap of footsteps around the corner, then a low threatening voice.

"Yep, you're the one from the robbery. The one who gave me trouble. I just had to be sure." That familiar voice, muffled by the wooden walls. "There's a few women in this place. I'd hate to take out the wrong one."

Cooper heard a female voice answer the outlaw, too low to be heard. Anna's voice, soft as spring.

His pulse stalled. He should have made certain the clinic was more heavily guarded. He could use the backup right now. Then again, with the jail under attack, every deputy was needed there.

A faint scuffle sounded on his left. Cooper spun, guns steady, to see Thomas Campbell, one of the men injured in the stage robbery. The cowboy was already out of bed and armed. Wearing only a pair of drawers, Campbell padded unsteadily forward.

"Corinthos wants the woman," he spoke low. "She made him angry or something. Do you need a gun at your back?"

"You bet I do." He knew Campbell's reputation with a gun, a rough-and-tumble foreman on a local ranch who knew what he was doing. Grim, Cooper thought of what lay ahead. He didn't want to make one mistake. It could cost Anna Bauer her life. "I'll go first."

"You're the boss."

Cooper padded down the hall, careful not to make any noise. When he was close enough, he leaned against the wall. He couldn't see Corinthos through the opened door, but he could hear his voice, then Anna's. She was begging him to leave her child behind.

Then Corinthos stepped into the threshold, pushing Anna in front of him. Surprise flashed in the outlaw's cold eyes when he stepped into the hall and spotted Cooper. Cooper aimed, but he didn't dare fire. The outlaw had Anna clutched against his chest like a shield.

"Let the woman go, Corinthos."

"Looks like the local sheriff thinks he can stop me. But will you sacrifice the woman?"

"I want her unharmed."

The outlaw lifted one revolver, pointing it to Anna's side. Rage shot though Cooper's chest. With no time to think, he squeezed the trigger. Sparks flamed, and thunder echoed in the narrow hallway. The bullet lodged into Corinthos' bandaged shoulder. The Colt flew from the outlaw's gloved hand and clattered to the floor.

Victory. Cooper grabbed Anna and spun her to safety into Campbell's arms. Now it was just the two of them, him and Corinthos.

"You are a gutsy devil, Braddock." A cold brown gaze battered his. "But this ain't over yet."

"I say your outlaw days are through." Cooper rolled the man around and clipped handcuffs at his wrists. "I've got a jail cell with your name on it."

Corinthos swore in pain as Cooper pulled him around by one arm, the injured one.

Finally. Cooper had the man who'd been terrorizing this town and stealing from its hardworking citizens. Now they could have peace. Satisfied, he pushed Corinthos against the wall.

"Outside." Cooper gave the outlaw a push. The big man stumbled past Anna. She leaned against the wall, white-faced and looking scared. Her large blue eyes were as round as saucers. He wanted to reach out and comfort her, hold her against his chest and assure her she was safe.

Now where did that urge come from? Wherever it was, he'd better squelch it.

"It will be all right." He tried to reassure her with as much of a smile as he could manage, as he would for any civilian in this town. "I kept my word. I might make a bad marriage prospect, but I'm not a bad sheriff."

"And I'm grateful to you yet again. That man tried to take Mandy, too."

Cooper studied the red welt marking her right cheek. Her hair had come down from its knot, disheveled and tousled. Her dress was ripped at the collar. Besides the fear, gratefulness shimmered in her luminous eyes, so round with an emotion he didn't want to think about. He didn't want to think that Tucker was right in how Anna Bauer felt about him.

"Is your girl hurt?"

She shook her head and tangled curls brushed along the soft angles of her face. "I hit him with the pitcher. I'm afraid I can't afford to replace it." Tears sparkled as they slid down her cheeks, tears of relief, he guessed. She must have been so afraid.

Not many women would go up against a man as dangerous as Corinthos. Awed by her strength and courage, Cooper lowered his eyes and gave the outlaw another hard shove. "Anna, I'll be back. Wait for me."

She said nothing. He ordered Campbell back to bed, he was bleeding fresh into his bandage. Cooper holstered one revolver and kept one hand at Corinthos' neck.

"Be smart, Braddock," Corinthos snarled. "You arrest me, and my men will bust me out. You'll have more gunfire on your streets.''

''That's the chance I'll take.'' He managed to push open the back door. He gave the outlaw a shove. ''I intend to put an end to your career in these parts, Corinthos.''

''Then I truly pity you. You don't know how wrong you are.''

A man had to stand for something, and Cooper had learned the hard way the kind of man he wanted to be. But not everyone thought as he did, not every sheriff used his badge to protect. Anna's soft face flashed into his mind, and the terror and pain Corinthos had caused the innocent widow and her child. Yes, he was glad he would be able to put this outlaw away.

''Drop it right there,'' a gravely voice ordered. Two armed men slid out from the shadows in the alley.

''I got your leader.'' Cooper pressed the Colt hard into Corinthos' neck. He was sorry his men were all at the jail, fighting to keep hold of the injured outlaw. Gunfire sounded from the direction of the jailhouse.

''Hold on,'' Corinthos said to his men. ''Braddock will see reason. I know he will. Our good sheriff doesn't have much of a choice.''

Cooper saw it all in an instant. Three men, revolvers drawn, all facing him. He couldn't outshoot all of them, no matter how good he was with a gun. But how could he let Corinthos go?

''Think about those girls of yours.'' Another voice, this time from behind.

Cooper felt the cold press of a pistol at his neck.

''Think about how much they need a father. One wrong move, Braddock, and they'll be orphans.''

Cold fury flooded his chest. Cooper clamped his jaw

shut. Sweat broke out along his brow. The last thing he intended to do was leave his daughters without a father, and yet his honor smarted. Allowing these outlaws to simply ride away went against everything he believed in.

"Maybe now you will listen to my proposition, Braddock." Corinthos gestured with his handcuffed wrists at one of his men.

"I'm not interested in anything you have to say." Cooper bit back the sour taste in his mouth. He would not be bribed, would not compromise his honor. It made him sick even to think about it. The man they called Dusty took the jangling ring from his belt and Cooper couldn't stop him.

"Listen up, Braddock. Your very existence depends on it." The cuffs clicked apart and Corinthos tossed them into the dust at his feet. "You know what I want."

"I'm no criminal." Sheer anger pounded through him.

"Braddock, you can just turn the other cheek and let us do our work. It's as simple as that. Think about how much your girls need you alive and well. As I see it, you don't have much of an alternative."

What these men proposed speared black fury through his chest, hot and all-consuming. The revolver bit into his neck, reminding him he could do nothing but watch as Corinthos turned to face him, a victorious sneer bright in those cold eyes.

There would be another time to prove his honor.

"This here's for the slug you put in me, Braddock." The outlaw's fist hit Cooper square in the face.

"You made yourself a bigger hero today, brother," Tucker commented from the corner where the doc's nurse was tending the gash along his ribs.

"What do you mean?" Cooper winced as the doc stitched the cut over his eye. "Corinthos got away."

"You saved your bride." Tucker's grin broadened. "Even got punched protecting her. Already the entire town is abuzz about it. You're such a hero."

"They ought to be furious at me because I couldn't bring down the gang." The doc tipped Cooper's head back to get a good look at his swelling eye. He swallowed a groan of pain.

"They'd rather know more about your wedding. At least now, since the gold shipment we hauled up the cliff is locked away in the bank's vault and Corinthos' man is still safe in our jail." Tucker chuckled. "You almost fooled me with your act, blaming Katie for writing those letters. That's priceless. And just like you. You're too tough to admit you have a softer side."

"I have no softer side." Cooper's face flamed. "Am I gonna live, Doc?"

"Looks like it." He turned to wash his hands in a basin. "But you're going to have quite a shiner."

"Black eyes don't bother me."

"Makes his softer side less obvious," Tucker teased.

"Watch it. I can still whoop you." Cooper stood with another groan. Bringing down Corinthos and his gang might be harder on the body than he thought. "Thanks for patching me up, doc. You know where to send the bill."

"What about your bride's?" The doc reached for a towel. "Frankly, I would treat her little girl whether she had the money or not. But you'll soon be her husband and responsible for her bills."

Cooper kept Tucker silent with a glare, knowing

darn well his brother would have something to add. "Yes, doc. Anna's medical bills are my responsibility." He could do no less. But this notion of marriage, well, time would prove that false soon enough. But if the doc thought they were to be married, who else thought so, too?

His guts twisted. His daughters might need a mother, but nothing was that simple. He couldn't just marry a stranger to make unruly Katie and shy little Maisie secure. They had love. They had him.

The unmistakable sound of muffled crying came from the room within. He hesitated, uncertain if he should enter. When he peered through the threshold, he saw Anna at her daughter's bedside, her back to him, her shoulders hunched forward. Her slim body shook with the power of her tears. Alarm speared though him. Something was wrong with the little girl.

"Anna?" He stepped into the room, then hesitated. She must not have heard him, she was crying so hard. Lord, he felt sorry for her situation. Nothing could be more defeating than watching your child like this, not knowing if she would live or die.

He laid his hand on her shoulder, and she jumped at his touch. How he ached to fold her in his arms and protect her, hold her tight against his chest. The urge was stronger than before, stronger than he'd ever known.

But he held back. He couldn't let himself care for her. Maybe as a citizen to protect, but nothing more. Not the way a man cares for a woman. And never the way a husband cares for a wife.

"What's wrong with Mandy?" He asked the question, although he knew he wouldn't like the answer. The child lay so still in that bed asleep. She had been gravely injured, the doctor had said. There were no guarantees.

"She sat up and asked for a cookie. A cookie. I know now she's truly going to be all right." Anna's lush bottom lip trembled. More lustrous tears glistened in her eyes. "I hadn't dared hope. I mean, I prayed, I wished, but it almost seemed too much to ask."

"Corinthos didn't upset her, then." Cooper was relieved. The little girl was fast asleep. Her breathing came soft and deep, in a more natural rhythm. Even he could see the change.

Anna's eyes glistened up at him, her soft face shadowed with fatigue. "She woke up and was afraid, but that was all. No real harm done. Not like you."

Her hand came up and brushed near his bruised cheekbone. Her soft touch made his skin tingle. "Aw, it's just a black eye."

She pulled her hand back. "The men got away. I saw them through the window riding off toward the mountains."

"Against my will." As long as the Corinthos gang rode this country, his town and the people in it weren't safe. Especially Anna.

"Will he come back?" Not fear for herself, but for her daughter. He heard that loud and clear in her voice.

His throat filled. "Definitely."

She tucked her bottom lip between her teeth, her forehead crinkling, her face paling. "I hate being this afraid. Now that Mandy's recovering, I want to keep her that way."

"You have my word of honor, Anna. I'll protect her with my life."

"Because it's your job, right?" She brushed a tentative finger against the upper point of his silver badge.

"Because she needs it." He knew he shouldn't do it, but he held out his hand anyway. Anna wouldn't misunderstand. She was a fair and sensible woman. She seemed to accept their situation, that he wasn't looking for a wife. "Should we go find Mandy that cookie?"

"I don't have a penny on me."

"My treat."

Pride flickered in her eyes. Then she took a breath. "I'll accept for Mandy's sake. There's something else."

"Name it."

"I'm going to take you up on your offer. When Corinthos walked into this room, I realized I need you, Cooper. I need your help."

"Help, now that's something I can do. This sheriff is at your disposal."

Anna placed her small palm against his. Her heat scorched his skin, kicked through his blood.

Cooper had forgotten how nice it was to walk beside a woman, to simply hold her hand.

With every step they took through town, Anna wondered how much she could confide in Cooper Braddock. With muscles bulging beneath his cotton shirt, he looked able to defeat any outlaw. That he'd pledged to help her gave her some comfort.

But trusting a man wasn't something she could do. Cooper might be heroic, but he was still a stranger to her. If she'd learned anything in her life, she knew better than to lean on a man. She might accept Cooper's initial help in securing a place to stay, but that was all. She had always made her own way. She had her pride.

"We aren't going to the bakery?" Anna asked as

they strolled past the shop. The wonderful smell of baked bread scented the air outside the shop's front door.

"Mrs. Potts makes the best cookies in town. Besides, my sister left a satchel of clothes she wanted to give you, and I forgot to bring it this morning."

"She doesn't even know me."

"She thinks you're going to be her sister-in-law, regardless of what I say." He lifted one brawny shoulder in a lopsided shrug. "Maybe you can do me a favor."

"If I can." She would do nearly anything to repay Cooper his kindness.

"Then you tell her the truth about the letters. She refuses to listen to me."

Anna laughed. Walking beside him down the tree-lined street made her feel bright and happy. Then she heard a small rustling in a giant fir above. A bird, maybe. Then a limb shifted and a little girl's face peered out from amid the soft green needles.

"Papa." A loud whisper.

Cooper tipped back his head. "Maisie, are you still up in that tree?"

"Yep." More whispers. "Is Anna my mama yet?"

"Remember what I said about that?"

"She's not my mama."

Anna held her breath as the golden-haired slip of a girl deftly climbed from one limb to another. It was such a dangerous height and far to fall. But Cooper appeared unconcerned, as if little girls climbed trees every day.

"Did you eat all those molasses cookies?" Cooper lifted his daughter from the lowest bough.

"I tried, but Mrs. Potts stopped me." Maisie's pink gingham dress snapped in the breeze. She hit the ground skipping. "I'm sorry you ain't my mama, Anna."

"Me, too." Her breath lodged in her throat and she couldn't say one more word.

Sunlight slanted through the pine needles, dusting Cooper with a dappled, golden glow. He knelt to rescue a bedraggled stuffed bunny from the grass. His dark shirt, halfway unbuttoned, gaped just enough for her to see the muscled expanse of his chest. The sight of his suntanned skin left her reeling. What a man.

He's not yours, Anna. She couldn't let her daydreams become confused with reality. He might be a hero, but he didn't belong to her. It was in his eyes, in the distance he kept between them, slight, but unmistakable. He didn't want to like her.

Well, she didn't want to like him. She wasn't about to pine after a man who didn't want her. Even if he was heroic and brave, strong and noble.

His voice, rich as evening, rumbled over her. "Come inside, Anna. Maisie and Harry Bunny will keep us company."

"Give me Harry Bunny, Papa. Please!" Maisie jumped up, and Cooper snatched the stuffed animal just out of her reach. She giggled, then he handed it to her with a smile warm enough to melt the earth beneath their feet. The little girl shone at the attention, hugging the worn pink bunny tight in her arms.

Maisie looked up, noticed Anna watching her and ducked behind her father's knees.

Cooper started up a set of wooden steps. Anna saw the house for the first time, made of neat logs and chinking. Paned glass windows viewed the street and the trees, and a generous porch caught the shade. It looked so snug and cozy, the perfect home for a little girl to grow up in. A house straight out of Anna's dreams.

"You're awfully quiet." Cooper's voice vibrated across her skin, luring her like a fish to a fly.

Hooked and fighting it, Anna focused hard on the path beneath her feet. "It's been an eventful day. You have a beautiful place here."

"Did you think I lived in a cave?"

A teasing light lit his eyes. Maybe he was afraid she was wishing after his home, thinking she wanted what Katie had offered.

Well, this home had never been hers, and never would be. She had taken a big risk answering that handwritten proposal, and it hadn't worked out, that was all.

"A cave would suit you better, Mr. Tough Sheriff."

"Now, only if you could convince my family I'm tough." He chuckled, rich and deep. "They keep saying I have a softer side."

"I haven't seen the slightest evidence of that." She could tease, too. In truth, Cooper was the gentlest man she'd ever seen. So tender with his daughters, his love for them honest and heart-deep.

She followed him into the beautiful log house and froze stock-still in the middle of the parlor. "Now this is what I'd expect in a cave."

He quirked a brow. "Sure, it's a little messy."

"Messy?" Anna breathed in the sight. The polished wood floors, the honeyed-wood walls, the gray stone fireplace in the center of the parlor were nothing short of perfect. Children's toys littered the floor—a small cowboy hat, a set of blocks, a toy train. "It's a great home for little girls."

"Is that you, Sheriff?" a woman's sharp voice broke the stillness.

"Yes, Mrs. Potts." Cooper gestured toward the kitchen. Anna followed him into a sunny, spacious room with a cookstove and worktable along one wall, a big bright window and eating table along the other.

A plump woman turned from the stove and wiped her hands on her ruffled apron. "I suppose you'll be wanting coffee. And I just finished with the dinner dishes."

Cooper planted both hands on his hips, emphasizing the width of his capable shoulders. "Don't worry about the dishes. I'll do them."

"If you ask me, that older girl of yours ought to start being responsible for some chores around here. That's what she needs. Discipline." The hired woman banged the coffeepot on the stove, the harsh thunk echoing in the pleasant room.

Anna jumped. Goodness, was the housekeeper always this sour? No wonder poor Katie had taken desperate measures to find a mother. Then Cooper leaned close and gave her a secretive wink.

"I have to be forgiving of Mrs. Potts's attitude," he whispered, so close his breath felt hot against the side of her face and she could smell the man and pine scent of him. "Every other available housekeeper in this county refuses to work for me."

"Katie's become notorious?"

"Exactly." His whispered word tickled her ear.

Sizzles streaked down her spine. Anna took a steadying breath and willed her body to stop reacting.

The skipping tap of a little girl's shoes announced Maisie's approach from upstairs. She was still dragging her worn pink bunny. "Gotta get some more cookies. Me and Harry Bunny are hungry."

Cooper pulled out a chair at the blue-clothed table. "The plate on this table is half empty. It was full when I left for work this morning."

"I've been sneakin' 'em." Maisie's whispered confession wasn't guilty at all.

Charmed, Anna could not hide her smile. How she wanted to see mischief shining like that in her own daughter's eyes.

A crisp white curtain blew in with the breezes from the opened window, snapping sassily behind him. "Come sit down with us," he invited, his eyes sparkling with humor. "If you dare."

"I'm willing to live dangerously." Anna crossed the room, trying to avoid the muttering Mrs. Potts in the center of the kitchen. A kettle banged against the iron stove. Cooper's gaze met hers, and his lopsided smile drew her closer. He was like no man she'd ever known before.

"Maisie! I see that." Cooper turned around, half laughing.

Caught, the little sprite shoved an entire molasses cookie into her mouth while still holding another in her free hand. "Oops."

Mrs. Potts harrumphed from the stove.

"I really like cookies," Maisie confessed with a full mouth.

Anna's heart crumbled. Katie had wanted a mother who could make cookies. Cookies her little sister loved.

"Sit down here and eat like a civilized little girl," Cooper admonished warmly. "Not like some wild animal."

"I ain't wild, Papa." Maisie happily settled into a chair and bit into her second cookie. "But maybe I wanna be an animal and have feathers."

"You can see how rough my life is." Cooper rolled his eyes in feigned agony. "I don't know how I survive it."

"You look like you're suffering." Anna took the chair he offered, his nearness filling her head, leaving her weak.

Mrs. Potts banged the coffeepot down on a trivet, then marched away, mumbling something about manners.

A whinny outside the kitchen was Anna's first clue before the ruffled curtains parted and a pony's nose poked through the open window. A wide tongue lashed out and big yellow teeth snatched a cookie from the stacked plate.

"Katie," Cooper scolded.

"Hi, Bob." Maisie gave the brown-and-white pony an affectionate pat.

Bob nickered in answer before withdrawing her head and trotting away from the house.

Anna wrapped her arms around her middle and giggled. All the trauma of the past few days, the worries over whether Mandy would live or die, her penniless state, Dalton Jennings' threat, Corinthos coming after her, it all faded as wave after wave of pure merriment washed through her.

"That's it!" Mrs. Potts slammed shut the oven door. Rage lined her unpleasant face. "I've taken about all I can stand of this…this nonsense."

Anna felt the joy ebb away. She heard the scrape of Cooper's chair as he stood and wondered if she should leave.

"Mrs. Potts. Please. I know my girls are—"

"Wild, undisciplined heathens! Wanting to be animals. Hanging from trees. Ponies eating from the table." She tore off her apron with quick, angry movements.

"Perhaps another raise would make a difference?" Cooper reached for his billfold.

"No money is worth this headache day in and day out. Pay me my wages. I'm through putting up with your undisciplined children."

The back door flew open with a bang. Katie burst into the room, braids halfway unraveled, her boy's clothes rumpled and dirt streaked. "Hi, Anna. I've been out riding with Davy Muldune."

"He has a pony, too," Maisie added.

"Mrs. Potts, is there any way I can convince you to change your mind?" Cooper approached the disgruntled woman, showing her the color of his money.

"Now I know why you're a good sheriff. Because wild criminals couldn't be as difficult to manage as your own children." Mrs. Potts grabbed the bills from his fist before he finished counting. "I can only hope a mother's presence will have a positive effect on your Katie's unruly disposition."

Anna opened her mouth in protest. Far too many people believed she and Cooper were—

"Here's my advice, Mrs. Bauer. If you are not a religious woman, take up praying." Mrs. Potts stormed out and slammed the door angrily.

"Boy, and I didn't even try to run her off today," Katie confessed.

Chapter Six

"Mrs. Potts wasn't a happy employee," Cooper admitted with a slow, lopsided grin.

Anna watched Katie look at her out of the corner of her eyes, then don an innocent face. "Papa, what are we gonna do now without Mrs. Potts? Who's gonna take care of us?"

"Who's gonna make me cookies?" Worry wrinkled Maisie's brow.

Anna knew where Katie was headed, and she wasn't going to sit around and let Cooper think she would go along with the child's plans. "It's time for me to go."

"Wait! Papa, Anna can bake cookies." Katie's grin dazzled. "I bet even better than mean ole Mrs. Potts."

Cooper's jaw tightened. "You forget that's why we have Aunt Laura."

Anna met his gaze. She could only interpret that tight thin line along his mouth as disapproval, as if he feared she would take advantage of their situation. She headed for the door. "Thanks for the entertainment. I really needed a good laugh."

"Wait, Anna!"

"Yes, wait." Cooper's rum-rich voice called her

back. "You forgot something. I don't want to get a reputation as a man who breaks cookie promises."

Humor twinkled in his dark eyes. Mandy did need those cookies to feel better. She was an injured little girl.

"Thank you. Cookie promises are important to keep." Embarrassment wrapped around her heart, but it was gratefulness that lingered, that eased the ache in her chest. Not many men would keep their promises to someone else's little girl. "Mandy will be very happy."

"I try to keep all females happy." He wrapped more than a half dozen cookies in a big blue napkin, folding it neatly. "I'm truly glad your daughter is going to be all right."

"Me, too." Katie gave the back door a good shove. Anna watched the door slam shut and wondered if the child was trying to keep her from leaving.

"Can you make molasses cookies?" Maisie asked shyly, with cookie crumbs circling her mouth.

"I—" Oh, no. She could see what those little girls wanted. Not just a replacement for Mrs. Potts, but someone to fill in as a mother. Anna took a step toward the door. "I truly need to go. The doctor was kind enough to stay with Mandy, but I can't impose on him for too long."

"The doc is a good man. He won't mind taking care of a little girl for just a few minutes longer, I'll wager." He held out one hand. "Come sit down with me. At least now we can talk without Mrs. Potts grumbling at everything we say."

His grin sparkled. Those twin dimples carved deep into his cheeks, and the flash of his white teeth kept her spellbound. Somehow she managed to tear her gaze away but she kept looking back in quick snatches as she sat down. He handed her the napkin full of cookies, and she had to remind herself Cooper Braddock was not hers to dream of, to wish for.

"Girls, go play for a bit. I need to speak to Anna."

"She ain't gonna be my mama, Katie," Maisie whispered as she snatched two more cookies. "Papa said."

"I know." Katie put an arm around her sister's shoulders. Together they clomped out the door and down the back steps.

Anna reached for the pot of rich-smelling coffee and began filling the two cups already on the table, sparkling clean in the sunshine.

Cooper wrapped his fingers around the back of his chair, standing behind it, his dark gaze forceful, shrinking the distance between them. She could see in him the loving, laughing father. And she could see something else: a little mischief, darkness and a lot of loneliness. She knew about loneliness, too.

"Some say Corinthos always gets rid of anyone who can identify him."

She choked on her coffee. "Get rid of?"

He nodded slowly. "I think he'll be back."

She remained silent, chin bowed. Cooper could not see enough of her eyes to read her emotions. But those flyaway curls framing her face made her look like everything missing in his life. Everything he could not have. "You're safe as long as you're in my town, Anna. I just thought you ought to know."

"I already do." She lifted her gaze to his. It wasn't guilt as he expected but belief that glimmered there, brilliant as sunlight on water, an unshakable notion that he would protect her.

"The doc told me your Mandy is nearly ready to leave his care. I'll talk to Janet, get you that homey hotel room I promised. You stay as long as you need."

"Most men would be running from a woman seeking matrimony." She laid her hand on his arm, a sweet and light touch that shot arrows of heat down his spine. "This isn't easy for me. I'm used to providing for Mandy on my own."

"It must be hard being a widow with a small child." He well knew what it was like to be alone, raising daughters.

"Yes." She bowed her chin. "It hasn't been easy. But that doesn't mean I intend to rely on you. As soon as I am able to leave Mandy, I will find a job."

"But I have an obligation to help you."

"Mandy is my responsibility." Her chin shot up. Her eyes snapped with barely veiled anger. He'd said the wrong thing, that's for sure.

Cooper took a breath, wished he knew what to do. He couldn't hire her to replace Mrs. Potts. That would be unfair to the girls. They already were disappointed Anna wasn't going to be their mother. What would it do to them with her in the house all day, cooking their meals, caring for them, baking cookies and petting ponies?

"Don't worry." So soft, her voice. And such compelling, luminous eyes. What was it about her that tugged at him? "I don't want Mrs. Potts' job. I don't want you to think—"

"No one in their right mind would want Mrs. Potts' job. Or at least, no one I can coax with promises of very generous pay."

"There has to be someone you can hire. Katie hasn't frightened away *every* woman in Montana Territory."

"Every woman."

"Why haven't you married? Not that it's any of my business, it's just that, well, a man like you doesn't have to settle for a mail-order bride. You can pick and choose."

"Not with two daughters to raise." Cooper could just see them through the window, riding Bob around the backyard. Maisie was clinging to Katie's waist with both hands, nearly sliding off Bob's rump with each rocking step. "A stepmother is not the same as a mother."

"Surely that's not true."

He stared down at his hands, callused from years of holding a gun and riding a horse. "I know from hard experience. Laura and Tucker's mother married my father when I was six. She took care of us, but I was always a reminder to her that my father had loved another woman. I was never truly her son. It wasn't easy. I don't want that for my girls."

"But who wouldn't adore Katie and Maisie?"

She looked so sincere. He remembered how she'd laughed when Bob stole the cookie from the table, how charmed she'd been by Maisie's cookie thefts. And he laughed, the warm rich rumble reaching all the way down to his toes. "There isn't a woman I've come across who wants to take on Katie, at least not without a big stick."

"Well, not without a big stick." Her eyes sparkled with emotion, but with humor, too.

She was joking. Cooper tried to smile and failed for the ache she made in his heart. "How many women would unconditionally love a difficult child?"

"Difficult?" Anna tilted her head to peer out the window, causing those fairy-light wisps framing her face to shimmer. "Why, look how well she rides her pony. See how she takes care of her sister? No matter how many times Maisie slips off Bob's rump, Katie never lets her fall."

"Katie has a good heart. She just causes so much trouble."

"She's just a tomboy. There's nothing too troublesome about that. Besides, she'll probably grow out of it."

"I'd hate to wait until I'm old and gray before she starts acting the way a female should."

"And exactly how should a female act?"

"Not like that." He lifted long tapered fingers to gesture toward the window.

Outside, beneath the dappled sunlight from overhead maples, Katie let out a war whoop and Maisie shouted, "Katie, if we're Indians, I'm needin' some feathers."

Somehow, she would find a way to thank him, to thank them all for showing her something she didn't even know existed. This happy brightness of love and family.

She stood. "Thank you for the cookies and coffee. I have my own daughter to look after."

"I'll let you know about the room like I promised." He stood, too. How handsome he was with the light slanting through the window, backlit by the honeyed-wood walls.

Her throat filled, and she couldn't speak. She headed out the door. And even when she felt his gaze, solid and steady, watching her cross his yard and go down the street, she could not look back.

The clinic was quiet. Anna still remembered the low bark of Corinthos' voice, still felt his hand on her arm, just above the bullet wound. A bruise in the shape of a hand was all that remained, but she felt bruised deeper still.

Montana Territory was a rough place, sometimes dangerous. Towns had been carved out not by women and families come to find homes, but by those looking for gold. Times were changing, thanks to men like Cooper. But not all men were like him.

When she'd first heard footsteps in Mandy's room, she'd thought it was Dalton. But when she turned around, it was only another outlaw among many in this untamed territory. She shivered and walked faster. She was glad a man like Cooper was watching over her daughter.

"She's been asleep the whole time." The doc kept his voice low, turning from the bedside chair. He stood, his smile pleasant. "I'm so pleased with her recovery."

"It's all thanks to you." Anna clutched the bundle in her hand, the cookies from Cooper's kitchen.

"I'm not totally responsible." The doc blushed just the same. "I'll be in my office if you need me."

The doctor left, and she was alone with her child. Lemony sunshine slatted through the edge of the closed curtains, casting enough light to read by. Anna set the cookies on the bedside table, then reached for the borrowed book of fairy tales. The images of Katie and Maisie this afternoon, eating cookies and riding Bob, filled her with hope.

She wanted Mandy well again. Every child deserved to play without worries, without pain.

"Mama?"

"Why, look at you. You're awake." Anna brushed wispy gold curls from her daughter's eyes. "Guess what I brought you?"

"Somethin' good?" So much hope in that small voice.

"Cookies. Just like you wanted." Anna reached for the bundle and unwrapped it carefully. Molasses sweetened the air.

"Oh, boy." Mandy actually smiled, her eyes bright.

Anna lifted the top cookie from the stack and held one out to the girl. "They smell real good. I bet they taste good, too."

"Thank you, Mama." Mandy grabbed it and took a huge bite, despite her pain and injury. "It's real good."

Nothing mattered but Mandy and the eager light in her eyes when she reached for a second cookie.

"Papa, I can't find Harry Bunny." Maisie dashed out of her bedroom, pink nightgown flapping.

"I have him." Cooper handed her the well-loved animal on his way down the hall. Tucking in his girls at night was one of his favorite jobs as a father.

Maisie's hands clasped around poor Harry's ears. "Thanks, Papa. I don't sleep so good without my bunny."

She dashed off to bed, bare feet slapping the floor.

The room was full of little-girl sweetness—pink curtains and a tea party set scattered on the braid rug, adventure dime novels piled on the nightstand.

Katie jumped into bed and ducked beneath the covers. "I've been thinkin', Papa."

"That's a scary prospect."

"Aw, Papa. Stop teasin'." Katie shook her head, clearly disappointed. "This is serious."

He sat down on the foot of the bed. "Serious thinking. That's different."

"Mrs. Potts quit. And I didn't have nothin' to do with that today. But what about tomorrow?"

Boy, how innocent the girl looked. Cooper wasn't one bit fooled. "What about tomorrow?"

"Who's gonna make pancakes the way Maisie likes 'em?"

"Yeah," Maisie piped up. "I don't like 'em burned. And they gotta be faces or I don't eat 'em."

Cooper could see he had a big problem. "Aunt Laura knows how to make pancakes the way you like them, Maisie."

"Yeah, but Anna could do it, too." Katie tilted her head to one side, gaining enthusiasm. "I bet she could do everything Mrs. Potts did. She's got her own little girl. She'd know exactly how to take care of Maisie."

"I need takin' care of," Maisie agreed.

"Anna could be our housekeeper from now on." Katie shifted beneath the covers. "Papa, I would be extra good if she comes."

"Does that mean you'll sit quietly and embroider all day?"

"Keep dreamin', Papa."

It only confirmed what he already suspected. His eldest daughter would never become skilled in the needle arts. "You girls know Anna isn't going to be a part of our lives, as a housekeeper or anything else."

"But Papa, if you like her enough, maybe you could change your mind." Katie sounded so hopeful.

"I wouldn't count on it, precious." Cooper hated seeing her disappointment. "Trust me on this."

"It ain't gonna be easy." Maisie cuddled up on her pillow, Harry Bunny clutched tight.

"But can we still be friends with her?"

"Friends is fine. Just no matchmaking schemes, you hear me?"

"Oh, Papa." Katie rolled her eyes and pulled the comforter over her head.

Cooper left the room with good-night wishes, but he felt troubled. His girls were young and imaginative. They saw their friends' mothers, saw what they were missing in their lives. He understood the allure of a fantasy mother, a pretty and kind woman to bake cookies, ride a pony, tuck little girls into bed. Thinking of Anna, he knew exactly why his daughters wanted her for a mother.

If only it were that simple.

Anna's back ached from spending the night in the chair at Mandy's side. Morning felt cool. When she pulled open the curtains, gray light met her. Clouds blanketed the sky, casting a drab pallor to the land. Rain was on the way.

"Breakfast." The doctor's wife, Betty Mason, swept into the room. The silvered tray she carried rattled with each step. "My, but your Mandy looks better today. Look at that healthy color in her cheeks."

Mandy still slept, her breathing more regular, more relaxed. She still had to recover according to the doctor, but she was making good progress.

Betty set the tray on the small corner table. "I brought enough for two. I'm still holding out hope your little one will find her appetite."

"Me, too." Anna's heart warmed at the woman's kindness. "You do too much, bringing me meals like this."

"Nonsense. It's the least I can do for the woman

who's come to marry our sheriff.'' Betty waved away
Anna's concern with a gentle hand.

"I'm not—"

"Have you met Laura yet?"

"No, but I—"

"You'll just love her. She has been helping raise up
Cooper's girls for years, so I hear. The whole family
moved to town just last year when old Joc retired. It's
been a welcome change, I tell you. Let me know if you
need anything else. I'll be just upstairs.'' Barely paus-
ing for breath, Betty waved a cheerful goodbye and
hurried from the room.

Goodness. Anna stared at the empty doorway. She
didn't know how so many people knew she had come
to marry Cooper. It was amazing how easily misun-
derstandings occurred. Well, thank goodness only the
doctor and his wife thought she was Cooper's bride.
She would talk to them this morning so there would
be no more confusion.

"Are you Mrs. Bauer?'' A petite woman filled the
doorway.

Anna set Mandy's empty glass of milk on the nightstand, the breakfast dish empty in her hand. "Yes."

"I thought I had the correct room. The doctor just
pointed me down the hall without much direction.''
The middle-aged woman with bright red hair, streaked
with gray, lay a hand on her chest. "My, is that your
hurt little girl? Katie and Maisie told me all about her.
How she was hurt during the stage robbery.''

"Yes. She's recovering.'' Anna stood, setting the
plate and flatware aside. "You know Katie and
Maisie?"

"Who doesn't? My, with the older girl racing that

daredevil pony around town. Legends are built on that girl. I'm Janet Briggs. I own the hotel on Maple Street—the red building with the white trim and shutters. Sheriff Braddock asked me to set up a room for you.''

Why wasn't she surprised? Cooper must have checked with the doctor. Mandy was well enough to leave the clinic today. It was something, Cooper being a man of his word. She'd never known such an honorable man. ''Then he also told you I intend to pay—''

''It's only until the wedding, of course.'' Janet Briggs chuckled, patting down her unruly tangle of hair. ''How exciting. Our handsome sheriff bringing you here as his bride. Everyone is talking about it. I'll have my husband come help you move. What's a good time? Say before noon? That way you can get your little girl settled before she has her lunch.''

''But Mrs. Briggs, I'm not going to marry Mr. Braddock.''

''What? Well, of course it's the last thing you can think about with your little girl so injured. Heard tell she almost died, poor thing. No, that just shows you're a woman of good sense, waiting to talk of wedding plans after the child is strong.''

Mrs. Briggs patted her hand. ''Now, there'll be no more talk of Cooper. What's important is your girl. She'll be comfortable at my hotel, I can tell you.''

Anna hoped no one else in this town thought she was Cooper's bride.

Mr. Briggs cradled Mandy in his big brawny arms as he stepped out into the sunshine. ''I hope the trouble with Corinthos doesn't shadow your opinion of our town. Flint Creek is a nice little place to live.''

"It's certainly very friendly here." Anna thought of the doctor and his wife, providing a change of clothes and meals and concern. Of Janet making room for her in their hotel. And now Mr. Briggs was carrying her daughter down the boardwalk, careful not to jostle her, as if she were spun glass.

"It's the sheriff. He's done more for this town than anyone in the past year." Mr. Briggs waited for a horse and wagon to pass before crossing the dusty street. "Braddock has really helped clean up this town. Chased away all kinds of trouble bothering our families and our businesses. He's a good man, that Cooper Braddock."

"Briggs, are you spreading rumors about me again?" Cooper's voice, low and rumbling, shivered down her spine.

Anna looked up at that dimpled, lopsided grin. Today Cooper wore a blue shirt that made his eyes even darker and tan trousers that hugged his muscular thighs. Her breath caught, and she had to act unaffected. "I'm afraid Mr. Briggs has been telling me terrible things about you."

"Terrible things?" Those dimples deepened.

"Very bad things."

"The worst of which is how he rescued this little girl." Briggs stepped through a doorway and into a dark-wooded lobby. "No one around here thinks he's a hero."

"Neither do I," Anna teased.

Cooper shook his head, swept off his hat. "A man can't get any respect around here."

"Respect is one thing you have plenty of, Sheriff." Briggs stopped his joking. "Mrs. Bauer, I'm going to take your little one straight up to her room. You stay here and talk with your groom, if you need to.''

''My groom?'' Anna felt her jaw slacken. ''But I told Mrs. Briggs I'm not going to marry—''

The man was already out of earshot, climbing the polished stairs, a sleeping Mandy lax in his strong hold.

Embarrassed, Anna tried to face Cooper but couldn't quite look him in the eye. ''I tried to make it clear when Janet stopped by the clinic this morning.''

She couldn't let him think she was helping perpetuate such inappropriate rumors.

''I know. Don't worry. I'll talk to Janet and clear everything up.'' He towered over her, a solid presence. No blame sounded in his voice or shone in eyes as deep as dreams. ''I just wanted to make sure you were safely settled in. Is there anything I can do?''

''You've already done it. I want you to know I won't be dependent on your help for very long. As soon as Mandy's a bit stronger, I intend to find work.''

''I don't doubt your integrity, Anna.'' He always sounded as if he wished he could. ''You've proven yourself an honest woman. Besides, my girls like you. I keep hoping you'll inspire Katie to take up a needle and thread. I have something for you.''

It was only then that she noticed the satchel in his hand. His big, well-shaped fingers curled around the leather grip. He handed it to her. ''What is it?''

''I meant to give it to you the other day, when you came to my house for cookies. But you left so suddenly I didn't have the chance. My sister found some things to give you. Since you'd lost everything in the wreck.''

How kind his voice, how big his heart. Anna ached inside. He made her feel so much. That wasn't a good thing. Not at all.

"When I get time, I want to thank her for these clothes. I can't believe how kind everyone has been to me."

"I'll tell her." Cooper leaned close enough so that she could see the glimmer of warmth in his eyes, feel the solid presence of him. "Take care of yourself, Anna. I'll be watching over you and your daughter. You're safe."

"I never doubted it." And she didn't. Even when he strode away, through the etched glass doors and from her sight, she felt safe. Protected. She'd never known such a feeling before.

Chapter Seven

Anna pushed open the door and couldn't believe her eyes. Why, the room was cozy from the ceiling all the way to the braided rugs. A fire blazed in a small stone hearth. She set the satchel on the floor.

Mandy lay in the dark wood four-poster bed, plumped up by pillows. Mr. Briggs fetched an extra blanket from the matching wardrobe against the far wall.

"Just thought I'd get her settled, ma'am." He gave the wool blanket a flick, and it landed neatly over Mandy's sleeping form. "With Janet and me having nine children of our own, and now with twelve grandchildren, why I'm a mite experienced with tucking in wee ones."

Warmth filled her. She should have known Cooper would have picked a good place for them to live, looked after by such caring innkeepers. "I owe you, Mr. Briggs."

"Ah, pshaw, it ain't nothin' at all." Briggs sighed just looking at Mandy sleeping. "I can't tell you how much I miss having little ones around. The problem with children is that they grow up and leave you. But you just can't stop missing them.''

She thought a tear glimmered in his eye. ''Well, let me hurry down and check with the missus. Janet wanted to send up a good hearty dinner right away. The little one needs to eat if she's going to be up and running about.''

''Thank you, Mr. Briggs.''

He waved goodbye, hiding his face as he left. Like a home. That's what this place was. The small touches—a crocheted scarf on the carved bureau and matching doilies on the nightstand and beneath the kerosene lamps. The handmade rugs on the floor, the samplers and framed quilt blocks brightening the walls. Fond of needlework, Anna vowed to examine them after she'd checked on Mandy.

But when she knelt down by the bed, her daughter was sleeping soundly, not disturbed by the move and the change in surroundings. So Anna hesitated from brushing stray curls from Mandy's face.

A light knock sounded on the door. Mr. Briggs with the promised meal, no doubt. She crossed the room. But when she turned the knob and pulled, she was surprised to see a woman she didn't know standing in the hallway.

''You must be Anna.'' Her voice was warm with friendship. Her dark eyes sparkled in such a familiar way, Anna felt as if she knew the woman at once. ''I'm Laura Braddock, Cooper's sister.''

''Laura.'' Anna stepped back, but kept her voice low. ''Please come in. I want to thank you for sending the satchel of clothes. I haven't even gotten a chance to open it yet.''

''Well, maybe now can be a good time.'' Laura

swept into the room with a swish of fine skirts. Only then did she notice someone attached to the back of Laura's dress. A little face gazed up at her.

"Hello there, Maisie."

The child blushed at the attention. She released her hold on Laura's skirt and hugged her pink bunny hard with her freed hand. "We come to see your hurt little girl."

"She's sleeping right now." Anna couldn't help the way she felt for Cooper's girls, for little Maisie especially. She'd treasured those letters about the little girl she had hoped would be her stepdaughter and Mandy's bigger sister. Lost hopes now, but she could not turn off her heart. "Did you want to come sit down?"

Maisie nodded, a serious bob of her head. Anna held out her hand. She led the child to the rocking chair by the fire, close to the bed. Maisie held her bunny tight as she crawled up onto the cushioned seat.

"I love Harry Bunny," she whispered. "Katie says it makes me a baby, but she ain't always right."

"Every girl needs a bunny to hold on to," Anna agreed, wishing Mandy's bear hadn't been left behind in the wrecked stage.

"I sure hope these things fit." Laura kept her voice to a whisper, but a friendly whisper.

Anna turned to see that she'd already opened the satchel and was unfolding a beautiful cotton dress. Folds of sky-blue fluttered when Laura shook it, chasing out a few wrinkles. Lace edged the collar, a bow decorated the waist, and more lace trimmed the hem. "It's simply beautiful," she breathed.

"It was always a little small in the bodice and I hate wearing a tight corset just to fit into it." Laura blushed. "I've gained a little weight. Larry keeps taking me out to eat. I think it's Janet's huckleberry torte. I tell you, she cooks the best cake in this town."

Anna couldn't believe it when Laura reached down into the satchel and withdrew an equally nice dress. This one was lemon-yellow with flecks of leaves, and pink and blue rosebuds. There was a pink gingham with a matching straw bonnet. And a blue calico, sprigged with darker blue flowers, accented with buttons and satin. "Laura, I can't possibly accept these. Why, they are like new."

"And all a little too tight, believe me." Those friendly eyes sparkled with kindness. "I have plenty. It isn't right that you've lost nearly everything. You need help, and since we're going to be sisters-in-law, then it's the least I can do. Welcome to the family, Anna."

Laura wrapped her in the warmest, sweetest hug. Tears burned in Anna's eyes, ached in her throat. Hugging Laura reminded her of how much she missed her own sister. How she worried about her, about them all.

"There, now that we're properly acquainted, you let me look after your little one so you can take a break."

"I really can't." How horrible she felt. Laura was so nice and had extended her such a welcome. "We aren't going to be sisters-in-law."

"It's not the time to think of such things with your little girl hurt." Laura touched Anna's hand. "I can't imagine how afraid for her you must have been."

"It's better now that she's healing." Anna looked down. This was what she'd missed, sisterly understanding. She had to be careful or she would be thinking of Laura as a sister too, when in fact there would never be that kind of bond.

Laura's touch was light, but infinitely caring. "You

look exhausted. You've been with her for a while now? You get outside, take a walk, do a little shopping. There must be something you and Mandy need, something I didn't think of. Oh, a hairbrush. I should have thought of personal effects. My mind has been all a-jumble ever since I started planning this wedding.''

''When are you getting married?''

''Soon as I can.'' Laura radiated happiness. ''I'll tell you all about that later. Right now, do what you need to do. I'll stay right here until you return.''

''I couldn't impose. Truly, Laura. Cooper and I are not going to marry.''

''Of course not.'' Laura's eyes glittered with humor. ''Now, I swear to care for Mandy as if she were one of my own beloved nieces. You go talk to Janet and take care of what business you need to. Go on. Take some time for yourself. Taking care of a child is hard work.''

Anna's throat tightened. ''Well, I do need to run to the store.''

A rustle of sheets interrupted. Mandy was awake, her big blue gaze focused on Maisie in the nearby chair.

Maisie hopped down from the rocker, bunny tight in both arms. ''You got hurt, huh?''

A solemn nod.

''I fell outta my tree once and got a great big splint on my arm.'' Maisie held up her left wrist. ''It was this one. It done hurt lots.''

Mandy nodded again. ''I done hurt, too.''

''But you don't gotta bunny.'' Maisie's brow wrinkled with honest concern.

''I dunno where my bear is.'' Mandy's eyes teared up, but she didn't cry. ''I lost him.''

''Then you'd better take Harry Bunny.'' Maisie

thrust the worn stuffed animal into Mandy's chest. "Cuz you got lots of hurts."

Two little arms, one wearing a splint, one without, wrapped around that bunny and held on. "I'm lots better now."

Anna couldn't speak. With her unselfish act, Maisie had made their world a more hopeful place.

Mr. Briggs returned with a dinner tray, enough for Laura and Maisie, too. While Mandy napped, Anna tried on the dresses. It was determined they were three inches too long and an inch too large around the middle. Laura practically pushed her out of the room to go pick up some needles and thread.

Anna felt the first drops of rain as she crossed the street. They felt wonderful, refreshing. Droplets plopped to the earth and she didn't hurry. It was nice to be outside. Nice to stretch her legs, work the kinks out of her back. She hated leaving Mandy, but she did need a break. Just a few moments to herself. How thoughtful of Laura to give her what she needed. How on earth could she ever repay the Braddock family for their kindness?

The stove in the Flint Creek Mercantile had been lit to chase away the dampness in the air. Fire crackled as Anna closed the heavy glass door behind her.

A pleasant-faced woman looked up from the nearby counter. "That's a cold rain out there, isn't it?"

"Yes." Anna realized her hair was wet. She should have thought and grabbed her bonnet.

"You must be the young widow new to town." The lady stepped out from behind the counter. "Goodness, I heard all about your little one. She must be doing better."

"Yes, thank heavens. I'm surprised you would even know about it."

"News travels fast in this small town, I tell you. What are you looking for, dear? I'd be happy to help."

"I was hoping you would let me set up an account." Anna prepared herself for a rejection, but she had to ask. "I was robbed up on the mountain pass—"

"I heard. Sorry thing, that." The store owner clucked. "Happens all the time in these parts. Of course I'll start an account for you. Your name is as good as gold. You just tell me what you want."

"I am looking for a new hairbrush and a few ribbons."

"For your little girl?"

Anna nodded.

"Right this way. I keep a nice selection, not like the general store over on the other side of Main. No, I think a customer deserves a selection." The woman breezed to a stop in front of neat shelves. "Right here. If you need anything else, just holler. My name's Leslie McDonald."

Anna picked out two small hairbrushes, a few ribbons for Mandy, and then began looking around. She found toothbrushes and toothpowder, then went in search of needles and thread. When she found the sewing section, she came to a complete stop. Colorful calicos and sensible ginghams and bolts of every color beckoned her closer. Such a nice selection.

Then it came to her. A handmade gift would only be a small token of thanks when weighed against all the Braddock family had done for her. But it was something she *could* do. Anna began planning which colors to use, her heart almost happy.

* * *

"Met your pretty new bride today, Cooper." Leslie McDonald greeted from behind her counter.

"She's not my bride, Mrs. McDonald."

"Of course not." The clerk clucked at him. "Well, Mrs. Bauer is as nice as can be. No wonder Katie was so excited about her when she came in here today to check the mail."

"My daughter was here?" Suddenly Cooper realized exactly how Katie had managed to place an advertisement for a mother and collect all that correspondence. "I have something to send out."

"Another advertisement?" Leslie clucked, obviously gathering up gossip. "I don't blame you for not sending this one with Katie. Don't you know she'd pretend to lose it. Are you looking for another housekeeper?"

"I take it you heard about Mrs. Potts."

"Mabel Potts told everyone. A pony eating from the table." Leslie's face sparkled with mirth. "I'll post that letter for you right away, sheriff. The stage comes through this afternoon."

"I know. Thanks, Mrs. McDonald." He tipped his hat, not wanting to say more.

Maybe someone nice would answer his advertisement this time. But not someone looking for a husband.

He stepped back out in the rain.

"That's yummy, Mama." Mandy opened her mouth for another bite of Janet's huckleberry torte.

Anna cut another small bite with the fork, then fed it to her child. Mandy chewed happily. Her appetite was stronger this evening. A very good sign.

She read from Katie's storybook until Mandy was asleep. And then she brought out her purchases and spread the cloth out on the small table. She would start her quilt block from the center. She chose the light tan calico, made a sketch on an old newspaper Janet Briggs had given her. When she was pleased with the pattern, she placed it over the fabric, pinned it, then cut. Hours slid away as she worked.

Mandy slept safe and sound, recovering well from her injuries. A fire snapped in the hearth, rain tapped at the window, a clock ticked on the mantel. They were snug here in this comfortable room.

Yes, there was much to be thankful for.

The night was a miserable one. Rain thundered from the sky, falling like angry gray bullets. Cooper was soaked clear through to his skin, but at least they'd seen the stage safe to the top of the pass, where his jurisdiction as sheriff ended. There had been no sign of Corinthos or his gang tonight.

The town was dark, mostly asleep at this hour. Only a few windows glowed with lamplight. As the deputies accompanying him rode in different directions, heading home, only Tucker stayed by his side.

"You have to be worrying over pretty Mrs. Bauer, right, big brother?"

"Corinthos has been known to kill witnesses to his crimes. Like a lot of outlaws in these parts."

"Montana isn't the most civilized of territories, that's for sure." Tucker reined in his mount at the livery. "I'll volunteer for the night duty. Barstow can't guard Anna all day and all night."

"I was going to take the night shift."

"Don't worry about it. A bridegroom needs his rest." Tucker dismounted. "I'll guard your fiancée."

"She's not my fiancée." Cooper swung to the

ground. His joints ached from the cold and long hours in the saddle. "I'm not a bridegroom and I don't need rest."

"Of course you're not." Tucker knocked off the rain collecting on his hat brim. "You're too tough for romance."

"Damn right I am."

"Go home, big brother. Make sure my nieces are tucked in for the night."

He wasn't going to argue. Cooper headed home, knowing he could trust his brother to keep watch over Anna. As he headed down Maple Street, he saw lamplight in an upstairs window of the hotel. He thought of her, thought of how nice it had felt when he'd held her hand.

No doubt about it, he was lonely. Sure, he watched couples in town, noticed those who looked happy and those who did not. Wondered what made a marriage last, what made love stay. He didn't know.

His house was quiet. Laura was asleep on the sofa, the fire nothing but embers in the hearth. He knelt beside her. Yep, she was out for the night. With care, he gathered her in his arms and carried her upstairs.

He laid her down on his bed and covered her with the afghan on the back of the chair. He would take the couch for the night. His sister, who had survived taking care of Katie and Maisie for a whole day, ought to at least sleep in a bed. Tomorrow she would need her energy.

The thought of his girls warmed him, chased away the cold deep inside. He pushed open their bedroom door. Shadows filled the room. Rain sluiced down the dark window, drummed on the roof overhead.

Maisie stirred. "Papa, is that you?"

"Guilty as charged." He crossed the room, nearly tripping on the tea party set scattered on the rug. "You're supposed to be asleep."

"I'm tryin'." She sighed heavily.

"Where's Harry Bunny? You can't sleep without him."

"I done gave him away." Maisie rolled over on her side to face him. "Laura and me saw Anna today. Her hurt little girl ain't gonna be my sister either, huh?"

"No, she isn't."

"She can keep Harry Bunny anyway. I'm all grown up. I don't need him no more."

"You gave your bunny to Mandy?"

"Yep."

"That was a good thing you did, Maisie." Cooper's chest filled. "I know I'm not as good as Harry Bunny, but I can give you a hug so you can go to sleep."

"Aw, Papa. You're better than my bunny."

"Why's that?"

"Cuz you still got your hair. Harry's bald."

So Cooper was laughing when he took his littlest girl in his arms and gave her a good-night hug.

"My, your little girl is improving." Janet Briggs looked down at Mandy in obvious fondness. "Look at her. Soon she'll be running just like a child should."

"Thanks to your good cooking." Anna squinted against the afternoon sun. "It's good of you to let her play in your yard."

"This is where my children played when they were young." Janet stopped her sweeping, mopped her brow. "Oh, what fun we had when they were small. This yard behind the inn is fenced and safe, not up against the street like the front. Just right for a child to run around in and work off some of her energy.''

''I have to talk to you about the hotel bill. We've been here a while. I owe you some money. I can't let you think—''

''Why, the sheriff is paying for your stay.''

''That's what I have to talk to you about. Cooper is going above the call of duty making sure Mandy is taken care of, but she's better now. I can start worrying about other things, like paying for the roof over our heads, finding a job.''

''Goodness, you have such a sense of independence, don't you?''

''Mrs. Briggs, I know—''

''Janet. Call me Janet,'' the pleasant woman invited.

''I know you are under the mistaken impression that Cooper and I are getting married. But we aren't.''

''You've changed your mind?''

''Well, no. You see—''

''Goodness, this is terrible news. Does Laura know you've canceled your plans to marry her brother?''

''I—I never actually had them to cancel in the first place,'' Anna stammered. Heavens, telling the truth never used to be so difficult.

''You're not going to marry Cooper?''

''No, I'm not.''

''Hmm.'' Janet studied her, forehead crinkled, mouth pursed. ''You wouldn't happen to be looking for work, would you?''

''Are you still short-handed?''

''You come down to the kitchen tomorrow morning, if your little one is still doing well. You can keep an eye on her and work at the same time. It will be no trouble at all.''

"Thank you, Mrs. Briggs." She never expected such an opportunity, such a good solution to her problems. "Come on, Mandy. We have an errand to run."

The little girl ambled over to her, adorable in her strawberry dress and matching bonnet handed down from Maisie. Mandy's blond curls shimmered in the sun and when she looked up, her eyes were bright. "We goin' to see Maisie now?"

"Yes, we are." Anna took her little girl's hand. "Thanks again, Janet."

The innkeeper gave the back porch a sweep with her broom. "Don't you give up on our sheriff now, you hear?"

Chapter Eight

Cooper strolled in his front door that evening with great expectations. Mrs. Beasely had started just that morning, answering the advertisement he'd placed in the local paper. She'd been working on a ranch in the outlying area and had never heard of Katie Braddock. She took the job he offered her, claiming to be the best cook in Flint Creek County.

"Papa, Papa, come quick!" Maisie launched herself across the floor. Desperate fingers gripped his own. "Katie's in real big trouble."

"What did she do this time?" He had extracted a vow from his oldest daughter to behave. Laura had to prepare for her wedding. She couldn't spend all day doing housework and cooking for them.

He stepped over the play tea party in progress on his parlor floor and headed straight to the kitchen. He heard a loud angry voice, then the sharp rise of a very familiar one. He burst into the room. "What is going on here?"

"You have an undisciplined daughter, that's what." A red-faced woman turned to face him, caught in the act of taking a wooden spoon from the drawer. "When

I tell that girl to do a chore for me, I expect her to do it.''

"But I'm paying you to do all the chores around here, Mrs. Beasely." Cooper tamped down his anger, although the sight of Katie's face, pinched, her eyes filled with stubborn tears, made him nearly lose control.

"That's what's wrong with the girl. No discipline." A vein in the severe woman's temple stood out, pulsing with her anger. "Do you know what I had to put up with today?"

"No, but I have some idea." He shot a warning look at his daughter.

"Your littlest one ran around like a wild thing all morning. Then she spilled apple juice all over the floor trying to make a doll drink from a cup."

"Maybe I should have been more clear when I hired you. I expect my girls to play. They are children."

"Children ought to be treated like little adults, with responsibilities and punishments. Why, look at this one. She brought a snake in the house—"

"Not on purpose." Katie's chin went up; she was telling the truth. "I forgot it was in my pocket."

"It leaped out from beneath the table and flicked its tongue at me. Scared me half to death. Reptiles in the kitchen. And that pony. It tried to bite me."

"It was just a rough first day, but why don't we—"

"A rough first day?" Mrs. Beasely tossed the wooden spoon to the floor. It struck with a deafening clatter. "I've cooked on cattle drives, chased off every rough cowboy who thought he could push me around or worse. I have raised ten of my own children. But I tell you what, Mr. Braddock, I've never had such a miserable time trying to manage your daughters. I quit.''

"But Mrs. Beasely—''

"You can send my wages to my address." The woman grabbed her coat from the wall peg and stormed off.

"Can't we talk about this?'' Cooper didn't like Mrs. Beasely, but housekeepers in this part of the country were damn hard to find. "I could pay you more."

"An entire shipment of gold wouldn't be worth it." The woman charged through the room, heading for the front door. She nearly tripped over the tea party. "Goodbye and good riddance."

"Oh!'' He dashed into the parlor in time to see Anna dart aside as Mrs. Beasely barreled out the front door.

"Bad time for a visit?'' she asked, a pinch to her brow. Was that a smile touching her lips? Was she laughing at his plight?

"It was a bad time." He watched the mean Mrs. Beasely retreat down the street. "But it's better now that she's gone. Come in."

"I don't want to interrupt your meal. I just wanted to drop by before Mandy was too tired."

Cooper didn't miss the sight of the little girl standing behind her mother, hands fisted tightly in Anna's skirts. She was a pretty thing, just like her mother.

"I'm still playin' tea party." Maisie bounced into the room. "Wanna play?''

Mandy nodded, released her mother's skirt and headed timidly toward the array of play enamelware spread out on the parlor floor.

He tried hard not to look at Anna. He watched the girls, looked out the window. But she drew his gaze. She looked rested, less worried. And so beautiful, he realized. The pink gingham dress suited her, brought out the rosy tint to her cheeks and the deep blue of her eyes. Her hair shone gold and true. When she smiled, he refused to admit to himself how much he liked the sight of her.

"I wanted to do something for you, because you have done so much for me." She bowed her head. Curls tumbled over her brow, hiding her eyes. "It isn't much, I know. How can it be? You saved my daughter's life. But I wanted to do something."

She lifted one slim hand. She held Katie's book and a bundle wrapped in plain brown paper.

"Anna! Anna!" Katie roared into the parlor, shoes drumming on the floor. Her tears were dried, but her eyes were still reddened. "I can't believe you're here."

"I brought you something." Anna's gaze arrowed to Katie, and the warmth of her gentle smile filled the room like sunlight, changing it from twilight to day.

"Goody. Can I open it, Papa?" Katie accepted the present and was all ready to tear into the paper.

And it was appropriate that she did so. Cooper kept his distance, glad for the girl eager to take what he couldn't. "Go ahead."

The sharp sound of tearing paper echoed in the room. "Oh, boy. It's Bob." Katie held up a fabric hanging done in fine needlework and different color calicos. "And all of us, Papa."

Maisie jumped up to see, abandoning her teapot full of imaginary tea. "Looky! There's my outlaw tree."

He cocked his head, took a look for himself. What he saw made him stumble, made the air whoosh out of his lungs. She'd cut pictures out of fabric, pine trees and a log cabin, grass and sky, two little girls, a sheriff and a pony, outlined them all in thread. It was their home, their front yard, his family.

"How did you do the pony?" Katie asked.

"I drew a picture first on newspaper to make a pattern, then I cut it out. See how I used dark thread for Bob's mane and tail?"

"And knots of thread for her eyes." Katie sounded excited. She sounded…interested in the needle arts.

Cooper could have fallen over backward.

Anna hadn't wanted to stay for supper, but she couldn't turn down Cooper when both Maisie and Katie started to plead. Mandy looked tired but happy, and was having such a fun time playing tea party with Maisie, it was easy to relent. Mandy hadn't been able to play in a long while.

"I'm surprised you're this good of a cook," Anna admitted over a bite of mashed potato.

"Papa is a great cook," Katie piped up. "Except he ain't never home on account on his havin' to work."

"Mrs. Beasely's roast was tasty." Cooper pushed back his plate. "Too bad she didn't have a better temper."

"She didn't like tea parties," Maisie piped up.

"Well, what kind of person doesn't?" Cooper pressed a kiss to his daughter's brow before he reached for her empty plate.

Anna stood to gather the plates, too. "You treated me to supper, so I will do the dishes."

"Nope. You're our guest." Cooper's hand shot out, his fingers curling around her wrist.

Heat snapped up her arm. "I want to help."

"I'll do the dishes." Katie announced.

"You?" Cooper appeared to nearly drop the plates

he carried in one capable hand. "Do you even know how?"

"I've watched lots of times. I'll run next door and get Laura to help."

"Good idea." Cooper couldn't believe his luck. First an interest in needlework and now this. "Maisie, go with your sister. I'm going to take Anna home."

"Me, too?" Mandy looked up, worry crinkling her brow.

"You, too." Cooper's voice knelled with such warmth.

Throughout the parting wishes and goodbyes, Anna kept gazing at Cooper. Kept noticing the little things, like the shadowy stubble on his jaw, the laugh lines around his eyes, the way a jaunty shock of dark hair cascaded over his forehead. He lifted Mandy into the wagon seat with care, then held out his hand to help Anna.

She didn't need his help. But she placed her palm against his anyway, just to feel the heat of his skin, just to be close enough to see him laugh when Katie and Maisie dashed down to the house next door.

"I couldn't help but notice that you lost another housekeeper," Anna commented after he released the brake.

The wagon rolled forward, drawn by his handsome palomino.

"One in a long, long list, believe me." He cocked his head just enough to look sideways at her. "Katie does drive a lot of them away on purpose. She was old enough to remember her mother leaving. Katherine walked out the door and left Katie crying all alone with baby Maisie. I found them in the dark when I came home from work."

Anna bit her lip, aching for Katie's past and for Cooper's. "A child can't easily overcome something like that. How hard it must be for her to trust another woman again. Especially a housekeeper who might not stay."

"That's right." Cooper pulled the wagon to a stop in front of the inn. "What you did for us, making that wall hanging. It made a difference. Thank you. I think you have given Katie a reason to take up needle and thread."

"To appliqué fabric ponies?"

"If Katie becomes accomplished in the needle arts, you will have my undying gratitude." His mouth drew up in that half-lopsided grin, the one she was coming to adore.

It was time to go, before she did something foolish like lean closer, ache to know how that sexy, curving mouth would feel kissing hers. Anna ducked her chin, hiding her face so Cooper couldn't guess her thoughts. "Good luck replacing Mrs. Beasely."

"Good luck to you, Anna." He hopped down and offered his help.

She handed him her daughter. Mandy had fallen asleep, and her head bobbed as he cradled her. Anna's feet touched the ground before he could reach up to help her.

"You let me know if you need anything, anything at all." In the thickening twilight, she could see the sincerity carved on his face.

How it beckoned to her. Anna shivered and tried not to let it show. She could never let him know how she felt.

Troubled, Cooper descended the stairs. Tonight his girls had talked excitedly of Anna. Again, Katie had made the suggestion that Anna could take Mrs. Beasely's place. His boots drummed on the floor as he stepped into the parlor.

"Something wrong, big brother?" Laura turned from the hearth, where she'd tossed a few sticks of wood on the flames. The fire snapped greedily. She brushed bits of bark and moss from her skirt.

"Nothing a good housekeeper can't fix."

"Or a wife."

Was that laughter in his sister's eyes? "Are you laughing at me?" he demanded.

"Never. Not at you." She hid her smile with a duck of her head. "I'm heading home. I have a long day ahead of me taking care of your girls."

Frustration swirled inside him. He shouldn't scold Laura for teasing him; where would he and the girls be without her? "You know how much I appreciate your stepping in—"

"I know," she interrupted, snagging her cloak from the coat tree by the front door. "Do me a favor, Cooper. Marry that nice woman you brought here. Don't worry about an appropriate engagement time, or anything else. It would be best for the girls."

Her hand touched his sleeve, the affection of a lifetime, warm and certain. His throat ached. Emotions jumbled down deep. "I've told you before. I'm not going to marry Anna. There was a misunderstanding—"

"I know. Janet Briggs told me."

"What did Janet Briggs tell you?"

"That you and Anna had a falling out of some kind."

"*What?*"

"I know, it's none of my business."

"I'll say. I can't believe this." He tugged open the door for his sister. "My personal life is nobody's business. Why is everyone speculating—"

"Because you're adorable, dear brother. And we all want you happy." Laura breezed through the door, all smiles. "You will fix whatever rift you've caused between Anna and you, right?"

"What rift?" He shook his head, closed the door as she swept out into the night. The last thing he needed was advice on how to handle his nonexistent engagement.

Well, as long as Laura believed there wasn't going to be a wedding, then that was fine by him. Cooper lifted the curtain in the dining room, waited until a lamp lit inside Laura's cottage. She was safely inside, so he returned to the parlor.

There it was, Anna's handiwork gracing the end wall. It was a fine job, he granted her that. And a thoughtful gift. It had delighted the girls. In truth, it had touched him, too. He studied the fine work, the happy little girls with real thread hair, tied in neat braids. Such delicate work.

Hell, he couldn't see himself remarrying. He'd believed in Katherine, in her affection, in her fidelity. Look how wrong he'd been. Her abandonment had hurt him, but it hurt Katie more.

Children were a big responsibility. Children were vulnerable. Even if he did admit he was lonely. He didn't want to share his life. He could not risk his daughters' hearts on another woman, on a stepmother who would never love them as a real mother might.

He watched the fire burn until there were only embers.

*   *   *

Anna squinted against the bright sunshine. It washed over her sweet and new. Spring was in the air, shown in the broad-leaved maples and aspens just unfurling their leaves. Mountain air and pollen warred with the scent of dust from the busy street.

This was the third day she'd been able to help Janet in the inn. As long as her serving girl was out with a fever, there was work to be had. Anna hoped she could have work for the remainder of the week. What she earned in tips gave her some cash to call her own, and Janet was taking her wages in trade against the mounting hotel bill.

"Mama?" Mandy tugged on Anna's skirt. "We gonna play tea party?"

"We're not seeing Maisie today." She stopped at the corner to wait for traffic. How much fun the little girls had, nights ago now, playing pretend tea party on the floor of the Braddocks' parlor. "We're going to the store to pick up fresh eggs for Mrs. Briggs."

"Candy, too?" So much hope in those eyes.

Anna thought of the coins in her skirt pocket. "Why not? We deserve a treat."

"We sure do." Mandy squeezed Harry Bunny tight.

When the last of the vehicles passed, a prospector's donkey and cart, Anna led her daughter across the street.

She felt watched. She looked up and saw a lawman, guns strapped to his hips. He strolled the street in the opposite direction. He lifted his hat, and she smiled.

One of Cooper's deputies. The streets here felt safe, unlike the ones back home. Montana was dangerous country. Ruthless men still ruled here, but towns like this, decent and filling with families, were thriving.

"Mama, I want lemon candy." Mandy had apparently been giving her candy choice some thought.

"Lemon sounds good." Maybe she would get a stick for herself. It had been a long time since she'd felt so hopeful. There had been no sign of Dalton Jennings. Nor any more threats from the man who'd nearly kidnapped her. And Janet said she was well pleased with her hard work.

She reached out to tug open the heavy glass door and saw a man standing nearly in her way. Rough-looking, his chaps and leather shirt were coated in several layers of dust and grime. He looked like a prospector, like dozens of men who came down from the hills to restock their supplies, cash in their gold and return to their claims. But a red bandanna hung at his neck, loosely knotted.

A red bandanna just like the one the robbers on the mountain pass wore. A puff of wind snapped her skirts and she stepped back. His cold, lethal glare laughed at her. Anna swept Mandy up into her arms and dashed down the walk. When she looked back, he was still standing there, that mocking half grin on his cruel face.

There had been a deputy walking Maple Street, but he wasn't there when she turned the corner. Shaking, she forced herself to calm down. The man wasn't following her. He hadn't tried to harm her.

"Mama. My candy." Sorrow laced those words.

"We just have to wait a few minutes. Then I promise we'll get you a nice big lemon stick."

Well, there was only one thing to do. Anna crossed the street. At the end of the block she pushed open the jailhouse door and walked into the sheriff's office.

"Why, if it isn't my two favorite ladies." Tucker hopped up from behind a paper-piled desk, his grin cocky and sure. "My handsome brother is questioning the prisoner. I'll get him for you."

"No, Tucker." Mandy was getting heavy, so she set the child down gently on both feet. "I mean, I don't need Cooper exactly. You could help me."

"Me?" Tucker laid a hand on his broad chest. "I'll do anything to help a pretty woman. What do you need?"

"I saw one of the robbers. He was outside the mercantile. He frightened me."

"Barstow is out walking the streets. He ought to have noticed a known criminal was in town." Tucker reached for his hat.

"He was dressed like a prospector."

"Where's Davidson?" Tucker brushed past her and stuck his head out the door. "I don't see him. Wait, there he is." The deputy shook his head, scattering dark locks across his collar, just the way Cooper might.

"Trouble?" There he was, standing in the threshold, shoulders set, looking like myth. "What trouble?"

His concerned gaze pinned her. He looked ferocious enough to frighten any outlaw. This was the man who had climbed down a cliff to rescue an injured child, who righted wrongs, made the world a little safer. Just looking at him made her chest fill with so many conflicting emotions.

"She saw one of Corinthos' men."

"Stay here." He grabbed his hat, then laid a gentle hand on her shoulder. Determination tensed his jaw, but he was all concern. "We'll keep you safe, Anna."

She already knew that. She turned to watch him go. Her heart pounded from his nearness. She felt breathless and light. What was she doing? She couldn't do this again, fall in love with a man she couldn't have. She'd made that mistake before.

But as she watched Cooper stride down the street, a man of power and right, her stomach flip-flopped.

She didn't want to need him. She shouldn't read anything more into his willingness to help her. He was the sheriff. It was his job. That's all she was to him.

The jailhouse door swung open with a squeak. Cooper strode inside, still squinting from the bright sun. He saw Anna rise from the chair by the window, expectation written on her soft face.

"Deputy Barstow spotted him and he took off. He had a horse tethered nearby. Barstow and Tucker are riding out after him, but he got a good head start." Cooper slung off his hat and avoided her gaze.

"What do you think he wanted?"

"Could be any number of things. We still have the gold they want locked up in the town bank. We've got one of their lead men locked up in my jail. And there's you."

"Me." She looked down. How pale she looked. He'd heard through Laura, who felt a duty to keep him informed about Anna, that she was serving in Janet's kitchen. Maybe she was working too hard.

"You can identify him. It's a tradition with a certain brand of outlaw not to leave witnesses alive."

"When I bought the ticket to come here, they told me there had been a lot of trouble. I thought it was worth the risk. I thought—" She looked down at her daughter, sitting on the polished floor, Maisie's old bunny, the fur worn away, clutched in her unsplinted hand.

"I've made sure my deputies have been keeping an eye on you."

"Guarding me?" She looked alarmed.

"Something like that. We just want to make sure Corinthos doesn't get a wild idea and try to hurt you."

"Why do you think I came here? To get away from men like that, not to find more." Tears stood in her eyes, but she sounded angry.

He took her hands in his. A jolt of heat arched down his arms, burned in his chest. "There are good guys here, believe it or not."

"I believe it."

How blue her eyes, how true her voice. The loneliness inside him felt less just being with her.

He dropped her hands and moved away. "I'll have one of my deputies accompany you back to the hotel."

"We need candy," Mandy spoke up.

"To the store, then." Cooper managed a smile before he turned away.

The jailhouse door squeaked open for the second time today. Cooper looked up from his paperwork, heart pounding. But when he saw Katie, braids unraveling and trousers stained with mud at the knees, he relaxed.

"I've come to kidnap you, Papa."

"Don't you know that's against the law?"

"Oh, Papa, it's just for a picnic. Maisie really wants you to come."

"Maisie, huh?" He wasn't fooled. "I've got a lot of paperwork here, tiger."

Twin lines etched along her brow. "Papa. We're all counting on you. It's important."

He could see that. The need in his daughter's eyes.

Oh, it wasn't easy being a single parent. He could be a father, but there was no way he could ever fill his daughter's ache for a mother. "If a picnic's important to you, then that's what I'll do."

"Thank you, Papa. You won't be sorry. Laura made you a lemon cake."

His favorite. "With that lemon frosting?"

"Come on, Papa." She took him by the hand and tugged, barely leaving him time to grab his hat. "We don't wanna be late."

For what, he didn't ask. He was afraid to know. He sensed a plot.

Chapter Nine

Lee Corinthos downed more whiskey. Pain speared through his shoulder with every breath he took. His left arm was damn near useless thanks to that white knight sheriff. And it was taking too damn long to heal.

Dusty broke into the cabin. "It took me nearly two hours to evade those lawmen. They're damn good trackers."

"You had better not have led them here." Corinthos took another swig, let the liquor burn down his throat. "Did you see Palmer?"

"Couldn't get close to the jail. Too many deputies guarding it. But I saw the woman. She's stayin' at that fancy hotel there in town. She spotted me, and the sheriff's men gave me a bit of a chase. I was faster."

"Yes, our fine Sheriff Braddock." Corinthos leaned back on his bed. "Seems he has a troubled past. He might bend a mite easier to bribery than we figured."

"That so?"

"I've been asking around. Seems down in Colorado, Braddock was in cahoots with Black Eyed Charlie."

"No kiddin'?" Dusty's eyes rounded.

"His wife was in on it and left him for Charlie."

Dusty shook his head. "How come he ain't in jail? Did he run?"

"Couldn't find enough evidence. But some say our Sheriff Braddock was friends with the judge, being he had saved the judge's daughter from being kidnapped by a rowdy band the year before. Braddock collected on that favor, don't you think otherwise. He's been proving himself on the right side of the law ever since."

"Is he playin' both sides?"

Corinthos winced against a flash of pain. "I intend to find out which way Braddock will go."

"Surprise." Laura stood up from the blanket near the south fork of Flint Creek, a gentle stream, with lush green grass surrounding it and tall cottonwoods. "We thought it would be fun to have Anna join us."

"Fun." Yeah, he knew a plot when he saw one. He took one look at Anna's face, the surprise wide in her eyes and knew she hadn't been expecting this.

"Katie." He looked down accusingly at his daughter.

Katie shrugged her shoulders. "Laura said you and Anna had a fight or something."

"Shh." Laura jogged up to him, lowering her voice, glancing over her shoulder at Anna still seated on the red plaid blanket. "This will give you a chance to mend things between you two."

"There's nothing to mend, Laura." This had gone too far. "There never was going to be a wedding."

"Sure, go ahead and deny it. Tucker's right. You just won't admit you need anyone at all. So go talk to Anna. I've got to fetch something from the wagon."

He took one look at Anna, beautiful in a blue dress. "I'll fetch whatever you need."

"No. You go to your Anna." Laura dashed off, leaving him frustrated.

"Come on, Papa." Katie tugged him forward.

The only consolation was the panic on Anna's face. She bowed her head, trying to hide it. He settled down across from her on the blanket, firmly keeping the picnic basket between them.

"I didn't know you were coming."

"Neither did I." The worry soft on her face touched him in ways he didn't want to know or feel. "Laura has informed me she's gotten us together so we can settle our fight."

"What fight?"

Fine. He was beginning to see the humor in it. "The one that is keeping us from getting married."

A flicker of a smile brushed her lips. "I tried to explain."

"I'm sure you did. I just think Laura wants it to be true. Just like Katie does." He grabbed a cup. "Cider?"

"Please." Anna tried not to look at him. Tried to keep her gaze low. And when he handed her a full cup their fingers met. A jolt of longing telegraphed up her arm. She didn't want him to know how she felt.

He didn't want a wife. He didn't want her.

She would never allow herself to pine after a man she couldn't have. She'd learned that lesson from Mandy's father, one that had hurt like nothing else. "At least the girls are happy."

"Anna! Papa! Come see!" Katie called, the meal over.

"What do you think she found?" Anna asked as she

helped Laura gather up the plates.

"Let's hope it isn't another snake." Cooper winked.

"Katie found gold!" Maisie shouted.

"Gold!" Mandy chimed.

Anna hopped to her feet. The creek was so shallow, she could see the pebbles on the bottom. Only tadpoles and waterskimmers squiggled around in the clear water.

"There it is." Katie held out her pan. Small rocks and dirt lined the bottom.

Then Anna saw the tiny irregular-shaped nugget, not much more than the size of a grass seed. "Katie, I can't believe you found one."

"Wanna try?" Katie reached into the water and dirt in the bottom of the pan to rescue her nugget.

"Sure. Show me how." Anna knelt down at the water's edge, and watched as Katie submerged the pan. Cooper knelt down beside her. She felt the heat of his body, breathed in the man and pine scent of him.

"Only rocks this time." Katie dumped it back into the creek.

His presence washed over her. She tried to watch how Katie filled the pan, then rocked it. But all she could think about was Cooper, nearly touching her elbow, so close she could hear him breathe.

"Try it, Anna." Katie held out the pan.

It was cold from the creek. Anna held the tin disc in her hand and scooped it into the water.

"Shake it gently," Katie instructed.

Anna was more aware of Cooper at her side. She shook, sloshing water and rocks. Katie reached out to help. It was more difficult than she expected. When she saw plain old rocks and dirt in the bottom, she was strangely disappointed.

"Let me try it. I bet I can do better." Cooper's eyes laughed at her.

"You're so certain of victory?"

"Of course. I am the sheriff, aren't I?"

The earth felt as if it were spinning. Light-headed, reeling, Anna could only look at his face, at his smile. At his lips.

"Oh, Papa. You've done this before." Katie shook her finger at him. "I got more pans in the wagon."

"I'll get them." Cooper sounded abrupt. He moved away so quickly, Anna wondered if he'd sensed how she was feeling.

She vowed to try harder to hide her affections. She saw Mandy, playing ankle-deep in water. Despite the heavy splint still on her injured arm, she was giggling with Maisie because a tadpole swam near her foot.

"I gotta find me a better place to pan." Katie rubbed her brow. "Upstream a little. There, where the water is slower." She tromped straight up the creek, water splashing everywhere.

"We're outlaws and we're gonna find gold," Maisie announced. "Come on, Mandy."

He could hear them well before he saw them. The squeal of little girls, the splash of water, women's voices low but constant. Cooper checked his watch. He really ought to be heading back. He had a stage to meet at the pass. He wanted to be sure to stop any of Corinthos' men, or any other outlaws before they could hurt any more children.

He caught his first glimpse of her through the trees, through shifting cottonwood leaves, whispering in the breeze. She was radiant, all brightness. Her voice skidded across his skin like a touch. When he stepped into the clearing, he looked at her first, not at his girls, not at his sister keeping safe watch on them.

Anna didn't look at him with those unguarded eyes. She looked relaxed, settled on a boulder at the creek side, deep in conversation with Laura. He could hear snatches of Laura's words, then the music of Anna's voice growing clearer with every step he took.

A twig cracked beneath his boot. Anna's head snapped up. She looked up at him, and made him feel…how she threatened to make him feel.

Her eyes shuttered, leaving only polite regard. He ought to be grateful. After all, he was the one who didn't want anything to do with her. He was doing his job, protecting her, and doing what was right, making sure she had a place to stay. That was all.

"I have to be heading back." She stood, a swirl of blue skirts and elegance, avoiding his gaze. "Mandy needs to go down for a nap soon."

Cooper stepped closer. He could not seem to help it.

Laura elbowed him in the ribs and whispered, "Now would be the perfect time to hire her."

He wasn't going to hire her. He blushed, hoping Anna hadn't heard Laura's bold advice. But she was already turning to fetch her daughter in the stream.

"This is for you, Anna." Katie, trousers wet up to her knees, ran barefoot across the grass. Something was fisted in one hand. "Since you came and stuff. And didn't get mad because we didn't tell you about Papa."

"I suspected a plot." Anna's voice was merry.

"All the gold I found today. It's probably a whole twelve dollars."

"Katie, I can't take your gold." Anna knelt. So gentle, brushed by sun, caressed by wind. How his fingers ached to touch her like that wind.

"But Anna, I want you to have it. I never said I was sorry for what I done."

"You keep the gold. Buy something nice for you and Maisie." Anna reached out, as if to brush those errant curls out of Katie's face, but held back.

"Are you mad at what I done?"

"How could I be mad at you? You were only trying to take care of your little sister."

Her chin shot up. "I knew you'd understand."

Cooper had never seen Katie so vulnerable. He swore the girl almost hugged Anna, then changed her mind. She ran away, not looking back, to the creek.

"Thank you." He had to talk to her, had to tell her.

"For what?" She didn't know what she'd done, or how much it meant.

"You forgave her. You just—" How did he say it? "You care for her, for her feelings."

"Of course I do. Don't misunderstand. I'm not harboring any secret hopes. It's just that I left my home and traveled a long way. Stage travel isn't the safest thing to do. I risked so much, just to know the little girls in those letters."

"You wanted to love them."

"Yes. But I'll settle for friendship." There was no blame in her eyes, just honesty as crisp as morning, as true as dawn. "Well, I have to go."

"I need to get back to work, too." What was it about this woman that drew him? Cooper didn't know. He took a step closer. "Will you walk with me?"

She didn't move away, but the polite regard vanished. When she smiled, it felt as warm as magic.

"Yes. Just let me get Mandy and thank Laura for the meal."

"No problem." Laura sidled closer, as if she'd been listening. "I can keep Mandy longer, if you wouldn't mind. She's having so much fun with Maisie. I could drop her off at the hotel in say, thirty minutes or so?"

Anna tucked her bottom lip between her teeth, an innocent gesture that had Cooper's heart pounding. She had such well-shaped lips, a full upper lip, and a generous bottom one. Just right for kissing.

"Yes, Mandy can stay. It will be so good for her to laugh and play. Let me go tell her."

Cooper watched Anna hurry away with a swish of blue skirts. From behind he could see the delicate column of her neck, the slim set of her shoulders, the narrow cut of her waist. She knelt down to speak with her child. Mandy's face brightened. Maisie sparkled like a gem. More happy than he'd ever seen her.

"Look how Anna affects them." Laura didn't miss it, either. "See how Katie opens up. And Maisie just beams. They need her, Cooper."

Yes, they needed her. He could see that. But not as a mother. What he was thinking wasn't a good idea, not a good idea at all. Would his daughters understand? No, it was a bad idea. They would always be wanting and wishing.

"Thanks again, Laura." Anna caught up to them. "I guess I'll see you in a little while."

"And tonight don't forget." Cooper watched the delight on his sister's face. "Anna has agreed to join my sewing circle."

"Just in time to finish sewing on all those little doodads on your wedding gown?"

"Exactly." Anna didn't seem to mind. She waved

goodbye to the girls, their answering calls loud enough to scatter birds from the trees. She fell in stride beside him as the clearing disappeared, and they were alone in the forest.

"I'm glad to see Mandy doing so well."

"She's nearly recovered. Thanks to you." Wonder shimmered in her voice, such a high regard it made him feel bigger, better.

He was no hero, no man to look up to. He'd lost his honor once and it still haunted him. "I did what any of my deputies would have done."

"But you did it." She looked away. "I suppose I need to ask you something, since you and your girls are the reason I came to Flint Creek in the first place."

He looked down at the ground, saw the clumps of bunch grass and new sprigs of buttercups. He knelt and snapped a stem off. The happy little flower gazed up at him. "What's your question?"

"How would you feel if Mandy and I stayed here in town? Now, we could move on if you wanted, but if you don't mind, I'd like to stay."

"You don't want to go home?" She looked so stricken, he softened the question. "I mean, you must have family and friends you left behind."

"A sister. I miss her very much." Affection filled her voice, sweet like honey. "But I have no reason to return. It was a struggle for me in Ruby Bluff."

"I don't mind if you stay. It would make my sister happy. She admires your needlework, you know. And your Mandy has found a friend in my Maisie."

"I don't want you to think I'm fishing for marriage."

"I never thought you were." She wasn't manipulative. She didn't use others, didn't hurt them, wasn't cold like a winter's night. She was a spring morning, fresh and new.

He should ask her. He should just say it. Lay down the rules. Let her know he was asking for his daughters' sake. If they couldn't have a mother, then maybe they could have Anna for a housekeeper. If she would say yes. If he could make her say yes.

"You do know that all the women in Laura's sewing group probably believe the rumors," he found himself saying instead of what was on his mind.

"Janet and her friend Leslie at the mercantile both seem to think we've had some sort of an argument and the wedding is off." Her laughter breezed over his, light and wondrous. "I think it came from my attempts to explain why there wouldn't be any wedding."

"So, that's why Laura invited us both out here. And why she's so eager to keep Mandy." Fine, he could see the humor in it, too. "She thinks if we can talk it over, we'll make up."

"I had no idea. Why won't everyone believe us?"

"Do you really have to ask?" He stepped forward and watched the pupils in her eyes darken. Watched her take in a small breath, lifting the curve of her firm bosom. "You've met Katie. I suspect she's been part of the problem."

"Time will prove us right." Her lower lip trembled. He couldn't seem to stop watching it, so pink, so lush.

He caught her mouth with his. Her lips were soft against his, just as he knew they would be. She tasted of lemon cake and sunshine, felt like heated velvet.

She wasn't responding. He felt it, knew she would pull away. But she didn't. Her hand touched his chin, a light touch. His skin sizzled. His chest ached deep inside, where his heart was pounding like a war drum.

She tipped her mouth up. She needed this as much as he did.

He slanted his mouth over hers. He gently backed her into the solid trunk of a tree and curled his hand around the back of her neck. His tongue caressed her bottom lip. Then he dared to press it inside her mouth.

Desire twisted through his belly, low and deep. He'd been so long without a woman's touch, without this heavy consuming need that made him ache, made him want.

"Cooper." Anna broke away, already blushing. Tendrils curled around her flushed face. Her eyes were wide. She laid one hand over her mouth, over lips swollen from his kiss.

"Anna, I never meant—"

She started walking, then running. He'd made a terrible mistake. "Anna."

She didn't turn around.

He caught up with her. She was walking fast. Her jaw tensed tight. Slender hands balled into fists. She looked ready to fight. She looked ready to cry.

"Leave me alone, Cooper."

He couldn't. He'd insulted her. He'd hurt her. "I usually have more control than that. I'm sorry."

"I'm sorry, too." She didn't look at him. Couldn't look at him. "I can see myself back to town."

"But—"

She just kept walking. Heat flamed her face. She kept her gaze on the lane at her feet, dodging gopher holes and wagon wheel ruts. Graceful pines, solemn firs, happy cottonwoods with their whispering leaves surrounded her, but she could not enjoy the sight of them. Could not think of anything but how she'd behaved.

She'd let him kiss her. In a moment of weakness. She'd let her guard down, and look what happened. She may have answered an advertisement for a wife in the county newspaper, but she wasn't desperate. She wasn't. She had just been lonely. Had dared to dream of a happy home for Mandy. With sisters to play with and a pony to ride on.

She could still make a good life for Mandy. She was in a town where everyone believed she was a widow, not an unmarried woman with an illegitimate daughter. Not a woman whose family had turned their backs on her. If it hadn't been for her sister, Anna would have had no place to go.

No, here in Flint Creek, everyone believed the lie she told, a lie for Mandy's sake. If they were to stay, if she could find a job and a little house to live in, then Mandy could be happy here. When she played with other children, they wouldn't call her a bastard. Other mothers wouldn't pull their daughters away.

There was a lot to be grateful for. Anna knew that. They had a real chance for happiness here, on their own, without anyone to lean on. She couldn't ruin it. Not by kissing a man who didn't want her. Cooper was lonely. She could see it in his eyes. Sense it in the way he reached out to her. They had much in common, both raising little girls alone. But that was all. That was all there could ever be between them.

"Anna." He must have decided to catch up with her.

She was still embarrassed. She didn't know what to say.

"I don't know how to do this, so I might as well come out and say it."

"Well, I don't want to hear it." She really didn't. She just wanted to forget her behavior, forget her mistake, and forget how easy it had been to give in to her feelings for him.

"It looks like I'm short a housekeeper."

A housekeeper? What about the kiss?

"I have it on good authority you might know how to cook." His dazzling smile muddled her thoughts, made it hard to believe.

"Somewhat," she admitted.

"Then maybe we can work out a trade of sorts until your daughter is well."

Work for him? In his home? "I already have a job. It isn't steady, but it's a start."

"I need help. Some serious help. You've seen my daughters. I can't get anyone to work for me. Mrs. Beasely was my last hope. No one else has answered my advertisements."

"You want me to work for you?" First he kissed her, then he offered her employment? Now she was getting mad.

"I'm not working in your home, Cooper." She had more pride than that. How was she supposed to feel? She was falling in love with him. How could she spend all day in his house, caring for his children, cooking his meals and washing his clothes and hide how she felt? It would give the girls false hopes.

"I'm not taking no for an answer." His voice drew her gaze, a heady combination of strength and kindness.

Oh, his kindness only made her want him more. How foolish was that? "I would love to work for you Cooper, but I can't."

"Why?"

"I can't." She began to jog, refusing to look at him.

She wanted to say yes. She wanted another kiss. She knew she had to get away from him.

Every once in a while she glanced over her shoulder. Cooper strode behind her, a respectful distance away, chin up, alert, watching the forest. For those robbers, probably. Despite how she'd acted, he still did his job. He still made sure she was safe from harm.

Town wasn't far. She went straight to the hotel and was glad when there was work to do. She would keep her hands and her mind busy. She would not think of Cooper Braddock, not remember his kiss.

Chapter Ten

"Laura, I had a great time." Anna didn't know how to say what she was feeling. She'd been lonely for so long, with only her sister to call friend. She felt as if she belonged in Flint Creek in a way she'd never felt in the town she'd grown up in.

"I'm so glad you were able to come." Laura waved Janet on, bid goodbye. "Anna will catch up to you. I want to keep her for a few more minutes."

The last of the sewing circle ladies said goodbye, stepping out into the darkness.

"Your being here has been good for Cooper." Laura drew Anna back down on the sofa.

"I don't see why. I hardly know him."

"He's thinking about his future. Something he hasn't done since Katherine left him. That was his first wife." The fire snapped, crackling in the hearth. Laura lowered her voice. "He truly loved her. I mean, complete devotion. She was his world."

"Cooper told me some of this." Her stomach twisted. Really, it was not her business. She should not know something so intimate.

"When she left him, she nearly destroyed him. Kath-

erine had been sleeping with an outlaw, and she had
been feeding him information about when gold ship-
ments were coming and going, how many deputies
Cooper had assigned to the bank or to the stage. His
reputation was ruined when she left. He was even
brought up on charges.''

Anna turned away. ''Were they dismissed?''

''Eventually. But it was a tough time. All the while
he was caring for his girls. Katie was nearly destroyed
by Katherine's abandonment. Maisie was just a baby.''

''It had to have been hard.'' Anna knew about dis-
honor. ''At least he had you and Tucker.''

''Our entire family stood beside him.'' Sadness
weighed down her voice. ''Cooper had never even suspected his wife. Would never have believed it if someone had tried to tell him. He had absolute faith in her.
And she shattered it. She broke his ability to trust right
along with his heart.''

''He's a good father.''

''Yes. He has done everything he can for his girls.
He loves them. It's been because of his character and
his strength that his daughters are happy. That they
were able to make a family, despite Katherine.''

She only admired Cooper more. He loved his girls
so much. It showed in everything he did. How much
more he must have loved his wife, the mother of those
children?

No wonder he felt so strongly against marrying
again. No wonder he didn't believe a woman could
love a child not her own or a man over a lifetime.

''How did it go, big brother?'' Tucker asked.

Cooper sat down on the front porch steps, too tired
to go any farther. It was late. He'd had a hard afternoon

and evening spent riding shotgun with the stage. Long hours spent thinking of Anna Bauer. "No sign of Corinthos. I know he's out there. He didn't try to break into the bank?"

"No. Everything was quiet."

Well, they were lucky. But luck didn't last. Cool night air breezed across his face. "I shot him. Right through the shoulder."

"A nasty place to take a bullet."

"He won't be riding and robbing for a while. I just don't know when he'll pop up next. I want to be prepared."

"You have the jail and the bank guarded. You are keeping guards on Anna and on your girls."

"The outlaw threatened me. He could harm them."

"Won't be the first time they've had a deputy keeping an eye over them. Or an uncle." Tucker reached behind him. "Want some cookies? They're Anna's. She made them in Janet's kitchen. Maisie says they are the best ever."

"I'm not hungry." He didn't want a cookie. He wanted the woman. "Did the girls give you any trouble?"

"Katie had another nightmare."

Cooper hung his head, stared down at his hands. "She hasn't had one of those for a while."

"With Laura getting married and leaving soon..." Tucker sighed. "I'm glad she has Anna. Maybe she's what Katie has needed all along."

That's exactly what he'd been thinking.

Anna should have looked up at the violent jangling of the hotel's front door. She should have known by the pounding footsteps. She was just troubled. She'd dreamed of Dalton last night, that he'd found her. Moreover, yesterday's kiss still haunted her.

"Anna! Anna!" Katie and Maisie clamored up to her table. The teapot rattled.

"Hello, girls. Are you here for breakfast?"

"Papa already made us pancakes," Katie said.

"You gotta come, Anna." Maisie tilted her head.

Charmed, Anna had to ask. "Come where?"

His voice, inviting and rich, replied, "Come home with us. We need a housekeeper."

"We really do." Maisie affected a great sigh. "You gotta little girl so you know all about tea parties."

"Unlike that awful Mrs. Beasely," Cooper added.

She twisted around. His eyes glittered with humor. Oh, he thought he was clever. "I can't say no to these little faces, and you know it."

"I do." His grin broadened into a full-fledged, heart-stopping smile.

Her toes tingled at the sight. How easy to remember the feel of his lips on hers. Tender, oh, so tender. But she had a daughter to think about. She could not work for a man she wanted to kiss. "No."

"Please?" He said it low, rumbling. Enough to make her spine shiver.

"No."

"We really need you, Anna." Katie grabbed her hand. "You can bring Mandy with you every day."

"Cuz tea parties ain't no fun alone." Maisie sighed.

"I can play," Mandy shyly added.

"You're outnumbered." Cooper took the chair beside her, settling his big, iron-hard body into it. So close, she could see the dark flecks in his eyes.

"Please, Mama." Mandy clasped her hands together.

There were so many practical reasons to refuse. And yet only three reasons to agree. And those three expectant faces watched her.

"Janet usually needs me in the evenings. Let me speak to her first."

Triumph glittered in Cooper's eyes. "When can you start?"

"This is far from fair." Anna couldn't help telling him when they were finally alone.

Once they returned to the house, all three girls dashed upstairs, giggling and planning.

"I'm a desperate man. You can't hold it against me."

"I have some concerns working for you." She had to be honest. She had to let him know what troubled her.

"Is this about what happened yesterday?"

How could she admit how much he affected her? She didn't want him to know. It was only a mistake to care for him, for a man not looking for a wife.

"I can promise not to kiss you again, if that would help. When I give my word, I keep it."

"I never doubted that." Her heart leaped.

He turned away, staring hard at the wall hanging she'd made. "Katie picked the spot to hang this. Your gift meant a lot to her. With Laura getting married and leaving soon, Katie needs someone who makes her feel secure and valued. I saw how you treated her yesterday at the creek. You do that for her. That's all I'm asking of you, Anna. I want you to care for my girls."

But not you. Anna nodded. "You don't think they will get overly attached?"

"I'll talk to them."

"There's one more thing." Should she mention her problems back home? "What about the robber I saw in town? Will he be a problem?"

"Tucker lost his trail up in the mountains some-where. It's possible he or his leader will be back."

She watched his eyes darken, like a cougar's just before a kill. "I'm concerned I might bring that trouble here, to your home."

She was very afraid.

His footsteps knelled closer. "You aren't bringing more danger to my life than I already have."

"What do you mean?"

"Deputies guard my daughters, too. Katie isn't so easy with her pony-riding adventures, but my men manage. Don't worry, Anna. Whatever happens, I can handle it. I live for trouble." His smile was warm, but he stepped away, putting obvious distance between them. "You will stay, won't you?"

"For a while."

But there would be no more kisses between them. And that was the way it should be.

Anna stepped outside to rustle up the girls. The sun hung high in the sky, casting few shadows but plenty of warmth. Robins sang, the air smelled like pine. She heard a rustling overhead. "Is that you, Maisie?"

A limb shifted and a face peeked out from amid the dark-green boughs. "I ain't Maisie. I'm an outlaw, and this is my hideout."

"What? You're not a sheriff like your papa?"

"Nope. I'm bad through and through." She swung down from the sturdy limb and hung like a monkey. She hit the ground with a two-footed thud. "Is it grub yet?"

"Yeah, is it grub yet?" Mandy climbed down more carefully. "Us outlaws are real hungry, Mama."

"Is that so? Then it's a good thing I have dinner on the table." Anna held out her hand.

Mandy stepped forward, her fingers gripping Anna's tight. "Did you make biscuits?"

"Just the way you like them." Anna's heart warmed.

Maisie grabbed her by the other hand. "I'm glad you like outlaws, Anna."

"Me, too. You girls are my favorite kind. Hurry, go wash up." Anna watched the two outlaws race through the kitchen and giggle at the basin. Maisie dropped the soap, but held the towel for Mandy.

"Everyone at the table. Katie, where are you?"

"Here. I'm leavin' my snake outside." She tromped in wearing her trousers and shirt, streaked with dirt. "Do you like snakes?"

"They don't scare me." Anna felt a tug on her skirt.

Mandy leaned against her knee. "Don't ever wanna leave here, Mama. It's nice."

The smile that brightened Mandy's face made her heart full. Nothing mattered more than this little girl. Anna brushed back unruly curls from shy blue eyes.

This first morning spent in Cooper's cozy log house had been a good one. Already it felt too much like a home, too much like her dreams. Sunlit rooms and children playing in the yard.

"Sit her down right here, Anna." Katie pulled a chair from the table and patted the wood seat.

She gently steered her daughter to the sun-warmed spot beside Maisie. Then she began setting the bowls of food around the table.

"You can cook real good," Katie announced as she

grabbed a steaming biscuit. "Oops. I forgot. I gotta use manners. I'm gonna be on my best behavior."

"Katie don't got many manners," Maisie explained.

"Are you trying to impress me, Katie?" Anna began dishing up Mandy's plate.

"Well, I figure if you like us enough, then maybe you'll end up stayin'." Katie grabbed the bowl of butter-fried potatoes. "That's why I picked your letter. I got lots, you know. You already had a little girl so I figured you could take care of Maisie."

"I need takin' care of," Maisie explained as Anna reached for her empty plate. "And I need lots of taters."

Anna obliged by giving her two heaping spoonfuls. Maisie rewarded her with a twinkling smile.

"Do you remember the first letter you wrote me?" Katie asked when Anna sat down at Cooper's spot at the table. "You said you were a pretty good cook. I figure that's important cuz nothin's worse than eatin' burnt food."

"We get that lots with Papa," Maisie confessed.

"Lots." Katie rolled her eyes. "He thinks he cooks good, but he don't. We don't wanna tell him and hurt his feelings."

"Papas have feelings, too." Maisie sighed, her burdens great.

He was almost afraid to go home. He dreaded a scene like the last time he hired a housekeeper. Maybe Anna couldn't handle outlaw Maisie and wild Katie any better than anyone else. What would happen then? If Anna didn't want to stay, his little girls' hearts would be crushed. They adored Anna.

Maybe hiring her was a bad idea. She was so reluctant about it. Maybe she was right.

The house looked quiet. No little outlaw climbing in the tree outside. No Katie dashing by riding Bob. Those weren't good signs. Squinting against the sunlight in his eyes, he circled around the back of the house.

The sound of voices grew as he approached the back door. He recognized Laura's laughter. Then Anna's. "Girls, would you like some milk?"

Three chorused yesses rang with the sound of happiness. Cooper halted on the porch, with just the smallest view of the kitchen through the open door. He saw Anna at the work counter, a dish towel tied around her waist in a makeshift apron, carrying glasses to the table.

"Don't push, Maisie." Katie's voice.

"I gotta have room for Mandy." Maisie's answer. "I needa fork, Anna."

He heard the clatter of flatware. Curious, he leaned a little more so he could see the table. His chest tightened at the scene. He'd been so afraid…. Well, he was glad he'd done the right thing in hiring Anna.

"Do you girls remember the last time we picked huckleberries?" Laura leaned across the table and grabbed the sugar bowl.

"I do! Maisie kept eating everything in my bucket," Katie accused.

Maisie giggled. "Then the bear came."

"He was a old mean thing and he raised his big hairy arms like this—" Katie dropped her fork and waved her hands in the air.

"And he growled really, really loud," Maisie added, punctuating the story with a roar of her own.

"I said, 'Maisie, run,' and we did."

"Katie dropped the bucket so we didn't get no berries after all," Maisie added with a purple-juice-stained mouth.

Anna's chuckle shivered through him, light and warm and sweet. "Cooper."

He startled at her voice and realized it could lure him anywhere. Her gaze seared through him like flame to steel, melting the strongest of elements. He felt his body's reaction to her and he didn't like it, didn't want it.

"Papa! Papa!" Maisie flew from the table and into his arms, excited to tell him all about her day with Anna.

"Papa, Anna made a pie. It's the best ever. Come see." Katie's eyes gleamed.

Cooper knew that gleam. She was still matchmaking. Maisie's hug felt sweet, but she hopped out of his arms before he could savor it. In a blur of pink, she scurried back to her place at the table.

"Come join us." Anna's voice. She stood, her pink-checked dress rustling around her slender, shapely form. He wanted to feel her against him, hold her close in his arms.

"Cooper, are you smitten?" Laura's eyes laughed at him.

"With you? Always." He hoped the teasing would distract Laura's innocent comment. No matter how he explained Anna's presence and Katie's letters, his know-it-all-sister refused to believe him.

"Come join us," Laura invited.

"I'll get you some coffee." Anna moved from behind her chair, her quiet movements lending grace to his unadorned kitchen.

He pulled up a chair, and Laura handed him a slice

of pie. His mouth watered at the sight of the crumbly crust and the purple juice leaking onto the plate. The best ever, Katie said. He didn't doubt it.

"She can bake, she can cook. She can even get Katie to act ladylike," Laura whispered in his ear. "Looks like you've found a winner."

No, what he'd found was a problem. A beautiful, elegant, incredible problem. Right now that problem stood at his elbow. She set the steaming cup of fragrant coffee beside him, and her arm brushed his. Tiny flames skidded along his skin.

Anna's touch. He couldn't remember the last time a woman had affected him so much.

"Can I see you home?" Cooper's voice, so strong, so duty bound. Her heart fluttered.

"It's only a few blocks to the hotel."

"Just wanted to ask. Don't want to make our best housekeeper unhappy."

"Oh, I'm your best?" She laughed at that. "I'm a fair to middling cook."

"You make my daughters happy."

He avoided her gaze, but he felt so solid and substantial, she found it hard to breathe. He stepped out onto the porch. Gray-purple twilight enveloped him, brushed across his shoulders in a way her fingers ached to. "Not everyone can do that."

"Making a child happy is so easy."

"So you say." He sat down on the top step. The haze of twilight framed him in shadow. "I can't tell you how many housekeepers I've gone through. And how much worse it is with Katie testing every woman she comes in contact with."

Anna laughed, pleased to know Cooper was astute

and insightful not just as a sheriff but as a father. "Katie doesn't seem to be testing me. Yet."

"She doesn't have to. She picked you out herself."

Anna felt her troubles lift like leaves on the wind. She sat down next to Cooper on the top porch step. She looked out at the peaceful world, at waving green grass, silent pines and firs, the movement of an owl in the trees.

"That's why I decided to agree to marry you—I mean, her," Anna confessed. "Ponies, cookies and bedtime stories. I thought, what a sensitive father knowing what nourishes a child's heart."

Magic. It lived in her voice as sparkling as fairy dust, in her words as powerful as myth. Cooper's pulse kicked as the breeze lifted, stirring the rose-sweet scent of her skin.

Love and magic. That's what his girls needed. What was missing in this house.

"Maisie really could use a mother with the way she shadowed me all day," Anna said with a shrug of one slim shoulder. "I'm not saying that mother should be me. Surely you know that. But a child needs a woman's love."

"Wait a minute, I—"

"You're a great father, Cooper," she interrupted, all grace and velvet steel. And that strength in her surprised him still. "A child gets a different kind of love from both her parents. It's a benefit for a little girl to grow up with both types of affection."

His throat closed. Cooper fisted his hands. He knew she was right. He knew it through the years even as he made the conscious decision never to put their ability to trust at risk. Or his. "Not every woman is capable of loving a child not her own."

"Nor is every man."

The truth of his words struck him, solid as a rock. "I guess we're both raising little girls on our own. And it's far from easy."

"Oh, it's not so tough. With a little help." Her eyes clouded, and the radiance faded from her smile. Like fog obscuring the sun, he felt the change, the coolness. He sensed a grief and sadness.

He'd known his share of sadness, too. But today, this day, had been a happier day for his daughters. Because of her.

She tucked her lower lip between her teeth, drawing his gaze there. Every muscle in his body tensed. Cooper's breath caught, his pulse hammered wildly. How he wanted to kiss her, to hold her in his arms and taste her passion.

But he couldn't. He'd given his word. So he forced himself to be content with simply sitting beside her. Feeling her presence brush across him like the breeze, touching him in places he hadn't been touched. Not since he'd loved Katherine.

Chapter Eleven

Early morning sunshine slanted low through the boughs of the tall pines, diluting it like dust in the wind. Through the low rays, he saw her, the shiver of calico around her slim body, the braided coronet of gold crowning her head.

He stood, coffee cup in hand. The clop of the horse brought her closer, sure and steady. Birdsong tolled in the fresh air. Dew clung to the blades of grass in the yard and along the road, shimmering like so many diamonds in the new day's light, and all as if for Anna.

"Cooper." She dismounted, keeping one hand on her child still perched on the bay's withers. "Am I late?"

"No. I'm just up early." He set his cup down on the porch rail. He lifted a shy Mandy from the horse and into Anna's arms. "I should have thought to find you a mount."

"You've given us enough." She didn't say any more as she cradled her daughter in those slender, loving arms before lowering her to the ground. "Have you started breakfast yet?"

"Just the coffee."

Her smile dazzled. "Then I'd better get to work."

The wind blew wisps of dark honeyed curls against her cheek, caressing her soft skin in a way he wanted to. "I'll take care of the horse."

Anna avoided his polite and proper gaze.

Hell, he was troubled. Not just because Anna was in his house, looking as if she belonged here. But because his blood heated, because desires he thought long forgotten stirred to life when he looked at her.

For a man resolved never to want another woman, it was a troubling situation.

"Anna, are you cookin' pancakes for us?" Maisie bounded around the corner of the arched doorway. "Papa said you was comin' right after the sun. But it took forever and ever for the sun to wake up."

"I had to wake up, too." Anna set the canister on the worktable. Flour poofed upward into the air when she lifted off the lid. She looked down to see Maisie standing beside her.

"Wanna see my alphabet? I'm writin' real good."

Anna's heart fell to her toes. "I would love to."

"Don't go nowhere. I'm comin' right back."

A chuckle sounded behind her and with the way it shivered up her spine it could only belong to one man.

"She's hard to say no to, isn't she?" Cooper asked from the threshold. He dwarfed the pleasant kitchen, his masculinity and power at odds with the frilly white curtains and blue-flowered tablecloth.

One look at his handsome face, and Anna's foolish heart thumped. "Impossible."

She felt self-conscious beneath his penetrating gaze, as if he were trying to see more of her than she wanted him to see. She measured out the flour and retreated back to the pantry for the buttermilk.

Cooper didn't know what to say as she searched for the canisters of salt and sugar. A pan of fresh eggs sat on the floor, and she grabbed two of them.

"How about a cup of coffee?" Cooper's gaze followed her back to the worktable.

"Sounds perfect. I don't feel awake yet."

He grabbed a hot pad, turning his back. "Didn't you sleep well?" His question only made him think of her, hair unbraided, fanning out along his pillow.

She nearly dropped the salt canister.

"No. I had a few bad dreams. Nothing serious."

"Corinthos?" He poured the coffee.

"No." Images flooded into her mind. She could not stop them. Dalton Jennings robbing the bank. Holding a gun. Firing it. Mandy falling. It was only her fears, she told herself. Not a sign of what was to come. Not even Dalton would shoot a child. It was just her fears for Mandy's safety. That was all.

Still, the knot in her stomach didn't relax.

Footsteps pounded along the wood floors, announcing Maisie's return. She bounded into the kitchen in a swirl of pink calico. "Anna! Look. I spelled my name."

She abandoned her pancake batter to study Maisie's slate. "This is very fine work. You must be one smart little girl."

She beamed. "Papa says that, too."

Anna brushed a stray curl from Maisie's eyes. "Want to help with the pancakes?"

Maisie slammed her slate down on the worktable and dashed across the room to drag a chair back with her.

Anna caught Cooper's gaze. Intense. Measuring. She

fought the little flip-flops in her stomach. How her body reacted to him. She tried to remember he wasn't hers to want. She didn't belong here.

Cooper strode toward her, the knell of each step ricocheting through her body. His nearness dizzied her. He set the steaming cup on the table at her elbow. "Sugar?"

"Please." He opened the crock in front of her. So close she could smell the morning-soap scent of him, see the clean-shaven texture of his jaw.

He stirred in the sugar, then moved away. But the coffee kept swirling, spinning around in the cup. Just like her thoughts.

"Is Laura moving very far away after she marries?"

"Larry has a house on the other side of town. Not far. But she won't be next door, either." Cooper crossed the room, taking his coffee cup with him. "I've depended on her too much over the years."

"She doesn't look to me as if she's minded." Anna thought of Laura's open affection toward her nieces.

"No. But it's time for her to leave." Cooper unfolded the morning's newspaper, but didn't read it. "That's why I'm glad you're here. Laura said she was going to invite you to the wedding."

She bowed her head, concentrating on her work. She measured the sugar, then folded in the dry ingredients. "Yes. I'm agonizing over what gift to get her."

"Me, too."

She felt him watching her. His brazen and hot gaze stayed square on her back. When she turned to check the fire in the stove, he didn't look away. Her pulse jumped, wondering what he was thinking.

"I'd forgotten how nice it is to have a woman in my

kitchen.'' Low and caressing, that voice. ''Someone who can make everything right.''

''But Mrs. Potts was a girl, Papa,'' Maisie argued.

''Mrs. Potts wasn't just a woman,'' Cooper explained. ''She was scarier than a charging buffalo.''

Glad she wasn't being compared to a big woolly animal, Anna turned to her work with a smile.

Morning dragged by. Cooper didn't like paperwork, and especially not today. He kept thinking of the woman in his house. How she'd made his daughters laugh all through breakfast. She'd made him laugh, too.

''Do you want to go take the early dinner break?'' He offered Tucker. ''I can do the noon rounds.''

''What? I thought you went home for dinner right at noon every day,'' his little brother teased as he carried out the prisoner's empty tray.

''I'm behind in my paperwork.'' Cooper didn't look up.

''Sure. It wouldn't have anything to do with Anna Bauer, would it?'' Tucker sat on the edge of the desk. ''Don't try to deny it. A woman's gotten to you and it's driving you mad.''

''She hasn't gotten to me.'' Cooper wanted to wipe that damn jaunty grin off his little brother's face.

''Sure. She's just about the prettiest woman I've seen since Denver.''

Cooper grabbed his hat. ''I'm going out to check with the deputies I posted at the clinic. You'd do better if you attended to your work and not my love life.''

''Love life! Ha!'' Tucker chortled. ''I knew I could get you to admit it.''

Cursing his slip of tongue, Cooper strode out into the hot afternoon sun and slammed the door behind him. Dust hung in the air and he tried to calm himself, tried to erase Tucker's taunts. Right now Anna Bauer was in his house, taking care of his girls. He'd seen how happy they were. That's why he'd hired her, for his girls.

The busy street was filled with horses and riders, mules and wagons, teamsters hauling supplies and women carrying shopping baskets from store to store. A pair of boys darted past, kicking cans.

What he needed to do was to concentrate on his work. Protect the peace. Hunt down Corinthos. Worry about transporting the gold that had been on that doomed stage. He did not need to spend all day thinking about Anna.

But he couldn't help it. As he strolled through town, he saw a blond woman everywhere he looked.

He simply couldn't get her out of his head.

Her presence had transformed his house in the way no other woman's had. She'd made it warm and happy, as if she'd brought the morning sunshine with her. Her voice sounded like music. From the moment he'd seen her showing Maisie and Katie how to make smiling-face pancakes at the stove, he knew he was in trouble. And they'd tasted better than any breakfast food he'd had before, sweet, light, tempting. Something he wanted to savor.

Maybe he was getting his feelings toward the pancakes and Anna confused. His blood heated remembering the swish of her pretty checked skirts over slender, curving hips.

There was no denying the spark warming his blood when he looked at her. And that spark was a frightening thing. Cooper Braddock didn't want to need any woman. It was safer on a man's heart that way.

* * *

Anna heard the knock on the open back door. Looking up, she saw Laura step into the kitchen.

"Whew, it's starting to get warm outside."

Anna reached for a hand towel. "Come in and cool off. I have apple cider."

"Sounds good. No, I can get it myself." Laura found a glass in the cupboard. "I saw two little outlaws out front still trying to evade that pesky sheriff."

Anna's heart warmed. "They've been at it most of the afternoon. Katie is over at Davy Muldune's house."

"Into all sorts of trouble, no doubt." Laura's eyes twinkled. "I was hoping to steal the girls this evening. The closer this wedding gets, the more I realize my life is going to change. I won't be living next door to my nieces. I won't be able to come over and share supper with them any time I want."

"You'll be sharing supper with your new husband."

Laura set aside the pitcher. "I'm looking forward to that. I just want to spend more time with Katie and Maisie before I leave. Katie doesn't take well to separations. Not with the way her mother left her. She pretends differently, but I know it affects her."

"She's a sensitive girl."

Laura cocked her head. "Most people would say she's trouble. But you're right. She's a good girl, too, once you get past the reptiles and the mud. Look, you've got supper almost ready. Let me help you set the table."

Anna uncovered a plate of biscuits and set it on the counter beside the crock of new butter. "Why don't you stay for supper? Mandy and I can leave if you want—"

"No!" Laura gave the cupboard door a slam. "You ought to stay. Why, you practically belong here. Besides, Katie would never speak to me again if I chased you off."

Pounding footsteps echoed through the house. "Laura! Laura!" Maisie burst into the kitchen, wearing her play cowboy hat and carrying her little enamel teapot.

Mandy trotted in behind her, wearing Maisie's too-big pair of fringed chaps.

"We're needin' tea, Anna." Maisie folded herself into Laura's arms.

"We're parched," Mandy explained.

Anna rescued the teapot from Maisie's precarious grip. "I'll get this filled right up. Do you two outlaws need any grub?"

"We're needin' some cookies, too." Maisie hopped down, serious as a hanging judge.

"Cookies, Mama." Mandy sighed. "It's important."

"And right before supper, too." Anna tried not to be charmed. And failed miserably. "Here you go. Two each."

She heard the crock rattle. Little-girl giggles filled the room with happiness. Anna filled the play teapot with more apple cider. "Here you wild outlaws go."

"Thanks for the cookies." Maisie grabbed the teapot and headed for the door.

Laura stood. "You girls want to come hide out at my place? Anna, can I take Mandy for a little bit?"

Two excited cheers nearly deafened them.

She laughed. "I guess so." Mandy waved goodbye to her, happily trotting after Maisie and Laura. What a fun outlaw tea party they were going to have.

Cooper stood in the doorway, his shadow long and lean on the floor. She looked up into his laughing eyes. "What was that?"

"Laura's taking the girls." Anna considered the timing. She saw through the open window how Laura glanced back at the house, then hurried the little girls toward her cottage. "I think she just lied to me."

"She set us up." Cooper swept off his hat, hung it on the peg on the wall. "She told me to be home at exactly five o'clock. It sounded important."

Anna looked at the table. There were two place settings. Two. "I never should have let her get away with this. Does she still think we're having a fight?"

Cooper's half grin drew her gaze and held it there. "She's a good sister, but she's in big trouble now. I'll go fetch the girls. You don't have to put up with my company. Where's Katie?"

"At Davy's." Anna set the plate of chicken on the table. "I smell another plot."

"I do, too." Cooper glanced at the window. "A plot getting bigger by the moment. I'll be right back."

He loped out the door, leaving her with a steaming bowl of dumplings. Anna set them on the table. She could see him through the window, heard the low rumbling of his voice as he called out to Laura.

Laura's horse and buggy were parked in front of her cottage. Anna saw the little girls inside it. Mandy grinned broadly on the seat beside Maisie. Maisie was still clutching her teapot and wearing her cowboy hat. Laura waved as Cooper approached and slapped the reins against the horse's rump. They took off out of sight.

"I can't believe it." He strode into the kitchen. "My sister just kidnapped our children."

"Kidnapped?" Anna untied her apron. "I'm sure she's taking them somewhere to eat. It's suppertime. We just have to follow them."

"No." His fingers wrapped around her wrist.

Heat skidded up her arm, jolted through her whole body. She looked up into eyes dark and deep. "Mandy—"

"Will be just fine." Cooper led her to the table. "Laura told me you and I need time alone."

"We do?"

"We need to start planning our wedding." That half grin was back, tugging at the dimples in his left cheek.

"Our wedding? Does she still think—" Anna took a breath. Stared down at his fingers on her arm. He released her and she stepped away. "I've never given her reason to assume that. You must think that I—"

"I don't," he interrupted. He held out a chair at the table. "Katie and Laura planned this. You wouldn't have made a whole platter of chicken and dumplings if you were in on the plot. Although, it is my favorite meal."

"Katie asked me to make it." Anna collapsed into the chair. "I feel weak."

He laughed. "Now you know what I'm up against. I'll take you out to find your daughter if you want. But it would be a shame for all this food to go to waste."

"It does smell good. I haven't had chicken and dumplings in the longest time."

"That gravy smells tasty." Cooper's smile dazzled. "Come join me for supper."

"Laura and Katie will think they've won."

"But we're not getting married, so what's the harm?" Cooper's arm brushed hers as he pulled out a chair.

Her stomach fluttered at his touch. A lot of harm could come from spending time alone with him.

He held the platter of chicken for her. "I have a lot to thank you for."

"You do?" Anna set a chicken leg on her plate.

"Every night I used to come home from work in fear. What did Katie do today? Is the housekeeper going to quit? Do I have to give her a bonus to stay?"

"Do you still come home in fear now that I'm here?"

"No." He grabbed a chicken breast and dropped it on his plate. "Now I come home and see my daughters happy and well cared for and a delicious supper on the table. What you're doing for the girls means a lot."

"I'm not doing anything different from what Mrs. Potts did. Minus the grumbling."

"That's not true."

"Well, except for maybe my dried-berry pie. I have it on very good authority that Mrs. Potts couldn't make pie half as tasty as mine."

"I've never had a pie that good." He handed her a folded dishcloth from the pile on the shelf. "We haven't had a lot of things around here."

"What could your family possibly be missing?" Anna spooned up a couple of dumplings, then handed him the platter. "You have a cozy, beautiful home, more books than I've ever seen, laughter at every meal. You have everything that's important."

"That's where I beg to differ." Cooper ladled gravy over his meat and dumplings. "I didn't realize what we were missing until you."

"Me?" She laughed at that. "You mean you haven't missed the arguments and demands for higher wages."

"No." His voice rang low with sincerity. Honesty

burned in his eyes. "My daughters are happy. Have you noticed how Katie smiles instead of scowls? That she's actually behaving herself?"

Anna laughed. "See, I told you. Your girls don't need a housekeeper, they need mothering. You owe me a big favor for figuring out the solution to your problem."

"Now you are teasing me."

"Someone has to." She stared hard at the glass. She took a sip of cider so she didn't have to look into his eyes and feel his captivating pull. She had to remind herself he was only being nice to her, that any glimmers of warmth and caring were in her heart alone. He was helping her out of charity. He was helping her because it was best for his girls. Nothing more.

"Like I said, I can't thank you enough." The smile in his voice drew her gaze. Her whole body tingled just looking at him. She wanted his kiss, his touch, more. Things it wasn't right for her to have. "You've done more than the job requires."

"Then we're even, because I can't thank you enough for paying both the doctor and the hotel bills. That was beyond the call of duty, Cooper. Even if I do intend to repay you."

"Oh, I don't know. That call of duty is a pretty large one. I've been a lawman for a long time." He lifted his own glass. "It's more than walking around with a badge on my chest. I try to do all I can for everyone. It makes for a better town, and for a better life."

"Too bad you aren't more humble," she couldn't help but tease.

"I deserved that." He laughed. "Actually, being a lawman is a family tradition. My father was a marshal, but he's retired now."

"Does he live close by?"

"He and my stepmother live over near Billings. They have a cattle ranch there." His fingers brushed hers when they both reached for the butter crock at the same time. She drew her hand back.

He hesitated, then offered her butter. "You know Tucker's a deputy. Two brothers are sheriffs over in Silver Bow, and another is a marshal."

"Five boys? Poor Laura, being the only sister."

"Not the only. The youngest girl is still at home with Mother and Pa. I was the oldest."

"So was I." Anna tried not to think of all the hopes her parents had for her. And how she failed them.

"It's nice having you in my house, Anna. I hope you can stay with us for a while. Katie needs you."

Her heart thumped twice, just gazing into his eyes. How impossible it was not to care for this man of iron strength and courage, of kindness and humor.

"Mama?"

Anna turned from the open window. "I thought you were sleeping."

With a rustle of the sheets, Mandy sat up, nothing but shadow in the dark room. "Do you got bad dreams?"

"No, pumpkin." *Just troubled thoughts.*

"Will the man in the moon help?"

"That's what I'm hoping." Anna gazed out at the nearly full moon, high in the zenith. Silver light filtered through dark pine branches.

"Do you see him?" The ropes creaked.

Anna's breath caught as Mandy slipped from the bed wearing Maisie's too-big flowered nightie. Her bare feet padded against the floor.

"Let me hug you." Anna held out her arms, and her daughter stepped into them. The little girl felt so wonderful in her arms. She settled her daughter onto her lap and together they gazed at the moon.

"Is he watchin', Mama?"

"I think I see his shadow right there on the moon. He's keeping both of us safe."

"And Maisie and Katie, too?"

"All little girls." Anna had spun the story to help Mandy sleep when she was afraid of monsters in the dark. But now, she wished the story were true.

She wanted someone to watch over her. To keep Dalton Jennings away. To keep her from caring too much for Cooper.

Chapter Twelve

Cooper looked forward to mornings. Anna greeted him with a smile and he held out his hand to help her down from her horse—not that she needed it. The brush of her palm to his made his pulse beat crazily. He breathed in the breeze of her flowery scent and ached to feel her body against his. Never quite touching, she moved away. Desire beat fast and hard in his blood, leaving him wanting more from her each day.

Good thing he was a man capable of self-control.

One morning, when he was bringing in the eggs, she came out to meet him halfway. Bob, just escaped from the corral, rushed up and grabbed Anna's hat right off her head. She only laughed, and that started Katie's and Maisie's mad dash to capture Bob and rescue the straw bonnet.

Katie retrieved the hat, but it was missing a decorative ribbon and had a bite taken out of the brim. Anna accepted everyone's apology with a rippling smile and turned down his offer to buy her a new bonnet.

Another morning she made her smiling-face pancakes, to the delight of the three little girls. Mandy discovered huckleberry syrup tasted better without a fork and started licking the purple juice right off her plate. Maisie followed suit.

But Katie just shook her head and mumbled about having manners. Anna smiled down at his daughter, affection glimmering in her eyes like a jewel too precious to touch.

Or too rare to believe in.

She made him realize what he'd lost long ago, what his daughters had never known. The loving touch of a woman—of a mother. The beauty of her affection in their home.

Since their meal alone together, the tension between them was less. Anna liked that. She liked that he gave her a smile when he left for work. But that smile warmed her heart, left her thinking of him through the long day of work ahead.

She was in his house; she could not avoid thinking of him. When she scrubbed the parlor from top to bottom and polished every piece of furniture, she spotted a book on the small table—*The Last of the Mohicans*. It took no imagination at all to see him sitting in the wing chair before the fire and reading by lamplight after the girls were tucked in bed.

Or when she stepped into his bedroom to change the sheets, how could she not think of him lying there with his head on the pillow, a shank of dark hair falling across his forehead? It was impossible.

Some evenings he made it home for supper in time to sit with the girls and listen to their cheerful accounting of their day. Mandy had become Maisie's constant companion, climbing up into the hideout tree despite her splint. Katie recounted how she actually carted wash water or peeled the potatoes just because she happened to be talking with Anna at the time. Anna could see by the humor sparkling in Cooper's eyes that he wasn't fooled one bit.

When he sampled her dried-apple pie and moaned with pleasure, she blushed. Then his gaze kept straying to her mouth as if he were thinking of the pleasure of their only kiss. The memory still tingled along her lips, heated her blood.

It was harder and harder to fight how she felt. Harder to keep those feelings from showing. She hadn't forgotten the kiss between them. She certainly hoped that he had.

Taking the tray she'd fixed firmly in hand, she headed outside beneath the shade of Maisie's tree. "Are there any outlaws around here?"

"Shh!" Maisie's voice. "Mandy, someone's found our secret hideout. Could be the law."

"But she's got strawberry tarts."

Branches rustled overhead. Two faces peeked out between soft green needles. "Are you the law, Anna?"

Anna chuckled. "I bring food, not handcuffs. I figured it was time for tea."

"Outlaws gotta have parties, too." Mandy was the first to climb down, almost as nimble as Maisie.

Anna set the tray on the porch where little enamel plates and cups sat in a circle. Harry Bunny, Mr. Bear and Molly the Dolly sat patiently before their empty cups, waiting. "What you girls need is a tree house."

"How can you get a house up a tree?" Maisie dropped to her knees with a thud.

"One board at a time." Anna laughed. "Do you want me to serve?"

So she poured cool apple cider into little play cups and set fresh strawberry pastries on small enamel plates. The bear, the doll and Harry Bunny got tarts and tea, too.

"Hello, girls." His voice, rich and warm.

She hadn't imagined it. Abruptly, she stood, her tray empty. "Cooper. You're home early."

"I have to ride shotgun over the pass tomorrow. The outlaw we captured when you came to town is well enough to travel. Two federal marshals are meeting us in Sandy, just across the pass. We figure Corinthos might make a move."

"That sounds dangerous." Anna remembered that day like a cold chill shivering across her skin.

"We've been keeping tight guard on the town, so Corinthos can't bring violence onto our streets." Cooper swept off his hat, looking less like the invincible sheriff when he knelt down beside his outlaw daughter. "Those look like mighty tasty tarts. Think Mr. Bear will mind if I steal his?"

"Mr. Bear is awfully hungry, Papa." Maisie's brow crinkled. "Try beggin' some from Anna."

Cooper tilted his head. His dark gaze settled on her. Anna's heart flipped over. His laughter trembled through her.

She shivered but could not look away. "Can I get you some tarts? Katie picked the berries fresh this morning."

"I'll take you up on that offer. These outlaws won't have nothing to do with me," he said with affection in his voice.

"That's cuz you're the law, Papa." Maisie took a big bite out of her pastry. "We don't want you to arrest us."

"I'll go easy on you this time." He gave Maisie a few tickles at her waist and she giggled. "But I'm taking in the lovely Miss Anna for questioning. She's a known cohort of two wildly dangerous outlaws.''

''Don't get throwed in jail, Mama,'' Mandy advised.

''I'll try to bribe him with my strawberry tarts.''

''I've a weakness for sweets,'' Cooper confessed. ''You might get away with it.''

So they were laughing when they reached the kitchen.

Anna reached down a clean plate and placed several pastries onto it. ''I have cider.''

''I can pour it.'' He still smiled with humor.

''I have supper ready in the cellar. Since it's so hot, I thought you might like cool baked beans, cold fried chicken and potato salad. I made biscuits.''

''I'm hungry already.'' His gaze brushed hers.

Did he know how he made her want? She watched his hands set the pitcher on the counter. Studied the strength in those fingers, powerful looking but so gentle. What would it be like to be touched by him?

''I've got work I can do, but maybe you want to be alone with your daughters. I can leave—''

''No.'' His answer came quick, almost harsh. ''I mean, I don't want you to leave. There's no reason.''

''Papa! You're home.'' The back door slammed open. Katie, wearing her cowboy hat and boys' clothes pounded into the room. ''I'm goin' berry pickin'. Davy and me found a really big strawberry patch out in the meadow. Wanna come?''

''We could all go.'' Cooper suggested. ''Would you and Mandy like to go with us?''

''Yes!'' Katie took off at a dead run. ''Maisie! Hurry up. Anna's goin' berry pickin' with us.''

''I guess she decided for you.'' On a grin, Cooper took a long drink of cider.

Anna couldn't help but wonder what was in store for them this afternoon. It was never uneventful around Cooper's daughters.

"Katie handles her pony well," Anna told Cooper as the wagon rolled along the rutted road.

"I never said she couldn't." Humor glittered in his dark eyes and no small measure of pride. "I just would rather she pursued more safe activities like sewing."

"Sewing is full of hidden dangers. Sharp needles. Pricked fingers. Cricks in the neck." Anna laughed. "I've been meaning to ask you something."

"I'm afraid to hear it, but go ahead." In front of the wagon, Davy and Katie led their ponies off the rutted lane. Cooper headed after them.

"How do you feel about tree houses?"

He cast her a sideways glance. "Tree houses?"

"You know, you take boards up into a tree and nail them together."

"I've heard of it before." Disapproval rang in his voice, but it wasn't real disapproval. Humor hid beneath it, as if she surprised him. "You want me to build Maisie a tree house?"

"Yes. I think she would be safer with a nice sturdy platform to stand on, something with rails. I would feel better about Mandy being twenty feet off the ground." Her voice rattled as the wagon rocked and jostled. The ground was uneven and rocky.

"It's bouncy, Papa."

"I noticed, Maisie." He looked over his shoulder. "You girls hold on. I don't need you pretending to be birds next, flying out of the wagon and onto the ground."

"We ain't birds, Papa. Really." Maisie, still wearing her outlaw hat, shook her head.

Cooper's laughing eyes met Anna's. "After Corinthos is safe in jail, I'll have more time. I could start it then."

"If you would allow me to get the lumber for you at the mill, I could build it."

"You?" He crooked one brow. "No, I think I'd better do it. Constructing a building isn't like making a quilt."

"That's right. Hammering is a manly art. Women should stay in the kitchen." But she was laughing. "I know how to hammer, Cooper. I built Mandy her own playhouse back home."

"You built a playhouse?"

"And it was square and plumb, too."

"This I gotta see." He halted the wagon, set the brake. "I'll approve the lumber. But I will help you build it."

"You don't believe me." She accepted the hand he offered and eased down onto the ground. "You just wait and see."

"We want down, Papa!" Maisie held out both hands. "We gonna get lots of berries."

"You're going to *eat* lots of berries." He lifted Maisie down. "I remember last time we went picking."

"We ran into a bear then." Katie knelt down to tether Bob to a wheel spoke. Davy did the same. "Hope we don't run into no wild animals this time."

"Don't worry. I think we're safe." Cooper lifted Mandy gently to the ground. "You girls make so much noise, you've scared away half the bears in Montana Territory. They're living up in Canada now."

"Oh, Papa." Katie grabbed buckets from the wagon.

The patch of wild strawberries wasn't far. Bees buzzed over fragrant blooms and birds scattered when they approached. Bright red berries glistened in the sunlight, sweet and plump.

Quiet Davy dropped to his knees and started picking. He had extracted a promise from his mother for a strawberry pie. Cooper tipped his hat brim low against the sun, crouched down by a plentiful patch and went right to work. Anna worked her way around the low branches of a thick fir. Strawberries grew on the sunny side, so fragrant, her mouth watered when she picked them.

"Hey, you're stealing my berries, Maisie." She caught the little scamp's hand in her pail.

Maisie took a big bite of a berry.

"She always does that." Katie rolled her eyes. "Maisie's better at eatin' than she is at pickin'."

"It's cuz I'm little." Maisie explained.

"Come over here with me. There's a patch right here. You and Mandy sit in the clover and you can eat everything you pick." Anna tugged a low bough out of the way. Mandy and Maisie dashed into the hidden patch of berries, eager to eat all they could. A big cougar uncurled itself from its sunny nap.

Maisie screamed. Mandy shrieked. The mountain lion looked terrified. He snarled and then ran, crashing through the bushes, crying out as he went.

Cooper reholstered his drawn gun. "The poor cougar was just taking his nap and you girls terrified him."

"Did we really scare him, Papa?"

"Didn't you hear him roar?" Cooper reached out and hugged his daughter tight against his broad chest, clearly glad she was safe. "I bet he's telling all the other cougars in the area, watch out for that outlaw Maisie. She sneaks up on a guy when he's napping.''

''Oh, Papa.''

''He's probably running for Canada right this minute. He's going to go join the bears you scared off last berry-picking season.''

Anna's heart had only just started to beat again. The girls were safe. And it was starting to be funny. Mandy was laughing, Katie was rolling her eyes. Davy looked completely puzzled.

''I'd best go check that there aren't any more dangerous wildlife around.'' Cooper winked, releasing his girl. He stood, all might and man. ''I'll be right back.''

''Did you hear that cougar roar?'' Maisie asked, eyes glittering.

There was no fear and Anna could already hear the story that could come from it, that would be told around the table that evening. Of the cougar that roared and how Maisie ate all the berries.

Lee Corinthos gritted his teeth against the pain in his shoulder. Damn that Flint Creek sheriff. ''It's my damn shooting arm,'' he complained as he rolled a thin cigarette. ''If I'm going to be in a gunfight, I gotta be able to use my best hand.''

''Then stay back and supervise.'' Dusty reached for his well-oiled Colt and spun open its chamber. ''We can't let that marshal get his hands on our man Palmer. He musta been hurt pretty bad for them to wait this long to move him from that jail.''

Corinthos dragged deep, savoring the rich tobacco. ''My plan stands. We take out the witness, the one who took the bullet to the chest. Then we set up an ambush in the pass. I want the chance to talk to our fine Sheriff Braddock.''

''Think our contact will come through?''

''He'd better. I pay him enough. Check on the men. Make sure their guns are loaded and they've got enough ammunition to take on an army.''

Corinthos blew out a ring of smoke and leaned back against the tree. Thunder boomed along the mountain peaks, echoing in the valleys. Dry lightning flashed against the low crest of the sky.

A storm brewed within him as well. It was time to bring the mighty sheriff to his knees.

Breakfast was a somber occasion. It was the day Cooper was leaving for four whole days. Anna had been doing extra work in the evenings for Janet, and had made arrangements to stay in the house with the girls.

Anna cleared the table as Cooper drew his daughters close to say his goodbyes. He didn't need to tell her about the danger ahead. She was afraid for him, even knowing how competent he was, shoulders wide, guns strapped to his lean hips.

He stood from the table, all steely man. ''You look troubled. Are you worried about staying with the girls so long?''

''No. I'm worried about you.'' It was the truth, and personal. She shouldn't have said it.

''This is my job. I've been facing this kind of trouble for a long time and lived to tell about it. I'll be home, all in one piece. I promise.''

''I hope so, because your daughters need you.''

He laid his big hand against her jaw and tipped her head back. His lips hovered above hers, not touching, but hot and dazzling all the same. Every inch of her body responded.

The back door flew open. Cooper backed away from her.

Tucker burst into the room, all business. "We've got trouble. Meet me at the jail."

Was it Corinthos? Did this signal more danger for Cooper? For her and Mandy?

She began shaving the bar of gray soap into the wash basin, but the sense of foreboding remained, cold and hard in her stomach.

"Damn." Cooper rubbed his forehead, sick at what he'd seen. Campbell, who'd bravely helped him save Anna that day when Corinthos burst into the clinic, had been murdered.

"This means trouble." Tucker led the way out of the room. "The outlaws are back on the move."

Cooper squinted up at the sky through the front street window, the thunderheads already growing. A haze clung to the horizon, a fire from a lightning strike, no doubt. The storm last night had kept him awake. "Corinthos must be nearly recovered from that bullet wound I gave him. It's lucky he can use his firing arm at all."

"The badder they are, the harder they fall."

"That's the damn truth." Cooper swiped the beaded sweat from his brow, then grabbed his hat. "Lemonds, thanks for letting us look."

The undertaker fisted his hands. "Campbell was a darn good friend of mine. When is this crime against decent people gonna end? That's what we pay you for. We want to be safe in our own homes."

Cooper saw the grief in the man's eyes. Campbell hadn't wanted the deputy's protection. He didn't live

in town. And he'd been killed in his cabin some time
at night. When he hadn't reported for his shift on the
ranch, one of the hands came looking for him.

"Don't let Lemonds' words bother you," Tucker
said the instant they were out on the dusty street.
"You're doing a damn good job. Only a few of the
stage runs have been hit on your watch. And the only
trouble in town was when Corinthos tried to take Anna
from the clinic."

"Still, one man's life is too much." Cooper clenched
his teeth, grinding with fury. "That outlaw told me he'd
be back. I suppose he thinks I'm going to look the other
way, but I can't. Anna's next on his list."

"You don't know that." Tucker stared off at the
mountains where the gang roamed free.

"But I feel it. I want you to stay here and watch
her. Take one of the deputies and rotate shifts."

"Whatever you want, Coop."

He'd failed once, and he knew the price. It would
not happen again. He would keep her safe. He'd given
her his word. "Let's get the men mounted and ready.
We've got a stage to defend."

As he unlooped the reins and swung up on his stallion, he thought of Anna and the girls alone in that
house. What would have happened if Corinthos' men
had targeted her or his family instead of Campbell?

He'd enjoyed her company yesterday. He had
thought about her last night in the long hours when
sleep would not come. He remembered that kiss, like
a ghost on his lips, not quite tangible. He had been
without a woman's touch for a long time.

A cool wind blew from the north. He felt it brush
his face, tangle his hair. He headed his palomino down

the street, trying to run away from emotions he didn't want to feel.

"I'll be keepin' an eye on you and the girls, ma'am," Deputy Dickens said from the front porch. "Just in case. The sheriff ordered it."

Even when he wasn't here, he honored his vow to keep the girls—and Mandy—safe. Anna couldn't help but admire the man. "I have some strawberry tarts left-over from yesterday. Would you like some?"

"I'd be mighty obliged, ma'am." The young law-man grinned. "I haven't had a woman's cooking since I left home. Want some help with those boards?"

"No, thanks. I've got it under control." Anna leaned each board up against the thick tree trunk. "Katie, did you find your father's hammer?"

"In the stable with his other tools. Here's that rope, too." Katie dashed to a stop. "Do you really know how to hammer?"

"My father taught me how." Anna looped the rope. She gave it a toss. It snaked over a tall branch. She grabbed the end and tied it firmly around the board, stabilizing it.

She felt Katie's touch on her shoulder. "I hate it when Papa leaves. I'm glad you're here to take care of us, Anna. I'm glad you're gonna stay."

Maisie nudged close. "You ain't gonna leave us like Mrs. Potts?"

So much need in those eyes. Katie grew still, and Anna saw the children's unmistakable concern. "Why would I do that? This is the best job I've ever had. Doing anything else would be boring."

Mandy snuggled close, too.

With every mile up the mountainside, Cooper's un-
easiness grew. He hated riding like a sitting duck out
in the open, waiting for trouble. He'd sent Locke and
Barstow up ahead to scout. He had eight men riding
with him, alert, watching for Corinthos and his gang.

Tiny hairs prickled along the surface of his arms,
down the back of his neck. They would try to take back
their man before the pass, he figured.

He sensed the attack before it happened, knew from
experience the silence that preceded violence. He drew
his men around and faced the steep, sharp embankment. The pass was tight, the perfect place for an ambush.

He whistled, calling Barstow back.

He heard the horses first. The tap of a shoed hoof
against rock echoed in the canyon down below. The
coach shot forward, fleeing for safety. Cooper ordered
his men to split up, half to defend the coach, the other
to join him routing the outlaws. He had two deputies
guarding the rear. And they had the advantage—they
weren't surprised.

"Braddock." A snap of a twig, and the hard nose
of a gun jabbed him square in the back. "If I shoot, I
cripple you for life, if you're lucky."

"Corinthos. How the hell—"

"Shut up and listen. Call your men off."

"No, I'm not backing down—"

"You're in no position to argue, Sheriff." Corinthos
laughed. "I may only have one good shooting hand,
but that's all I need to bring you down."

"We're not backing down, Corinthos." Barstow's
voice, brash and deadly.

If the men put down their weapons, then they were
all dead.

"This is the second time I've got the advantage." Corinthos swung him around and backed him up against a tree trunk. "You and I are gonna make a deal, *Sheriff*." Corinthos said the last word with a sneer.

Rage flared in Cooper's chest. There had been no gunfire. None of his deputies had been killed. Someone had let Corinthos by. One of his own deputies.

"No deals."

The outlaw cocked his Colt. "I'm going to have my men take Palmer off that stage without any trouble. And then you and I are going to come to an agreement about that gold you've still got locked up in the town's bank."

"I make no agreements, Corinthos. I don't bargain with criminals."

"High-handed talk from a man who barely missed being hung himself."

Cooper closed his eyes.

"I did my job. I found out everything I could about you. Black Eyed Charlie is a good friend of a friend. He told me about your pretty young wife who played consort to him behind your back."

Cooper couldn't swallow. "I didn't break the law."

"That ain't the way I heard it. I wonder what the good people of Flint Creek will think if they knew the man they hired to protect them has a history."

"I'm not going to back down because I was a fool to love the wrong woman years ago. It's in the past. People will understand that."

The outlaw's eyes flashed with greed and twisted power. "A man can lose his honor a second time, but he doesn't get it back. What will happen to your daughters then?"

Cooper watched his deputies, guns drawn, keep close

eye on Corinthos' armed men. Palmer was taken without incident.

He hated being powerless. It was almost worth his life to stop Corinthos right here and now. Almost.

After the outlaws rode away, Barstow strode close, kept his voice low. "I heard what Corinthos said, that he wants to strike a deal. I worked for Joe before you came to town. He backed down and let that outlaw do anything he wanted."

"Don't worry," Cooper growled. "This time there will be no bargains."

Chapter Thirteen

"That's a good start to a tree house," Tucker commented when he stepped out from the night shadows. "I wonder what Cooper's going to think when he sees you've turned his girls into carpenters."

"He already knows." Anna pushed open the gate to join him in the shadowed front yard. "I'm glad you're here, Tucker."

"Aw, shucks, it's the least I could do."

"I heard about poor Mr. Campbell from Leslie at the mercantile."

He stiffened. "No one was trying to hide the news of his death from you. It's just…I don't want you worrying, Anna. I can take care of you while Coop's gone."

A humid breeze puffed over her. The charged air smelled like rain. Dark clouds covered the moon. There would be no wishes made tonight. "I feel like I've brought trouble here."

"What trouble? Corinthos has been a menace to towns like Flint Creek for too long." Tucker shook his head. "Besides, us Braddock men are tough."

"That we are." A shadow moved in the night. Cooper rode out of the grove of tall trees, nothing but darkness and might.

Her heart soared. "Cooper, I thought—"

"Me, too." He dismounted. His gaze was only for her.

"What went wrong?" Tucker stepped forward to take the palomino's reins.

"Corinthos surprised me."

"Surprised you? The toughest sheriff in Montana Territory?"

"Go ahead and tease. I'll tell you about it later. We probably have a problem with one of our deputies." Grim, Cooper's jaw set tight. A muscle jumped at his temple. "You'll hang around tonight?"

"Just as I promised." Tucker led the stallion away.

Anna felt Cooper's rage. What had gone wrong up on that mountain? "It's late. Did you get supper?"

"I grabbed a bite at the diner. I had a report to write up and I was starving." He tossed his hat through the air. It caught the porch rail post, swirling to a stop atop the carved knob.

"Something went wrong."

"Damn right it did." He raked his hand through his hair. Dark locks swept his wide shoulders, tangled in the hot breeze. "Corinthos had a gun to my back."

"Did he hurt you?" Her voice broke.

"No, my pride got the worst beating. He took back his injured man. Unless I wanted a slaughter of my deputies, I couldn't stop him. He wants me to look the other way while he does whatever the heck he pleases. He's gotten to someone on my payroll."

Her jaw dropped into a surprised O. "Who?"

"If I knew that, he'd be in jail." Cooper nodded toward the path worn through the lawn. They started off together. He walked slow. Her nearness swept across him, charged as the night air. A storm was brewing, in the sky and in his heart. "Don't worry. I vowed to protect you and I will."

"I don't want you to die for me, Cooper. That isn't right." She looked down to the dark forest floor at their feet. "I couldn't live with that."

"Who said anything about dying?"

"But he had a gun on you!"

"Whoa, wait a minute." He wrapped her into his arms, sheltered her against his chest. She leaned into him, nestling her face in the hollowed curve of his throat and chest. She seemed to fit just right in his arms. "No need to worry, Anna. Nothing's going to happen to me."

"That's right. I forget what a great sheriff you are."

He chuckled, and it vibrated against her ear. She snuggled against him, feeling his iron-solid male heat, breathing in his scent. She felt as safe as heaven clasped in his arms. She shouldn't be here. She should step away.

"I realized what I had to lose." His voice vibrated through her as if it were her own. "My daughters. Everything I've worked for, worked to stand for. I guess we're all vulnerable in some way."

"It's called being human."

He didn't like it. He didn't like feeling so alone. He could have died on the mountain tonight. He could never have the chance to pick berries again, see his daughters at the breakfast table, feel happiness when they came rushing to greet him at night.

And he would not have Anna in his arms. Never have the chance to close up the loneliness in his heart.

To fill it with something better. He wanted something better.

"Anna?"

She gazed up at him. Her lower lip was tucked between her teeth, drawing his gaze there. Every muscle in his body tensed. Cooper's breath caught, his pulse hammered wildly. A sharp need drove him. How he wanted to kiss her, to taste her passion.

He leaned forward. Her eyes widened round as the moon. With a simple tilt of his head, their lips met.

The heat of the kiss captivated him. Gentle. Demanding. She tasted sweet like strawberries, rich like coffee. He slipped one hand to her shoulder, then curved the other around the back of her neck. She felt so slight, but her warm velvet skin teased at feelings he'd buried so long ago.

A brief flash of lightning split the sky above and he could look into her forever-blue eyes. Sure, he had the girls to light up his life, but he needed different kinds of affection, too. He wanted to need someone just a little bit.

But she stepped away. "Cooper, I—"

"I lost my honor once. I can't do that again." He would say anything to keep her with him, to stop her from leaving him alone in the darkness. Thunder cracked overhead, splitting the silence of the night.

"I know you won't give in to Corinthos' threats, Cooper." So sure her voice. She laid a hand on his arm, light but so gentle it nearly undid him. He'd had no one but family to trust then.

But he knew he could trust her. Just this once. Just a little. "He's threatening me with something that happened in my past, something I'm not proud of."

She remained silent, waiting. The wind ruffled her

hair, lifting the sweet scent of her straight into his nose. She filled his senses and made him feel. Deep down in his chest, emotions ached.

"I'm not giving in. I did nothing wrong. The charges were dropped. I would never aid and abet a criminal. It's against everything I believe in."

"I know this about you. And anyone who looks at you knows it, too. You are a man of honor. A man like Corinthos can't change that."

"No. But I could have died tonight. Without telling you how glad I am you're here. For the way you treat my daughters. For the way you make me feel."

Even in the dark, he found her mouth again. For a brief moment Anna wanted to step away. But the feel of his lips slanted over hers, gentle and full of need, urged her to stay. He needed her. She needed him too. She didn't want to admit it.

He laved his tongue across her bottom lip, and she moaned. He caressed and nibbled. How sweet it felt. She tipped her head back, opening to him. It hurt to be so vulnerable. She dared to lay her hand along his jaw, to feel the luxury of his textured male skin.

Moaning low in his throat, Cooper drew her arms up and placed them around his neck. She snuggled against him, breathing him, feeling the steely wall of his chest.

He felt like a dream, all solid man, just as she knew he would. Her breath quickened. Being in his arms made her feel as if she'd never been held, never been touched before.

Her hands played with his collar-length hair, and she wrapped a few locks around her fingers. He moaned, deepening their kiss. She felt the hard length of his arousal against her hip.

"Anna." He breathed her name, spoke against her lips.

No one had ever wanted her like this.

A sharp snap of a twig drilled through her senses, made her aware of the world again. Thunder crashed overhead. Tree limbs rustled, just a ways up the path. She heard footsteps. Felt her heart tumble when Cooper stepped back sharply.

"Is that you, Tucker?" he called out, one hand moving toward his revolver's grip.

Tucker stood in the path, both hands planted firmly on his hips. "This proves it, big brother. I knew you were lying about those letters all along."

Anna was angry. Cooper had left the house by the time she arrived the next morning. Was he avoiding her? She'd needed to talk to him. He had to know how she felt, where she stood. He'd kissed her, even when he'd promised not to.

Laura returned at the end of the day to watch the girls. Cooper was working late. Anna was finishing up the dishes when she heard him outside. Ready to do battle, she pushed open the screen door.

He didn't turn at the sound of her step. He sat on the top back porch step, his elbows on his knees, staring off at the mountains. The thickness of twilight cloaked his features, but even in the darkness she could see the square line of his jaw, feel the intense brush of his eyes on her.

She breezed past him and emptied the washbasin in the flower bed. "You've been avoiding me."

"I knew you'd eventually figure that out." His attempt at humor failed. He looked miserable. "I broke my word to you."

"I know." She was angry about it, even if the kiss last night had been wondrous. "I can't work for you. I have my pride, Cooper. And self-respect."

"You have every right to feel that way." He sighed, rubbed his hands over his face. "I'm sorry."

His free hand brushed her cheek, blazed fire across her skin, and desire consumed her like flame. Brilliant, intense, immediate. Her whole body trembled, aching to know more of his touches. To lay her hand against his whiskery jaw, to explore the ridge of muscle across his wide chest. She kept her hands to herself, but she trembled. She'd never known the power of such want.

"Please. Give me another chance to keep my promise to you. Or Laura will think we're having another fight."

Anna fought against the smile, and lost. His gaze twinkled at her, glinting with humor, but dark with truth. He respected her. He needed her.

How was she ever going to resist him?

The next day, Anna set the tray of refreshments on the table in the center of Cooper's parlor. For once the toys were picked up off the floor. The play holsters, cowboy hats, chaps, stick ponies and the tea party set now littered the porch and front yard.

Sheila Muldune had brought her daughter to play with Mandy and Maisie. Carol Fykerud had brought her daughters of the same age. Through the open window, Anna could hear the delighted screeches of little girls playing outside.

"I don't know what I'd do without all this help." Laura looked up from her sewing. "How do I thank you all?"

"It is our pleasure." Sheila Muldune looked up from

her hemming. "These little dresses are going to look too beautiful on the girls."

"If I can get Katie to agree to wear hers." Laura's eyes twinkled. "Anna, the dress Sheila is working on is for your Mandy."

"What?" Anna lifted the pile of fabric from the seat of her chair.

"I didn't want to leave her out. I can't tell you how much fun I've had getting to know her." Mirth bubbled in Laura's voice. "She will be my niece soon."

"Have you and Cooper set a wedding date yet?" Carol Fykerud reached for a glass of fresh lemonade.

"I was wondering the same thing." Sheila's voice shivered with excitement. "Will we have a second wedding soon?"

Anna blushed. "I thought you understood. Cooper and I—"

"Were caught kissing in the dark the night before last." Laura's laughter started everyone laughing.

Anna didn't think it was funny. "It was a momentary lapse—"

"Sure. Momentary." Sheila shook her head, disbelieving.

"I'm his housekeeper. Like Mrs. Potts was."

"You're nothing like Mrs. Potts." Laura took a sip of lemonade.

A movement fluttered outside the curtains. Then Bob poked her head through the window. Her nose flared. She gave a low whinny, scenting the cookies on the serving platter. Her long tongue reached out. Carol Fykerud gave a scream, startled by the horse lips at her elbow. Then she sank back into the chair, laughing.

"She likes molasses cookies, too." Anna grabbed

two cookies and crossed to the window. "Here you go, Bob."

The pony crunched happily. Anna held the second cookie out to Davy's pony, who was more polite and did not stick her nose into the parlor.

"Did you see that?" Leslie dissolved into laughter.

Anna was at least glad the topic of conversation had taken a turn for the better.

Cooper hated that work had kept him late. There had been an incident at the saloon. By the time he'd resolved it, the sun was already setting. He wanted to see Anna. He just wanted to see her.

But he knew she'd gone home when he reined in and dismounted outside the stable. The horse she borrowed from the hotel's owners wasn't grazing in the shade of the big maple. Pal nosed him, already impatient for his supper. Cooper ran his hand down the horse's honey-colored, hot velvet neck. The animal leaned into his touch. They'd been riding together for seven years. The loyal stallion swung his head, making a second demand for grain.

Cooper laughed. "All right, boy. Anything you want but the Richards' filly."

He trumpeted at that. He glanced at the direction of the neighbor's stable.

"Women are nothing but trouble and not nearly as loyal as you." The cynical remark tasted sour in his mouth because he knew darn well it wasn't always true.

He thought of Anna's sunny presence in his kitchen. The woman had nearly fallen down a cliff to rescue her child. She was loyal to a fault. Not at all like Katherine had been.

Cooper led the palomino into his roomy box stall. Fresh straw littered the floor. He slipped off the saddle and blanket, peeled off the bridle and then forked fresh hay into the feeder.

Pal stomped his right front hoof and swung his head up and down in protest.

"All right. I'm getting the grain." Laughing, Cooper dipped a bucket in the nearly full barrel. Molasses, sweet corn and oats scented the air. A swallow chirped in the rafters above, protective of newborn chicks. Cooper ducked his head as the father bird, red-bellied and sharp-beaked, dove at his hat and chased Cooper out into the yard.

"Hi, Papa," Maisie greeted from her open second story window. "You missed molasses cookies."

"Is that what you and Anna made today?"

The little face bobbed, and blond curls bobbed, too.

As he tugged open the screen door, he was met with the wondrous fragrance of supper. Anna must have left a plate for him warming in the oven. His mouth watered. His stomach rumbled. He grabbed a towel and opened the stove door.

"Anna sure can cook," Katie reminded him, as if that fact had been in question.

Startled, Cooper nearly dropped the food-stacked plate. "I didn't see you there. I can't remember the last time you were this quiet."

"Oh, Papa. This is surely trying my patience." Katie dropped the hoop on the table with a thud. "I ain't no good at this. Anna says I have to try to have patience. I'm much better at riding ponies and stuff."

Was Anna responsible for this mysterious, girl-like change in his oldest daughter? Afraid to break the spell,

Cooper pulled out the chair across from her. "I'm better at riding and stuff, too."

His mouth watered around the mouthful of mashed potatoes. Sweet, creamy, rich. Even after sitting in the oven.

"Anna sure can take care of Maisie. I reckon I done good picking her out."

"I reckon you did." Chuckling, Cooper attacked the spicy baked beans, by far the tastiest he'd eaten. "Anna is the best housekeeper we've ever had."

"Papa, that's not it at all." Katie lifted her chin, both hands tightly fisted. "Maisie oughtta have a mother. She's not like me. She ain't tough, and she needs someone to cuddle her."

"There won't be any more women coming to town hoping I'll marry them, will there?"

"Stop teasing, Papa. This is serious." Katie snatched her sewing from the table. "Laura's up in the attic crying."

"Crying?"

"Some mushy stuff, I guess." Katie headed upstairs leaving him in his transformed kitchen.

Everything was clean. From the polished floors to the blackened stove to the glass in the cabinets above the work counter. No dust, no cobwebs, no dirt in corners or crumbs on the table. The curtains looked freshly washed and pressed, crisply fluttering in the pleasant evening breezes.

Anna's touch. He finished the plate of food Anna cooked, then walked through the house Anna had cleaned. Her careful work was everywhere, even along the dirt-free banister that now glistened like a polished stone.

He hesitated on the last step and squinted through

the dimness of the attic. He spied Laura kneeling at an opened, dust-coated trunk.

Katie said she was crying. And in the lemony haze the last rays of daylight threw into the tiny room, he could see it was true.

"I hear you're getting married tomorrow." The words meant to sound light were leaden instead.

She fingered a thick fold of lace. "I'm getting out while I still have the chance. It's been torture helping raise those nieces of mine."

Her words, meant to tease, sounded infinitely sad.

His throat filled. He understood all she didn't say, ached with what he could not. "We're going to miss you, Laura. Especially the girls."

"I know." Tears stood in her eyes. "But it's time for me to leave home, big brother."

He sat down on a crate beside the trunk. "What are you up to?"

"Going through Mother's things." Laura sighed. "Father saved some of her favorites for me. They've been packed up for so long, I can't remember what I have."

Cooper's throat tightened with the pain of memories and separations. Mother's fine tablecloth. He recognized it now. And the set of china come all the way from England. "I want you to be happy, Laura."

She lifted a saucer and rubbed the heel of her hand across it. "Larry loves me. I know he'll be good to me."

Cooper only nodded. Love. He couldn't believe in something so hard to hold, to see. He'd tried to once, but only found illusion and trickery. "Larry better treat you well, or I'll hog-tie him in jail and give him my special torture treatment."

"You're terrible." Laura threw a doily at him.

He caught the scrap of lace before it smacked him in the nose. "If you ever need anything, you know where I am. I'm always here for you, Laura. Just like you've been for me and the girls. No matter what."

"I know, and that's why you owe me, big brother." Her hand covered his. "One day I'll have children of my own and believe me, when I need a baby-sitter, I'm hauling all six of them right over here for you to look after."

"Six? You expect me to take care of all those children?"

"Anytime I want to go gallivanting around." She winked, all laughter and happiness and sadness.

He knew, because he felt the same way. "Laura, nothing would bring me greater pleasure."

The day of Laura's wedding dawned like any other. Cooper ambled downstairs, buttoning his shirt to find her in his kitchen instead of Anna, making pancakes for the girls.

"Shouldn't you be getting into that fancy wedding dress of yours?" he said, trying to hide the sadness that ached inside. His little sister was leaving them.

"Who cares about a fancy dress?" Laura teased from the stove, all sunshine, all smiles. "I told Anna to come in an hour later. I'm spending my last morning of freedom with my nieces because I'm going to miss them the most."

"Papa! Papa!" Maisie dashed across the kitchen, swinging some white thing violently in one hand. "Look what Aunt Laura got me."

"A new bridle for Bob!" Katie squealed from the table where she ripped open brown wrapping paper.

"It's a bride hat." Maisie plopped the object on her head, the gossamer fabric floating down over her face.

"A veil." He knelt down. "It's beautiful on you."

"Laura's leavin' today, so she's makin' bacon." Maisie sighed.

"Don't you leave, Laura." Katie dropped the bridle with a clank and a thud. The merriment drained from the room. "You have to stay here. You're supposed to take care of us when Papa can't."

Tears of regret shimmered in Laura's eyes.

Cooper stood, held out his hand. "Katie, Laura deserves a family of her own. Don't spoil her special day."

"She's got us." Katie's hands balled into tight angry fists. "A bridle ain't gonna make it better. I don't want nothin' but Laura."

"Katie!" His rebellious daughter had gone too far. "You apologize to your aunt—"

"Cooper." Laura swiped her eyes. "Gifts can't make up for my leaving. Katie, I just wanted you girls to have something to remember my wedding day. It's a happy day for me."

"Why? So you can leave us to go kiss Larry?"

"I don't want to leave you." Laura's voice broke.

"You fix it, Papa. Don't let Laura go." Katie tugged on his hand.

"Oh, tiger." He pulled Katie to him and held her tight. How little she felt in his arms. How vulnerable. She'd always been sensitive about goodbyes. "You have me. And I'll always make certain there's someone to look after you and Maisie."

"But not someone who loves us like a mama." A sob rent the air. "You won't marry Anna and now Laura's leaving. What's Maisie gonna do?"

Katie's genuine pain darkened the sunny kitchen like a swift black cloud. She broke away from his hold and bolted from the room.

Cooper pulled himself to his feet. He hadn't been the only one hurt when his wife abandoned them. Katie had been devastated, inconsolable.

Sorrow trembled in Laura's eyes.

"It's not your fault," he said. And it wasn't. It was his. He hadn't seen this coming. He hadn't thought how hard Katie would take her beloved aunt's departure. Even if she was only moving from the cottage next door to a grand house three streets away.

He crossed the yard toward the stable. Each step kicked more pain through his chest. He tried to squeeze out the mumble of a guilty conscience, but he failed.

He pulled open the stable door to hear Katie's sobs echoing in the rafters, the aching sound of a little girl's heart broken and bleeding.

Yep, there was no denying it. Housekeepers and a loving aunt could never heal the scars in his daughter's heart.

Only the strength of a mother's love could do that.

Chapter Fourteen

Anna held tight to Mandy's waist and wished she would quit fidgeting. The mare they rode was steady and dependable, but she was going to wrinkle her pretty dress. The wedding was a few hours away. Anna had hoped her child could stay presentable and mud-free, at least until after Laura's ceremony.

"Looky! It's Bob!" Mandy's admiration for the pony shimmered in her voice.

"That can't be." The sun was in her eyes and she couldn't see. The crook in the road cast them in shade, and she gazed down the street. Homes perched along the wide lane, towered over by giant firs and pines. The craggy purple peaks of the mountains looked down on them all.

Then a movement caught her eyes. She saw the streaking pony and the girl clinging bareback. She saw at once the sturdy four-foot-high fence and Bob's reckless gallop. "What's Katie doing?"

Anna saw the pony hurl over the cut-timber fence. Then toppled in midair. Anna watched in horror as Katie flew over Bob's head and fell directly into the panicked animal's path. The pony hit the ground, first stumbling and then rolling.

"Katie!" The girl could have been crushed. Anna kicked the mare into a trot, then a lope. She grabbed Mandy and slipped to the ground. Fear for the fallen girl pulsed through her, and she stumbled along the side of the rutted road.

Katie! Where was Katie?

Bob squealed in panic, then clamored to her feet. Anna left Mandy and the mare by the side of the lane. She launched herself between the slats of the fence. The pony danced around in the tall grass, panicked. Anna soothed the frightened animal with her voice, then snatched the reins.

"Katie?" Two quick knots and Bob was safely tethered. The tall grass obscured everything. Then Anna saw a corner of red fabric and fell to the ground.

Katie. She lay motionless, unconscious, her body sprawled at an unnatural angle.

Anna rested a hand on the girl's chest. A pulse beat beneath her fingertips. Thank God she was breathing.

"Katie!" Cooper shouted.

"Over here!" Anna's voice wobbled.

Seconds felt like minutes as she waited for help. She brushed tangled curls from the girl's forehead and saw a small cut trickling blood along her hairline. Anna pulled a clean handkerchief from her skirt pocket and pressed it gently to the wound.

"I saw it from the parlor window." Cooper approached, his booming voice startling grasshoppers, birds and the wind from the seed-tipped grasses. "Katie, you scared me near to death. Don't you know you could have been killed? I've told you before, no j—"

"Cooper. She's unconscious." Anna touched his

knee as he stomped to a halt before Katie's prone body. Looking up the length of him, he seemed taller, broader, stronger. He stood between her and the sun, the glint of rays hiding half his face, but she still saw his enraged fear.

"Don't worry. She's alive."

He dropped to his knees. The earth shook. He wiped his right hand over his face. His furious expression changed to shock, then he was all action, all protective father. His capable fingers brushed over arms and legs. Then he trained his grave, all-business gaze on her. "It doesn't look from here as if any bones are broken. I need to get her to the house."

"Let me help." Anna held Katie's head while Cooper gently lifted her motionless body. There were no groans of pain and no struggles toward consciousness. Cooper settled the girl tight against his chest. She lay as limp as a doll.

Mandy huddled in the grass, crying, and Anna reached out for her hand.

The owner of the field loped out of his stable. "Sheriff, I saw that girl of yours fall. I was in the back pasture." He wheezed, out of breath. "I'll race and fetch the doc if you want."

"Thanks, Eric."

"Papa!" Maisie cried out from across the street, apparently afraid to leave her own yard. Her ruffled pink dress and a white bride's veil fluttered in the crisp morning breeze.

"This way. Hurry." Cooper urged.

Anna struggled to keep ahead of him to open the gate, then the front door. She took Maisie by the hand and led both crying little girls into the house. She left them in the parlor. She hated doing it, but Cooper needed her help. She rushed ahead to open doors. Her heart broke watching him gently lay his injured daughter on her twin bed.

"She still hasn't woken up." He turned to her, his face lined with worry. "I hope the doc hurries."

"She took a bad fall, Cooper, but she'll be all right. I know it."

"I hope you're right." How broken he sounded.

Anna rested a hand on his forearm, felt the iron muscle, his hot skin and the light dusting of downy hair. This man, larger than life, able to defeat any villain, felt vulnerable at her touch.

"Katie was upset over Laura's visit this morning. When we were ready to head over to the church to help set up for the ceremony, she got all worked up again. She tore off astride that blasted pony." His throat worked.

"Katie will be fine. You have to believe that."

"She does have a hard head." So affectionate, those words. He brushed a hand over the still girl's ashen brow. "I should have insisted she do more on her needlework."

"Let me go heat some wash water. Seems she landed in the mud. And I did, too."

"Laura's wedding." He said the words with regret.

Then she understood. "When Eric returns with the doctor, I'll have him go by the church."

His mouth frowned in thought. "I want Laura to marry that banker and not worry about us. She has a new life now, new priorities. I don't want her to worry. Katie will wake up any minute."

But his arm trembled beneath her hand. He was as terrified for Katie, Anna realized, as she'd been when Mandy was hurt.

"She deserves to know. You stay with your daughter, Cooper. I'll be right back. Make sure she doesn't get chilled."

Brightness burned in his night-dark eyes. He knelt down and laid one strong arm around his daughter, cradling Katie as if she were the most precious child in the world.

Anna had never before seen the strength of a father's love, of a man's protective tenderness for his family.

Footsteps pounded down the hallway. Anna moved aside to let the doctor get closer.

"Tell me what's wrong, Doc." Cooper sounded like thunder, afraid of nothing, dominant and powerful.

But she knew the fears haunting him.

Anna turned and slipped out of the room unnoticed. All the troubles she'd endured and would yet face, they were all nothing as long as Katie opened her eyes and could ride her pony again.

She was warming wash water when a knock rapped at the back door. The door swung open, to reveal a woman's pale and worried face.

Anna reached for a hand towel. "Laura. I'm glad you got my message."

"How's Katie?"

"Still unconscious. The doctor had hoped she might be awake already. But—" Anna couldn't say the words.

Laura, wearing a beautiful dark-blue dress with matching hat, stepped into the kitchen. She must have come directly from the church. Her wedding was scheduled to start in less than ten minutes. "Larry and I have decided against going ahead with the ceremony. Katie is more important. We can always reschedule."

"Aunt Laura!" Maisie flew across the room, veil shivering behind her, Mandy trailing. "You ain't wearin' your bride hat."

"Not now, dearest." Laura laid a hand on the girl's tousled head. "Why don't you go play in your tree?"

"You mean my outlaw hideout?" Maisie hesitated. Clearly worried.

"I saw a sheriff sneak past the window looking for you," Anna improvised. "You girls had better hurry before he drags you back to jail."

They hurried on their way, eager to evade the make-believe sheriff.

"Katie doesn't seem to have any other injuries." Anna led the way through the house. "The doc is hopeful she'll open her eyes soon."

"I'm glad you're here." Laura stopped at the foot of the stairs. Tears sparkled in her eyes. "The girls adore you, and that's why I didn't stop to think. I never realized Katie would take my wedding so h-hard." A sob choked her words.

"This isn't your fault, Laura."

She took Anna's hand, a gentle welcoming touch of new friendship. "I'm so happy they have you. The girls need you so much."

Laura's words echoed in Anna's mind when she brought lemonade to the outlaw brides out on the porch, still evading that pesky sheriff. Later, after the wash water was warm and she'd cleaned the dirt and blood from Katie's face and arms, Anna couldn't shake the unmistakable, heartbreaking truth.

Laura was right. The girls needed her far too much. She wasn't here to be their mother; she was just hired help. And what if Dalton came for her? She would have to leave. How could she break those little girls' hearts?

* * *

"I made you some dinner." Anna hesitated in the threshold, balancing the loaded tray.

Cooper wiped his hands over his face. "I'm not hungry."

"I think a meal is just what we all need." The doctor rose from Katie's bedside. "Still no change," he answered her silent question. "That beef stew smells excellent."

Anna blushed at the kind praise. "I just want to keep you happy. Katie's pretty special to us."

"I know." Warmth shone in those intelligent eyes. The doctor was a good man. Anna knew beyond doubt he would do everything he could for Katie. "Cooper, I suggest you keep your energy up. Likely as not, that girl of yours is going to open her eyes and you'll need your energy to chase after her."

"After I hang her from a tree for jumping her pony over that high fence."

"Poor tree," Anna teased as she set the tray on the low chest of drawers between the two beds. She unloaded the steaming bowls of stew, the plates of warm biscuits and fresh butter.

Cooper's hand caught her wrist, his touch heavy with need. "I'm glad you're here to watch over us."

Her vision blurred. Anna ducked her head and hurried from the room.

The day slowly bled away without improvement. The doctor remained, worried about Katie's head injury. If she did not awaken soon, he feared the worst. Cooper rubbed his face with his hands. She was so pale, so still. The day faded to dusk, then to the first shades of night.

Before he heard the light pad of her step, Cooper felt her presence, like the veiled starlight dusting the quiet room.

"You're still here?"

"Where do you think I would go? I care about Katie. There's no way I could go home. Not now." She moved in the shadows. He heard the clink of enamelware, smelled the rich aroma of fresh coffee. "Laura has taken Mandy and Maisie home with her for the night, so we can concentrate on Katie."

His joints ached from long hours in the hard-backed chair. He'd hardly touched the food she'd made, but the notion of coffee, hot and soothing, felt just right.

Anna set the tray on the little chest of drawers. She brushed close to him, the sweet rose scent of her tickling his nose, the hem of her skirts rustling past his thigh.

He couldn't remember the last time someone had brought him coffee before he could ask for it.

"I heard the doc leave. What did he say?" Quiet fear in those words.

"A head injury is bad news. I've tried to be positive, I've tried not to picture her just fading away, never waking up."

"You can't think that. You can't begin to allow such a possibility. Katie will be fine." But despite her brave words, fear shook in her voice.

"I have to be practical, Anna."

"Life is too hard to be practical all the time." She sat down in the brush of starshine across Maisie's empty bed. "Sometimes a person has to make wishes and keep a tight hold on them."

"Is that what you do?"

"I've made a lot of wishes in my life, on the first

star of the night and the last of morning, on rainbows and waterfalls and full moons.''

"Does it work?" He sat down beside her.

He watched Anna's gaze fall to the child tucked in bed. "Sometimes."

Sorrow vibrated in her voice, quietly as if she were trying to hide it. Why hadn't he realized it before? Anna had journeyed here intent on loving his girls from the very start. Back home, had she made starlight wishes for their future together?

She met his gaze, direct and honest. "It will work this time. See that star, the bright one right through the trees?"

"The shimmering one." Just like her. He leaned close, breathed in all her gentle goodness and light.

"When I make a wish on that star, it always comes true."

"But you just said—"

"This is a special star." Soft poetry that voice, spinning a tale he wanted to believe. "It's Sirius, the Dog Star. He guides the great warrior Orion across the night skies and protects him."

"And little girls, too?"

"Especially little girls." Like magic, she smiled.

"Then I guess we'd better make a wish."

He was tired of being alone. Tired of standing tall without anyone to lean on. The doc's warning had scared him more than anything had. He didn't want to be alone, stand tough, be strong. He needed her.

She'd stayed at his side and gone without sleep to care for his girl. Anna could have left for her hotel room and a snug night's sleep because Katie wasn't her daughter, wasn't her responsibility. But she'd stayed, knowing they needed her. Knowing Katie needed her.

"There. Wish made." Anna opened her eyes. "I always read to Mandy when she's ill. Let me do the same for Katie. Maybe she'll hear my voice and wake up."

"If anyone's voice can reach her, yours will." Grim, Cooper watched his daughter sleep. If she didn't wake by morning's light, the doctor feared… Well, the possibility was too dreadful to think about.

"Let me choose a book from the shelf. Would you pour me a cup of coffee?" Anna knelt to study the titles.

His hand shook, rattling the pot as he poured. Silver light dusted through the window, illuminating his movements. Remembering her story, his throat filled with unspoken fear.

What would he do if he lost his Katie?

"I bet this is her favorite." Anna sat down by Katie's side, as she did not long ago for her own daughter, and tilted the book to read by starlight—a dime novel called *Captives of the Wild Frontier.*

Anna closed the book. Cooper returned to the room with a new pot of coffee and a plate of oatmeal cookies.

He faced her, his dark eyes empty and shielded. "I can't lose her."

"I know." Anna could see the pain beneath, and she knew from experience how much it hurt. She ached to comfort him, to be comforted by him. To know the shelter of his arms, to lean against the iron-hard breadth of his chest. To find some comfort from all this fear.

"It's my fault. I never should have agreed to that damn pony." He rubbed his hands over his face.

"But a girl needs a pet to heap her affections on."

"I thought I was enough, that I could be what Katie needed in place of a mother. I was arrogant enough to think that no matter what happened, my love could fix it."

"And it can. You're a good father, Cooper. The best one I've ever seen." And she ought to know. Affection burned in her heart. Affection for him. For the courage in his soul, the love so deep for his daughter.

"I suppose I should pay you extra for that compliment," he teased, but that brief sparkle of humor quickly extinguished. "Compliments can't change the truth. I'm not enough, and I've known it for a while. I haven't given my daughters the one thing they needed most of all. Now look what's happened."

"It does no good to blame yourself." Anna wished she knew how to make everything better for him and for Katie. "A parent can't be everything to a child, no matter how hard you try, no matter how good your intentions."

"But you realized your daughter needed a new father, and you tried to find her one." He reached out, and his hand caught hers. "What happened to your husband?"

"Cooper, this isn't the time. Katie is hurt."

"And she might never come back to me." His heated hand gripped her more tightly, his skin rough and male-textured. His big fingers threaded through hers. "Please, I want to know."

But what would he think of her? His free hand brushed her cheek, blazed fire across her skin, and desire consumed her like flame. Brilliant, intense, immediate. Her whole body trembled, aching to know more of his touches. To lay her hand against his whiskery jaw, to explore the ridge of muscle across his wide chest. Anna trembled. She'd never known the power of such want.

"Did you lose him in the war?"

She accepted the cup he offered. "Yes, James died in battle." She winced against the memories, raw and sharp. But she could not lie to this man she cared for so much. "James came from a very fine family, and they refused to let him marry an immigrant farmer's daughter like me."

How it hurt to remember. "We were engaged and we tried to elope. They found us and stopped the ceremony. They sent him off to the war and I—"

She stopped, lowering her gaze so she wouldn't have to see the disapproval in his eyes. "I found out too late that I was pregnant. James died before I could write to him."

"And you lied about it to all of us." Incredibly, his voice wasn't filled with more than surprise.

"Yes." Her hand trembled. She sipped the coffee before she spilled it. "I wanted to protect Mandy. I wanted to give her a new start where she wasn't an illegitimate child no little girl would play with. I have to be honest. I wanted the same thing for myself."

He let out a shaky sigh. He was silent a long while. "It hasn't been easy for you."

She looked up. No blame marked his face. Just understanding. "How can you act as if I'm—" She couldn't say the words. "How can you be so accepting?"

"I have my mistakes, too. My failures."

"You? Why, you're a big strong sheriff who never fails anyone." And a compassionate man. Inside, she sparkled with unending affection.

But his face was shadowed. "You have no idea how wrong you are about me."

Anna met his gaze and saw eyes filled with doubts. But she had none, not about him. "A dishonorable man doesn't love his daughters the way you do. Or protect a town from murderous outlaws. Or help a woman alone with an injured child."

"I'm not what you think—"

"Anna?" Katie's voice, scratchy and low.

Thank God. Anna set down her coffee and knelt beside the bed. Cooper was already there. Their hands brushed. Their arms met. She felt the hot length of him from shoulder to hip.

"Where's Bob?" Katie tried to sit up.

Anna pressed her back...and so did Cooper. His big hand covered hers as together they forced the girl into her pillows.

"I want you to rest, tiger." His voice vibrated through Anna, quivering along her nerve endings, tingling in her fingertips.

"P-papa, is B-bob all right?"

"She looks fine. It's you I'm worried about."

"My head hurts."

"And it's no wonder, trying to jump that damn fence." Anger, relief and love tangled in his words.

Katie began to cry. "You ain't gonna take Bob, are you, Papa? Anna, don't let him."

"Little girls shouldn't be racing around on the backs of animals."

"Cooper." Anna took Katie's hand. "I had a pony when I was young."

"You did?" The touch of the girl's fingers to hers, needy and trusting, released a flood of emotion. Affec-

tion for this child rushed through her, feelings she
didn't have the right to.

"This isn't helping my cause," Cooper whispered.
His words tickled Anna's ear, and she fought the flicker
of want rushing into her blood. "Maybe you could
mention how you learned to sew at that age."

Anna laughed. "Sorry to disappoint you, but I'm on
Katie's side."

Although weak and in pain, the girl would be fine.
She gripped Anna's hand with such force, such delib-
erate, unveiled need. And Anna knew with a certainty,
as Katie closed her eyes and drifted back to sleep, she
couldn't be what Katie needed. Staying would only
make matters worse.

The lamp on the chest burned steadily, fighting
against the darkness of night.

Anna pushed open the door. The lamp on the bureau
tossed a glow across Katie's bed. "Here's your chocolate."

"Ain't Papa comin'?"

"He's downstairs making more coffee. I think he's
awful tired from being so worried about you." Anna
set the tray on the chest between the beds.

"Were you?"

"Absolutely." She sat down on the edge of the mattress tick. "Just because a girl acts tough, she can still
be hurt or scared."

"Are you tough, too?"

"I sure try to be." Anna reached for one mug and
tested the temperature. "Here, drink up."

Katie pulled a book from the edge of the table.
"Chocolate tastes better with a story."

"Always." She scooted closer and opened the book.

Katie nestled against her, and sweetness filled Anna up. Leaning back into the extra pillows, she began to read.

The light at the end of the hall drew Cooper's gaze. His body heated at the sight of her. Brushed by a single lamplight's glow, she stood beside the bed, smoothing the covers beneath the girl's chin.

Anna's blond curls tumbled over her shoulders, glinting in the gentle light. He could see the soft roundness of her breasts, the flare of her hips. What would it be like to have her beside him in his bed? He felt a hardening, a thickening in his groin.

"She's finally asleep." Her whisper shivered over him, warm and alluring. "She fought to keep her eyes open."

"She's always wanted a mother to fuss over her." Cooper tried to sound normal, but his pulse was racing through his veins. He could face dangerous outlaws without a flicker of fear, but the very idea of getting Katie a mother terrified him.

"What little girl doesn't want to be cherished?" Anna leaned one slim shoulder against the door frame.

"You've certainly treated her as if she's your own." He choked on the emotion that flooded his chest and constricted his breathing. "No one has ever cared for her the way you have. There are some things you can't buy, can't pay a housekeeper to do for a child."

"I'm not just any housekeeper."

"You sure aren't."

"I'm a housekeeper who owes you my daughter's life. And you've shown me a kindness I know I can never repay."

"Not a kindness." He wanted to break his word again, to hold her against his chest, love her as if his heart had never been hurt, find comfort when he'd denied that for himself for so long.

He needed her. He'd never needed anyone so much. But how could he take the risk?

Chapter Fifteen

"You have company." Mr. Briggs knocked on her door. "That sister-in-law of yours."

"I don't have a sister-in-law." Anna tugged open her door to see the kindly man standing in the hallway.

"Well, you'll be married to her brother soon enough." His eyes laughed at her. "I'd send her up, but she said she's in a hurry. Want me to watch over Mandy?"

The little girl looked up from her play. A brand-new tea party set of her own, bought with Anna's tip money. "Can you play tea party, Mr. Briggs?"

"I've been invited to a few over the years." The gentle man winked at Anna. "Does Harry Bunny mind if I have some tea, too?"

Anna's chest warmed. She wasn't alone. She had made friends, and had found people to care about here in Flint Creek. She found Laura in the lobby, seated in a plush wing-back chair by the window.

"How's Katie?" She accepted Laura's hug, glad too for her friendship. "I wanted to drop by the house and check, but it's Sunday. I didn't want to interrupt."

"You are part of the family, Anna. Goodness."

Laura's hand squeezed hers. "Katie spent the morning sitting quiet in the parlor. She's got quite a headache, but she's going to be fine. Cooper had a talk with her this morning, and she wants me and Larry to marry."

"Katie *wants* you to be married?"

"We've rescheduled the wedding. Which reminds me why I came." Laura knelt down and handed Anna a paper sack. "I gave each of my nieces a gift, a goodbye gift, I guess. I wanted Mandy to have one, too. It's a veil, and it matches Maisie's exactly. Now both little girls can play bride together."

Anna reached into the bag and tugged out the sheer veil. "Laura, how can I begin to thank you?"

"You already have. By coming to Flint Creek. By being the mother Katie and Maisie need."

"Laura, I'm not their mother. Cooper and I aren't—"

"Oh, I know." Laura gave her a quick hug. "But you will be. And it has made all the difference in their lives. I'll see you at the wedding."

Laura swept from the lobby, leaving Anna with a full heart.

He watched dawn come, almost as slowly as his resolve. His decision hadn't been easy, but it was the right one for his girls. Laura was there, she'd insisted on staying until Katie was stronger. He heard her clinking in the kitchen, making breakfast for them all.

She was getting married today, her ceremony rescheduled at Katie's request. His talk with the girl and the promise he made weighed heavily on his shoulders. It was the right thing to do. He knew it, deep down.

"Papa, do outlaws get married?" Maisie hopped out

onto the porch to ask, wearing the veil Laura had given her. And the play holsters and hat, too.

"I suppose some do." He knew full well there would be an outlaw bride in the tree later today. "Are you going to get dressed up for church? Or are you going to go rob all the wedding guests?"

Maisie giggled. "Outlaws don't go to church, Papa."

"Then go dress up like a little girl. We don't want to be late."

"I *am* a little girl, Papa. I don't gotta pretend." Laughing, she dashed off.

He listened to the footsteps fade. Then he stood and went upstairs to get dressed himself. His sister was getting married today. And he would be giving away the bride.

"Is Anna here yet?" Katie fidgeted in the scratchy lace dress.

Cooper glanced around the church. It was half full of people and cheerful anticipation of the wedding to come. "I don't see her."

"There she is!" Katie pointed toward the vestibule.

"Anna! Anna!" Maisie dashed down the crowded aisle and flung herself at Anna's knees. Anna hugged the child gently. He froze stone solid at the sight of her. She was beyond beautiful, like a rainbow after a storm. Gold curls framed her face and a soft blue dress hugged her slim shape.

Then she smiled. Her eyes shone bright, just before she dipped her chin. He found himself walking toward her without consciously thinking of it.

"Are you gonna ask her now, Papa?" Katie asked.

"Not now." He wasn't ready. Would he ever be

ready? But he was a man of his word. And he'd made a promise to his daughter.

"Katie." Anna's hand brushed the curve of the child's face. "Your eyes are black and blue. Are you feeling better?"

"Gotta headache. But not as bad. The doc said I can't ride Bob for a while. Until my head stops hurtin'. I don't think that's fair."

"He's just watching out for you. Just the way your father does." Anna looked up. Her eyes laughed at him. "Did you chain Bob inside the stable?"

"Handcuffed her, too." He winked.

"Papa, you mean hoofcuff." Maisie rolled her eyes. "Pony's don't got hands."

The minister touched his sleeve. Cooper wanted to stay, wanted to watch the mirth sparkle in Anna's eyes, hear more adorable things his daughters might say. But Laura was waiting. It was time.

"I'll keep the girls with me," Anna said without asking. Maybe Laura had spoken to her.

"The front row, on the bride's side." The minister warmly took Anna's hand and led her away. The three girls followed. "I don't see much of the Braddock girls in my church on Sundays. I trust that will change."

Laura was waiting for him. She looked nervous.

"Do I look all right?" Laura fretted. "I think my hair looks wrong. I should have worn it up."

"It's perfect." He gave his sister a hug. "You look perfect."

Tears filled Laura's eyes. "Don't tease me. I feel so nervous I'm about to explode."

"You'll be fine. Larry will take one look at you and know he's marrying the finest woman in Montana Territory."

Tears slipped down Laura's face. "I'm so happy. I can't tell you how relieved I am to know the girls will be taken care of. Thank you for having the courage to find a wife, Cooper. To write those letters. To ask Anna to come to our town. I can truly get married without any regrets."

It was time. Cooper escorted his sister down the aisle and handed her over to Larry, the bookish banker who looked just as nervous as Laura did.

Two lives joined with a single love.

"It was good of you to have a reception here in the hotel," Anna told Janet as she added fresh potatoes to the buffet trays.

"It was the least I could do since she had to cancel earlier." Janet glanced over the food. "We need more rolls. I'll go get them. Make sure Mr. Briggs keeps cutting that prime rib nice and thick."

Anna laughed. She settled a stack of clean plates on the table.

"Anna." Sheila Muldune took a plate from the stack. "I want you to know I made Davy swear he wouldn't tempt Katie to go riding. They can go on their gold-hunting adventures on foot, like the real prospectors do."

"I'm sure Cooper will be glad to hear that." Anna laughed. Sheila held the same views on ponies as Cooper did.

"Anna. How can I ever thank you?" Laura wrapped her in a hug. Her face was flushed with pleasure. She radiated happiness. "You made this possible." Laura pressed a kiss to her cheek. "Just think, the next wedding in this town will be yours."

"Is a date set yet?" Carol Fykerud asked.

"There is no date." Really. Anna felt a tug on her sleeve.

Katie stood behind her, a plate in her hand. "You gotta go talk to Papa, Anna. He's got something to ask you."

She spotted Cooper talking to Tucker over in the corner. They both sat at a small table, hunched over empty plates. Cooper sat with his elbow on the table, his fist propped against his cheek. He looked so handsome in his black suit. The dark fabric stretched across rock-hard shoulders, outlined his powerful form. Her fingers ached to run along the widths of those shoulders and across the breadth of his chest.

"I'm working tonight, Katie."

"But you work for us." Distress rose in her voice.

"I help Janet out now and then for the extra money."

"You don't need money. You got us." Katie took her hand. "You gotta talk to Papa."

"I will. I promise." She could see how important it was. Katie could be dramatic, but her feelings went heart deep. "Let's wait until the rest of the people have filled their plates, then I promise I'll go talk to your papa."

"Promise?"

"Don't you worry. I'll always keep my promises to you."

"I love you, Anna." Katie gave her a quick hug and dashed off to join Davy Muldune.

Tears burned in her eyes. Anna turned back to her work, but her gaze kept straying to Cooper. And to the little girls, all three of them, she loved so much.

"Papa, Katie wants to know if you're gonna ask her now." Maisie propped both elbows on the table. "So, are ya?''

"I never should have said anything." Cooper took a stout drink.

"Whiskey?" Amusement tugged at Tucker's mouth. "You never drink. I'd love to know what you're going to ask Anna."

"Katie won't tell me cuz I can't keep no secrets. So, are you gonna ask, Papa?"

Cooper drained the glass. Katie sent Maisie to prod him because no one could resist Maisie. "Fine. Go tell Katie. I want you girls to stay here."

"I'll keep an eye on them." Tucker winked at him. "I hear you two have yet to set a date. Pick a good one."

Nerves churned in his stomach. Cooper crossed the hotel dining room. Voices and laughter, sounds of celebration and friendship filled the air.

"Your wedding's next, huh, Sheriff?" the mayor called out to him.

"Look, he's blushing." The livery owner sounded pleased. "I guess that means he'll be a groom before the Fourth of July."

Anna stepped around the buffet table. Her gaze latched on his. She looked embarrassed. "I've never known a single rumor to have such a long life."

"Come outside with me." He held out his hand.

Her gaze searched his before she laid her palm against his. Her skin felt warm and sweet. So different from his. She was soft and silken. Her rose scent filled him, made his heart beat faster.

A strong wind had come up, and it tore the door open. They stepped out into the night together. Her fingers felt so tentative in his, as if he loosened his hold she would slip away from his touch.

"I'm glad Katie has accepted Laura's leaving her." Anna sounded sincere, as concerned as always about the girls she had traveled so far to love.

He held that thought close to his heart. He'd seen how Anna sat by Katie's side, refusing to leave until she woke up, until she knew the girl would be all right. How she'd read to her, the same way she'd read to her own daughter. How fairly she treated his girls, not favoring them above her own in any way.

"I made a pact with Katie," he confessed.

"A pact? What did you promise Katie?"

"Something important to her. To all of us." This could work, Cooper realized. If he could gather his courage and just ask the question. If Anna said yes.

Lamplight from nearby windows cast enough glow to see her by, to glint in the dark-gold locks of her braids, unraveling in the hard wind, fanning around her shoulders. She looked as magical as a sea nymph beckoning lonely sailors. Or sheriffs. Cooper tried not to imagine how her luxurious curls would feel against his naked skin.

He cleared his throat. If Anna said yes, then she would be his to touch.

"I promised Katie you." He blurted out. "Be my wife, Anna. Be a mother to my girls."

"You want me to marry you?" She stumbled.

He reached out to steady her. Her elbow was so fine, so delicate. He ached to hold her against him again, taste her kisses and more.

"Is it because everybody thinks—"

"No, Anna." He pulled her against him. How many lonely nights had he spent alone in his bed, convincing himself loneliness was better than the alternative. He'd been wrong.

If Anna said yes, then she would be his to touch. To hold close at night. To make love to until sleep claimed them both.

"I'm asking you because I want you."

"You want me? But you don't want a wife. Isn't that what you told me?" The truth was there, shadowed in his eyes, and they both knew it.

"Yes, but I've changed my mind. I want you for my girls. Face it, I'm outnumbered. Two small females are just too many for me to handle. I need help. Take pity on me. Say yes."

"Oh, Cooper." Her heart felt ready to crack in two. She never imagined he would propose. Never thought he would want her.

"I won't lie to you. I don't believe in romantic fantasies and happy endings. But I do believe in duty and commitment. And that's what I have to offer you."

"But I had hoped…" She hesitated, struggling to speak past the emotion tight in her throat. "You want a marriage of convenience."

"Yes." His grip on her hands tightened. "Isn't that what you wanted when you accepted Katie's proposal? You have everything my girls need—a mother's love. I have a secure home and future for yours."

Promises knelled in his voice, as bright and hopeful as church bells on Sunday. How could she refuse? How could she accept? She loved him. But he did not share her affections. What kind of marriage would they have, his duty and her yearning heart?

"Say yes, Anna." Maisie's whisper came from nowhere.

Cooper turned around, searching the shadows.

"There you are. What are you doing out here? Tucker's supposed to be keeping a watch on you."

"He's here too, Papa."

"What?" Cooper had been so nervous speaking with Anna he hadn't even noticed the noises on the street. Or the ones in the shadows next to the hotel.

"We've been listening, big brother." Tucker strode out into the lamp-lit street.

And Laura, too. "Sorry, Cooper. We just couldn't stand to wait any longer. You were taking so darn long. I can't believe you didn't propose properly before this."

"Say yes, Anna." Katie took her by one hand.

Maisie by the other. "You gotta be my mama, Anna. Don't nobody have outlaws in their kitchen but you."

Mandy came up and leaned against her knee.

Anna gazed up at him with helplessness in her eyes. And a slight look of panic.

Something was wrong. He'd thought they got along well together. They laughed at the same things, loved their daughters in the same way. Why couldn't they have a logical practical agreement to raise their children together?

"I'm outnumbered," she said. "How can I say no?"

"Now you know how I feel every day of my life." The knot in his guts eased when she smiled, then she started to laugh.

The door to the hotel popped open. He heard Laura say in a victorious voice, "She said yes!"

Cheers rose in the distance, but the sound of his pounding heart drowned them out.

Anna was truly going to be his wife.

She waited until the last plate was dried before she asked Janet to do her a favor. The motherly woman was more than happy to keep an eye on Mandy while she slept. She understood Anna might want to speak with her groom.

Rain scented the air, but hadn't fallen yet. The night felt charged, as if a lightning storm were building. She saw the deputy shadowing her. Because of Cooper, keeping an eye on her, keeping her safe. He was a man of honor, a man who kept his vows. She knew she could trust him with her life. He'd already proven his worth.

Then why was she disappointed in his proposal? Every step she took brought her closer to his house. She didn't even know if he would be awake. Maybe she should go home. Maybe it would be better—

A light glowed on the Braddocks' front porch. The strike of a match, then the butt of a cigarette. No, maybe a cigar.

"Anna?" He'd spied her in the dark, started walking toward her, a slow amble that left her heart beating.

If she married him, she would share a bed with him. Her stomach flipped. The thought of his hands on her skin, touching and caressing, made her hot, made her want.

"I needed to talk with you." She took a deep, steadying breath. "With our audience tonight, there was a lot I couldn't say."

"Come sit down. Did you want anything?"

"No." He sounded so warm, so friendly. But his voice sounded thin, as if he were uncertain, too. His hands caught hers. Crackling heat telegraphed up her arms at his touch.

She settled down beside him on the top porch step. She could feel his strength and his honor even in the dark, even without looking at him. His presence affected her, made her blood pump with need for him. The need to curl up in his arms and hold him until her fears and loneliness faded.

She didn't want to be a woman married for her usefulness. She'd fallen in love with the Braddock girls and their father.

But he didn't love her.

"There are a few things I wanted to speak with you about. I didn't want the entire town to hear." She kept her voice low so her words would not carry. "You've gone a long time without even considering marrying again. I know you must have some reservations now."

"This is a marriage of convenience, Anna. Not a love match. My reservations are few."

"But you have reservations."

"Yes. I'm not ready for this. In all honesty, it isn't easy for me to think about handing over my life to a woman, to trust her with my future and my daughters' hearts."

"I see." She bowed her head. "I had hoped there was some affection on your part."

"I want a practical arrangement." Shrouded in the dark, his shoulders braced, he looked like a warrior of old, an undefeatable knight who stood for all that was right. "You take good care of my girls, that's what matters."

"I am more than that, whether you see it or not. If I marry you, if I pledge to honor you, then I will. I will always do the best by you, because I know you are the kind of man who can be both strong and tender, a man I can believe in. It's important to me that you know that, that you have faith in me."

"Anna." He felt… He didn't know how he felt. She

muddled him, made the clear light of day hard to see. She made the wall around his heart crack. She talked of honor when a woman ought to speak of needlework, cooking and gossip. As if a woman's word could be as strong as a man's.

And yet maybe it was, he thought looking at her, at the fury tight in her shoulders, clenched in her jaw. She looked like a cougar tensed for attack, ready to defend what she believed in, who she was.

His heart tugged. He needed her. Far too much. She made it too easy to care, to feel, to want. He reached out and pulled her to him. Somehow his mouth found hers. She was heated velvet and passion. She did not satisfy his need, but made him want more. He wanted her naked beneath him, all fire and passion.

Cooper closed his eyes. She made him care. He had to guard against caring too much.

As if in answer, giant raindrops pelted from the sky, falling like hail. Lightning flashed, thunder shook the windowpanes.

"Summer storms are amazing." Transformed, Anna stood. She held out her arms, leaned back and swirled around in the rain. In moments, she was drenched, but her happiness was contagious.

He wanted to hold her in his arms. He wanted to take her upstairs and lay her across that bed and love her until dawn broke.

"I'm about to break my promise to you." He took her hand and folded her against his chest.

"Again?" Laughing, she tipped back her head. Rain drenched him, too, but he was not cold. Because he had her in his arms. "I suppose this time I'll allow it."

His lips found hers before he could change his mind. A playful kiss, one based on physical desire, that was fine. But this, it came from a deeper place, the part of his heart tucked safely away. Anna could touch him there with the brush of her gentleness and fire, with her goodness as pure as rain.

He moved away before he lost more of his control. Before he began to believe in the fairy tales she'd been reading to his girls, of castles and princes and happily-ever-afters.

Romantic love was a dreamer's invention. He wasn't foolish enough to believe in a fantasy a second time. He needed to remember that. Duty was one thing. Need was another. He would never again fall into the trap of believing in something that didn't exist.

Chapter Sixteen

Anna set down her hammer. "Why, it's the new bride. How's married life treating you?"

"Very well."

"I heard the good news from Leslie when I went to pick up the mail." Laura breezed up to the outlaw tree.

"What good news?"

"That you were out with my brother awfully late."

"*What?*"

"Deputy Barstow confirmed it. Tucker rushed over from work to tell me." Laura's eyes twinkled.

Mortified, Anna felt the heat creep up her neck. Images of last night flashed through her mind—leaning against his solid chest, letting him kiss her in that mesmerizing way. Her blood bubbled just thinking of it.

"Laura! Laura!" Maisie hung from a sturdy bough. "Come see our hideout."

Mandy readjusted her play veil. Now that her splint was off, she reached out and hung beside Mandy. Anna moved the sack of nails aside and helped Laura up the ladder and onto the floor of the tree house.

"This is impressive." Her eyes sparkled. "What does my brother say?"

"He still can't believe I'm teaching his girls how to hammer." Anna tucked the nails in her pocket and the hammers in the waistband of her apron. "Thirsty?"

"Yes. It's hot today. Summer is almost here. The perfect weather for a June wedding." Laura descended the ladder. "Tell me. You two must have set a date."

"We haven't even discussed it." Anna climbed down the ladder. Her feet touched the ground. "Come into the kitchen. Katie is still hurting. She's taking a nap."

"A nap?" Laura's voice dipped. "Amazing."

Anna looked at the two outlaw brides up in the tree, play veils swinging with the afternoon breeze. "Do you girls want anything?"

Maisie lifted the cowboy hat off of her head. "Big pieces of cake."

"With lots of chocolate frosting," Mandy added.

"Yeah, cuz brides get hungry."

Anna waited until she was inside the house before she started giggling. She heard play shrieks from up in the tree. Apparently the outlaw brides had been discovered by that pesky pretend sheriff.

"What's so funny?" Cooper towered in the threshold, the sun at his back, haloing him in gold.

Her heart stopped at the sight of him. Memories from last night—the way he'd touched her, the way she'd touched him rushed over her like a hot breeze. He smiled, and she remembered being wrapped in his strong arms, sated and more satisfied than she'd ever dreamed.

"Your daughters are adorable," Laura spoke up, breaking the silence, reminding Anna she was standing there staring at Cooper.

She lowered her gaze and headed to the counter. She found the knife, lifted the lid off the cake plate.

"Laura, you look happy." He towered above Anna, his arm brushing her shoulder. "I'm home early."

As if her body remembered last night all on its own, her heartbeat tripled. Heat crept through every inch of her body. "An easy day at the jail?"

"My biggest challenge was a panicked request from Mrs. Fykerud. I was called upon to handle a wild animal attack."

"Here in town?"

"Yep. An elk ran out of the woods and charged her clothesline. Her freshly washed red flannel long johns were in jeopardy, and I came to the rescue."

"Why, not even a woman's laundry is safe in this town." Anna's chuckle came rich and easy.

"I'm sorry to say many pairs of underwear were in tatters by the time I arrived on the scene, but I was able to rescue her red flannel petticoats before they met the same fate."

"And the elk?"

"I chased him away with a wet mop." Cooper swept off his hat. "Sometimes my assignments are truly dangerous."

Anna tipped her head back, laughing. Gold curls tumbled over her shoulders. Cooper took a step back, unprepared for the rush of need pounding through his blood. He remembered her in the starlight, the taste of her, the feel of her. Even though he'd vowed not to want her, not to need her, there it was, a craving so great he could think of nothing else.

She enchanted him. It was that simple, teased him with everything he'd vowed never to have again. He'd thought when he proposed to her he could keep his needs and his emotions detached. But he'd been nothing short of a fool.

"Larry said you are going to be moving the gold soon." Laura's voice was solemn.

He'd forgotten she was in the room. That's how Anna affected him. "The mine that owns the gold has hired enough armed men to finally see it safely to Virginia City. They should be here tomorrow. It was just confirmed today. That's why I'm home early. I'll be gone for a week riding with the shipment. We're keeping this information quiet. Not even half of my deputies know."

"Larry will be relieved to have that shipment out of the vault." Worry crinkled Laura's brow. "It's only because of how you protect this town that the Corinthos gang hasn't tried to rob the bank."

"Or tried to harm me." Anna smiled up at him. A hot flame of pure want licked down his spine, engulfed every inch of him.

"I'm going to leave you two be." Laura grabbed her bonnet. "Anna, the sewing circle is meeting at Sheila's next week. We're starting a wedding quilt for you."

"For me? But I—"

"I know. You and Cooper are the most private people I know. We're making you a quilt. End of argument. Bring the girls. Sheila's daughter is hosting a dress-up party. Now, I just need to grab a few last things from my cottage and start for home."

She left them alone, with only Anna's layer cake between them. "She misses her nieces. I think that's why she dropped by today."

Even her voice made him hot with desire, the sound of it, the gentle caress of it. "Don't kid yourself.

Tucker has been trying to pump me for information all day. He probably got Laura to come over here and see what she could learn from you.''

Her eyes sparkled, but he remembered how they had gazed up at him last night, wondrous and luminous. ''Laura didn't get any information out of me. Would you like a slice?''

She held the knife, ready to cut him a generous piece. ''Yes.'' He wanted much more than a slice of cake.

Then little girls dashed into the room, talking over one another to tell him of their day, of the tree house, the garden, the tarts Anna made.

Happiness. He couldn't remember a time like this, his girls secure, his home cozy. And it was because of Anna. All because of her.

''I'm not so good at indoor stuff,'' Katie confessed as she helped dry the last of the supper dishes.

''Maybe you and I could find something to do. Just until your head feels better.'' Anna lifted the last of the pans from the rinse water and dried it. ''How is that quilt block you started?''

''Lost somewhere in my room.'' Katie shrugged. ''Anna, how can you stand to sew?''

''Well, I try to make things I like.''

''Like the wall hanging you made us?'' Katie thumped the kettle down on the counter.

Anna knelt and placed it on the lower shelf. ''You like ponies. We could do something with that.''

''Like what?''

''Well, we could make a quilt.''

''Of ponies?'' Katie sounded doubtful.

''How about of the things you like to do? Every

block could be about something different. Maybe one could be Bob. Another about your gold-hunting adventures.''

''And we'd make it to look like your wall hanging?''

''We could do it together.'' Anna took the wet dish towel from Katie. ''Go in the parlor and get back to your story. I'll see you in the morning. Maybe we can go shopping for fabric pieces then.''

''Ain't you gonna buy stuff, too? You and Papa gotta get married. You're gonna need a real nice dress. That's what Laura did.''

''Fine. You can help me pick out the material. Go play.'' Katie had been shadowing her, as if she were afraid to let her out of her sight. Finally the girl relented, perhaps afraid she would feel obligated to perform more household tasks.

''Want an escort home?''

''I'll be fine, Cooper.'' She hung up the towels to dry. Her back was to him, but she could feel his gaze like a touch to her body.

''Will you be able to stay with the girls? I should have asked you, given you more notice.'' He raked his hand through his hair. A dark lock fell across his forehead.

Anna's breath caught as her gaze slid downward over the linen shirt stretched taut over delineated muscle. She remembered the hot velvet feel of that skin, the solidness of the man.

''Are you going somewhere tonight?'' she asked.

''Tucker's on guard duty outside. I'm going to keep him company.''

He looked tousled and incredibly male. He buckled on his gun belt with sure, capable movements of his suntanned fingers. Last night, she'd wanted more than his kisses. Her blood heated, sharp and fast.

"Do you have a date in mind?" Cooper snared his hat from its peg, dropped it on his head in a slow masculine movement. "Everyone is expecting a wedding."

All but her bones melted at his slow smile. She took a quick breath. "When you return from protecting the gold shipment?"

"Yes." His dark eyes sizzled. "The sooner the better. I would hate to start any more rumors."

"What? You're not staying late at the Braddock house?" Janet Briggs looked up from her knitting. "I remember when we were young and in love, Frank."

"I brought her flowers every evening." Mr. Briggs set down his newspaper. "I got home late many nights."

"Oh, Frank." Janet blushed. "Our Anna doesn't want to know about that. I'm just glad you and Cooper are in love, dear. I can't tell you how highly he's regarded in this town. Everybody wants to see him happy."

"And see those girls of his with a mother." Mr. Briggs held down the cookie jar for Mandy to take a handful. "We'll host the reception, of course."

"Oh, I think a big ham for the reception would be nice." Janet's face lit. "What do you think, Anna?"

"That sounds expensive. And a lot of trouble." Especially for a marriage of convenience. Anna worked at the knot in her bonnet ribbons.

"Nonsense. You feel like one of our own, Anna." Janet's voice dipped. Affection shone in her eyes, unmistakable and steady. "You and your girl have given us a taste of what we've missed all these years."

"Since our children grew up and flew the coop." Mr. Briggs cleared his throat, his eyes misting. "It's been darn good to hear a little one's laughter."

"And it's a long time since Frank has been able to play tea party." Janet set aside her knitting and stood. Her hug was sweet and light, but touched Anna deep inside. "A pretty young widow like you, all alone, well, we just can't help feeling protective. We can't help caring for you as if you were our own. I hope you'll let us do this for you, host your reception."

"Don't get us wrong." Mr. Briggs cleared his throat again, but was unable to dislodge the emotion thick in his voice. "We don't want you and Mandy to leave us. But we're glad for you. We hope you bring the whole troop of Braddock girls for a visit now and then. To put some laughter in our lives."

"I think I can do that." Anna's throat ached. She had friends here, in this town. And she now had family, too.

"And one more thing." Mr. Briggs stood. "I want to walk you down the aisle."

Tears filled her eyes, but not tears of sadness. They came from the heart. From a place where happiness lived. "Mr. Briggs, I would be honored."

A shadow moved in the night. Moonlight cut through the grove of pines. Cooper laid a hand on his Colt. He spotted small dark eyes and a flash of dirt-brown fur. Just a coyote.

He relaxed, released a breath. He was a patient man, but he hated waiting. Corinthos' threat gathered over his head, dark as a storm. Cooper knew he wouldn't back down, wouldn't hand over his honor like goods to be bartered.

"Ho, Coop." Tucker's voice rose out of the dark yard behind him. A heady wind rustled the trees, covering the sound of his steps. "There's been no sign of trouble in town. You're right. If Corinthos is going to show up, it's going to be in the morning."

"I keep hoping he doesn't know about the gold." Cooper swiped the sweat from his brow. A hell of a storm was brewing, the air laden with humidity. "But unless I'm wrong, Corinthos will know. He's got one of my deputies on his payroll keeping him informed."

"I've worried about that, too." Tucker gazed out at the night, watching the shifting shadows. "The men are ready. We'll take the gold as soon as the bank opens and we'll ride."

"Tomorrow I'm going to end this with Corinthos." Cooper hauled a pouch of tobacco from his vest pocket. "There's no other way. He's going to come after that gold. By sunset, I'll have him in my jail."

"Without a doubt." Tucker rolled a cigarette. "Corinthos isn't as tough as you and me."

"Well, maybe me, but I don't know about you, Tucker." Chuckling, Cooper struck a match. "You're a real weakling."

"We'll see about that, big brother."

Cooper breathed in, savoring the smoke. He gazed at the house, thinking. The girls were in bed sleeping, the rooms dark. By this time next week, Anna would be here as his bride.

"I'll watch the house," Tucker offered. "I'm off duty, but I don't mind staying."

"I wanted to check the stables, see where my men are. Whoever is working for both sides won't be able to contact Corinthos during the day. Thought I'd stroll through town, keep my eyes open."

"You already know who it could be?"

Cooper tapped out his cigarette. "I know who it isn't. Not you. Not Barstow."

"Why not Barstow?"

"He's worried I may be as soft as old Joe. I suspect Dickens or Davidson. Can't hurt to see if either man is still in town."

"He'd need to contact Corinthos tonight."

"That's right." Cooper grabbed his hat off the newel post. "I'll be back if I need to bring in a bad deputy."

"And here I thought you might want to go see your bride-to-be," Tucker teased.

"You sound smug, little brother. I'm only marrying Anna for the girls."

"Sure. Go ahead and deny it, but you have a soft side, big brother. You don't hide it as well as you think."

Tucker thought he knew everything. Annoyed, Cooper headed down the streets. Well, maybe Tucker wasn't all that wrong. Cooper couldn't stop thinking of her, of how sweet she'd felt in his arms. He wanted more. He wanted to lay her down and love her until she moaned low in her throat, until she wrapped her thighs around his hips and sheathed him deep inside.

Distracting thoughts. Cooper cleared visions of Anna from his head, tried to pay attention to the night.

The town slept. Houses were dark, businesses closed and locked. He checked the livery first. Went down the aisle and counted up his deputy's horses. Davidson, Dickens, Barstow, Locke, Brewster, Collins, Johnson and Black. All were bachelors who lived within a block or two of the livery. He checked to make sure the horses were cool. They had not been ridden hard tonight.

Well, the night was young. He would wait.

* * *

A quarter moon hung low in the sky, its sterling light playing with the edges of the curtains, as if trying to peek through. With Mandy asleep at last, she parted the fabric.

The town was peaceful. It was a pretty place, with young trees lining the streets, flowers spilling out of window boxes, bright store awnings shading the boardwalks. It was a fine place to call home. She was getting married. Cooper flashed into her mind, strong as myth, mighty as legend. And so kind. Her heart fluttered. She remembered the way he'd touched her, the heat of his kisses against her skin. How was she ever going to protect her heart? He didn't love her. She feared he might never trust her completely.

A rider dashed down the street, following the old trail out of town. She reached for her sewing. Another new dress for Mandy made from another adorable pink fabric Leslie had ordered especially for the little Braddock girls. Next she would make one for Maisie.

The window pinged. She jumped, then saw a man on the street below. She would recognize the cut of those shoulders anywhere. Dark locks spilled over his collar. Even in the shadows, he looked invincible.

She opened the window. "Cooper."

"On patrol," he explained. Then he tossed down his hat and grabbed hold of Janet's rose trellis. The wood groaned beneath his weight.

"I could climb down," she offered.

He hiked himself up to the windowsill. "I'm the man. I get to climb the building."

"The same way you got to build the tree house?"

That made him chuckle rich and deep, his good humor as attractive as the rest of him. "Fine, you win. You built a darn good tree house. I'll be back to help with the roof."

"Are we going to add walls, too?"

"Sure. Why not? Even a few windows. Outlaws have to be able to keep watch for the sheriff."

How he drew her. His nearness made her dizzy, made her blood thud in her ears. Goodness, she felt as if she'd just run ten miles. "When are you leaving in the morning?"

"We won't move the gold until the armed guards are ready. But I'll need to be at work early."

"I'll be there to take care of the girls." Did she tell him how much she would miss him? How worried she was? She knew he was doing his duty, keeping his commitment to the town and the businesses. But she wished he didn't have to leave, that he would send a deputy in his place.

She loved him much more than she wanted to admit.

"You might try using the door, Sheriff," a voice called out from a neighboring window.

Anna blushed. "Mr. Briggs. Cooper and I are just talking."

"I know how it is between a courting couple. Just don't break Janet's trellis, Sheriff."

"Tell her to rest easy, Briggs." Cooper's grin dazzled. "I'm on my way down."

"Sure you are." Briggs laughed, then shut his window.

"Have you noticed how no one around this town believes us?" Cooper pressed a kiss to her cheek.

How she wanted more. "I've noticed that. Why do you suppose that is?"

"Because certain family members just can't seem to

mind their own business." He sounded amused, not angry as he started back down the trellis. "Beware the family you are marrying into, Anna."

"Yep, the Braddocks are an unworthy lot. Every single one."

His laughter touched her, made her long for the haven of his arms.

Lee Corinthos sat back with a smile. Satisfaction gleamed in his midsection like gems catching the sunlight. "So the mining company has brought in an army of guards?"

Davidson rubbed his brow. He looked nervous. He always looked nervous. "Even if we ambushed them in the pass, we couldn't win. Word is there will be thirty men."

"And only twelve of us." Dusty cackled, holding his whiskey bottle by the neck as if to strangle it. "Think the sheriff will look the other way?"

"We'll find out come morning." Corinthos took a long pull of whiskey, let the liquor burn down his throat. "I'll find out which way Braddock will go. If he won't bend, then we'll kill him and storm the bank. Once the guards take over, we won't have a chance."

Yes, it sounded like a good plan. Corinthos wanted that gold.

Chapter Seventeen

"I'll grab breakfast at the diner," Cooper said as he buckled on his holster by the back door. "I have a meeting with the mine president and his lead guard."

Anna set down her measuring cup. Flour poofed up in little white clouds. She hated knowing he was going to face that horrible outlaw. The thought of Cooper hurt…why, it nearly brought her to her knees. "You keep yourself safe."

"Don't worry." The gun belt hugged his lean hips, riding low, the holsters snug against his muscled thighs. "I'm going to outsmart Corinthos. Early this morning, Tucker and I arrested one of the deputies who was on his payroll."

"One of the deputies?"

He nodded, grim and steely. "That will give us an advantage today. So don't worry. You keep my girls safe, just like you're doing." He grabbed his hat and plopped it on his head with a flourish. There was something soft, like longing shadowing his dark gaze. "Goodbye, Anna."

"Goodbye." She wiped her hands on her apron and took a step toward him.

He folded her into his arms, against the iron hardness of his chest. His mouth met hers with a tender ferocity, possessive and gentle all at once. She ached for his touch, for more than this kiss.

He stepped back, breaking their embrace. True regret flickered in his gaze. Then he tipped his hat and strode out the door. Leaving her alone with her fears for him, with the yearning for him deep in her heart.

She went back to mixing pancake batter, thought of the girls upstairs. Thought of all Cooper trusted her with. His children. His home. His honor. He believed in her.

It wasn't love, but it was enough.

"Mornin', Sheriff." Corinthos sat straight in the saddle, hands gripping gleaming revolvers, cocked and ready.

"Not many outlaws ride through town in broad daylight." Cooper thumbed back the hammers on both of his revolvers. "Unless they're looking to be arrested."

"Now you're dreamin', Sheriff." Laughter flickered across those cold, deadly eyes. "I have word you're planning on moving that gold shipment without telling me."

"I bet Davidson kept you informed." Cooper's rage flared. "He won't be at my back, or haven't you noticed?" He didn't turn, but the line of deputies and armed men behind him, protecting the jail proved his statement. "There will be no one letting you in the back door, or shooting me or my lawmen from behind. Surrender now, Corinthos, while you still have your life."

"I don't intend to die today. But I do intend to kill you."

* * *

"Anna. Janet was just in here talking about the reception. Ham sounds like just the thing. I put in a special order for a few extra surprises myself." Leslie McDonald scurried out from behind the front counter.

"You shouldn't go to any trouble. Cooper and I will probably want something quiet and simple."

"Gotta have a pretty dress, Anna," Katie piped up. "That way Papa will see how beautiful you are and fall in love with you forever."

"Gotta have a big veil, Anna." Maisie swept hers out of her eyes.

"And lots of ruffles," Mandy added.

"See?" Leslie beamed. "It's unanimous. Come over and see the new silk I've ordered in. I was expecting this visit, you know."

"We wanted to look at your calico selection, too." Anna glanced at Katie. Katie rolled her eyes. Laughing, she led the littlest girls down the aisle after the cheerful store owner.

Leslie pulled out a chair at a cloth-covered table just as Carol Fykerud and her girls came over from the fabric row, bolts of red flannel in hand. "I heard a certain gentleman was climbing up to your window last night. Did he ever come down?"

Anna blushed. "Carol. He only came to say hello."

"Sure." Merriment sparkled in the woman's voice. "I had the privilege of being protected by your Cooper."

"I heard about your elk problem." Anna laughed, grateful for a new topic of conversation. "I heard you lost every last pair of red long johns."

"And me with four boys to sew for." Carol laughed.

A clatter and a horse's squealing whinny erupted on

the street outside. With laughter still in the air, Anna spun around and looked past the window display of braided Indian corn. She saw at least two dozen horses crowding the street. Voices rent the air. She couldn't make out the angry words, but she knew the sound of trouble.

Was it the gold? Was it Corinthos? Through the window she could see the rump of Cooper's honey-gold horse, white tail twitching in the breeze. She stood and saw the broad back of one wonderful man holding two guns at a group of mounted outlaws.

Cooper! Shivery fear wrapped around her chest. There was going to be a gunfight.

"Girls!" she said, too sharp. "Come with me."

"Oh, my! Oh, my!" Leslie looked faint.

Anna grabbed both little girls by the hand and headed for the back of the store. She wanted the children out of danger. "Katie. I want you here, too."

"That's Papa!" Her voice came from the front of the store.

Leslie cried out, "Oh, my! Those men are trying to rob the bank!"

"Stay," Anna ordered in no uncertain terms and left the girls behind the molasses barrels. "Katie, get away from the window."

"Papa!" The bell above the door tinkled as Katie escaped, heading straight toward the dangerous scene.

On a dead run, Anna caught Katie before she could step out onto the boardwalk. The girl fought her, crying, terrified of losing her father. Hurting for her, sharing her fear, Anna wrestled her back into the store.

"Don't distract him." She held the girl, tried to console her. "We have to stay out of his way."

Gunshots popped on the street. She could hear the

dull thud of a body hit the earth. The fear gripping her heart tightened. Unable to breathe, Anna ushered Katie to the back of the store.

Cooper was a good sheriff, she told herself above the sound of gunfire. He could take care of a simple bank robbery. But as she knelt down on the floor, holding the girls in a tight huddle, a bullet shattered the front window and ploughed into the wall behind them.

No man, not even Cooper, was invincible.

The outlaw's eyes flickered, then he fired.

Cooper shot twice. It was fast enough. He felt an arrow of heat spread across his temple. He saw the flash of surprise on Corinthos' face as the outlaw slid from his saddle and hit the ground, dead.

Cooper looked down. Red sluiced down his face, stained his shirt. He vaguely realized it was his own blood, but the shooting had only just begun. He aimed and fired, downing another outlaw. The horses milled. He struggled to keep his seat, to keep his head clear and his reflexes quick.

He didn't stop fighting until the dizziness claimed him. Weak as a kitten, he hit the ground. The revolvers slid from his grip.

''Coop!'' Tucker's voice.

He looked up at his brother's face, eyes dark with fear.

''Did we get them all?'' His own blood blurred his vision.

''Every last one.''

''Good. My head is killing me.''

''Is it over?'' Katie asked with wide eyes.

Anna poked her head over the tops of the molasses

barrels. She could only see a portion of the street, and a crowd of horses and men. At least there were no more gunshots. "I think it's safe. We'd better get you girls home."

Leslie popped up to inspect her damaged window. Anna took hold of Katie's hand before she could dash off, then wiped tears from Mandy's eyes and kissed Maisie's worried brow. Hand in hand they headed through the store.

The girls were silent, and Anna had to keep telling herself everything was fine. Cooper was a good sheriff.

"Oh, my!" Leslie gasped, turning pale.

Anna's gaze flashed to the street, to the scene of injured, maybe dead men lying prone in the dust. Oh, God. Tremors shivered through her and she turned the girls around. This wasn't something children should see.

"Let me take them upstairs for fresh lemonade," Leslie offered, pale-faced and clearly shaken by the scene outside. She took Maisie's hand. "I have molasses cookies."

Anna thanked Leslie for her thoughtful offer and handed over a reluctant Mandy.

"Anna." Katie bumped against her. "Anna, that ain't Papa, is it?"

Over the shattered window displays, Anna saw the riderless palomino, and the big, motionless man's body lying in the dust.

Heart in her throat, Anna could only stare. She saw Cooper's dark hair, tousled as always, the wide cut of his shoulder, and the shape of one big hand motionless and bloodstained. She started to tremble.

"It *is* Papa!" Katie lunged.

Anna held the girl tight. Wrenching sobs shook her

reed-thin body. Anna felt Leslie's hand on her shoulder. She turned and saw sympathy in those sad eyes.

"You go see after your man. I'll keep these girls safe and comforted. You come for them when you can."

Anna wasn't aware of letting go of Katie or how she found herself racing across the street. She darted between the curiosity seekers and people offering help. A few deputies kept peace and helped the fallen men. Anna spotted Tucker's dark hat, and saw him kneeling over his brother. Over her Cooper.

"He's still alive." Tucker pressed a blood-soaked handkerchief to his brother's head.

She fell to her knees and brushed a hand along the slope of his hairline. "Cooper."

"I'm fine. I think." He tried to sit up and failed.

"You need a doctor. Lie still." Her fingers came away wet with fresh blood. Panic beat through her. "Tucker, help me."

"He'll be fine." Tucker laid his hand on her shoulder. "Who do you think Katie got her hard head from?"

"Well, the bullet grazed his skull." The doctor turned from Cooper's bed, shoulders slumped from fatigue. It had been a long day for him. "He's going to have quite a headache for a while. But I'm going to let him go home with you."

Relief lanced through her.

Cooper looked up from his pillow. "I have a harder head than that outlaw thought."

"Go ahead and be proud of yourself." She held back the emotions, the love she would never confess to him. "You gave us all a scare for a while."

Noise echoed in the hallway, sounding like a herd of wild elk.

"Shh! Papa's sleepin'."

"Don't push, Maisie."

"He's got an ow."

Cooper tilted his head just a smidgen. Three girls stood in the threshold, studying him with wide eyes.

"Anna says you ain't dead, Papa," Maisie whispered.

"We brought you some soup." Katie straightened her shoulders. "Mrs. McDonald and I made it."

"She's a thoughtful lady." Anna took the covered bowl from Katie with a smile.

Pain lanced his head. But it wasn't too bad. Thank heavens for that.

"Someone didn't believe me when I said you would be all right." Anna settled down in the chair beside him.

"I wasn't either scared," Katie denied.

All of them were. Cooper studied the little girls peering across the blankets at him. His throat ached with the knowledge of all he had, of what he never wanted to lose.

Anna leaned close. She smelled like roses, always roses. Then the scent of hot chicken broth tickled his nose. He was surprised when his mouth watered. He felt like death warmed over and hurt like the devil.

"Just sip," she instructed.

The spoon touched his lips, a little too hot. Liquid sluiced into his mouth and across his dry tongue. Another spoon of broth nudged against his lips. He noticed the care she took not to spill. He saw the affection in her eyes, unmistakable and as breathtaking as sunset. No one, ever, had looked at him like that.

"Me and Mandy helped cook, too," Maisie spoke up. "But I closed my eyes cuz Mrs. McDonald killed her old hen."

"With an ax," Katie added. "I peeked between my fingers."

"Don't like chicken no more," Mandy added.

Silent laughter filled Anna's eyes and he saw, for the first time, what romantic love could be. Not something based on power and control, or on obligation like a debt to be paid. But a bright, selfless light. A strength far more powerful than any he'd known before.

"I can do it." He took the spoon from her, capturing her fingers beneath his. "Thank you."

She smiled, her caring as tangible as her touch. His heart lurched. If only he knew how to love her the same way.

Anna held his boot so he could step into it.

He grabbed the boot from her. "I don't need help."

"The doctor said you had to take it easy." She yanked the boot out of his grip and held it firm.

"Give me my boot." That lopsided, sexy grin spread across the corners of his mouth, bringing out his twin dimples. "I'm too tough to be pampered."

"No, you were just shot. Nothing serious." Anna held his boot. His foot slipped right in. "Now, lean on me when you stand."

"Yeah, or you'll fall down, Papa." Maisie added from the foot of the bed.

He chuckled, easy and light. Dark hair fell across his forehead, and his eyes watched her with a twinkling merriment that made her heart flutter. Made her wish she was already his wife.

She took his elbow in her hand, helping him rise.

He felt warm, all muscle, solid beneath her fingers. He leaned on her, just a little until he was on both feet. She breathed in the pleasant soap-and-man scent of him. He was stronger than he looked.

"Don't forget my hat." He grabbed his holsters from the stand and buckled them on.

Katie carried it to him, the worry lines still wrinkling her brow. "Here you go, Papa. I thought you was dead."

"Well, I'm pretty tough to kill." Understanding glittered in his eyes. He pulled his daughter close and held her.

Anna opened the door and led the way out into the warm kiss of the sun. A healthy breeze kicked up a swirl of dust. Horses clopped by, their steps echoing in the alley.

"Good to see you, Sheriff." A man on the street, whom Anna didn't know, lifted his hat as he rode by.

Cooper nodded, tipping his hat.

"Oh, Sheriff." A door jangled open. Mrs. Barclay hurried out of the bakery. "Thank you for what you did, for saving us from those terrible Corinthos men. Our town is now truly safe."

A small amount of pleasure sparkled in Cooper's eyes. "Just doing my job, ma'am."

Farther down the boardwalk Leslie McDonald rushed out and hugged him. "Oh, look at that bandage. I'm so thankful you weren't killed."

"It was just a nick, Leslie," his low voice rumbled.

"Head wounds bleed like the devil." She patted his hand. "Because of you and your deputies, we can all live in peace. How can we ever thank you?"

"You already have."

And so it went, one passerby after another, one shop

owner after another thanking him, expressing their gratitude.

Pride for him simmered in her heart. Pride for this man who'd stood so strong for justice, for honor and for all that was right.

"Hello, hero." A voice called from down the street.

"Tucker!" Three girls raced toward him, clattering down the boardwalk like elephants. Tucker was holding up three sticks of lemon candy.

"Call yourself a hero. You're the one who stayed in your saddle during the gunfight." Cooper looked a little pale, but his smile was just as wide as ever.

"I was always the better brother," Tucker teased as he surrendered his lemon sticks to the three eager little girls. "I've got news. Are you too injured to head over to the jail?"

"The doctor said to take it easy," Anna spoke up.

"Big brother, she's acting like a wife already. You're in real trouble."

Laughing, Cooper's fathomless gaze fastened on hers. He made the air impossible to breathe. "Having a wife isn't going to be so bad."

"Not so bad?" she challenged.

"Not bad at all." Cooper's hand covered hers, drawing her eyes up to his. She saw the truth in those eyes, dark as the night and twice as bold. He wanted her. The same way she wanted him.

"I won't be long," he promised. "Probably some paperwork I have to fill out. There's the matter of the gold shipment."

"You're not as tough as you think, Cooper Braddock. So if he faints, Tucker, will you bring him home?"

Both men laughed. She laid her hand in Cooper's.

Her pulse surged when his fingers closed around hers. A perfect fit.

His head hurt, but it wasn't bad. He'd hurt worse before. Cooper headed down the street with Tucker, leaving Anna and the girls behind.

"Federal marshals rode in less than an hour ago." Tucker kept his voice low as they headed for the jail.

"For Corinthos' body? Or to help with the gold?"

"The mine president is grateful to us. Now we can move the gold without threat of that gang. We're going to try leaving early tomorrow. Think you'll be ready to ride? I could go in your place. That would give you more time with your Anna. It would be sad to separate you two lovebirds. Of course, it could be for the best. Janet Briggs' trellis may not survive many more midnight climbs."

"Stop with the teasing and the advice." Cooper rubbed his brow, encountered the white swath of the bandage. "I can do fine on my own, little brother."

"Well, up until now you've needed everyone's help." Tucker's eyes laughed, then sobered. "The marshals have come on business. Seems they are tracking a fugitive through this area."

Cooper pushed open the jailhouse door. "A fugitive?"

Two men stood up in the office. Their badges identified them as U.S. Marshals. The guns at their hips stated they meant business. "Yes, a fugitive, Sheriff. As you know, we've had trouble keeping our lawmen honest in this territory. We're after one of your own. A sheriff from down south."

"I haven't seen a notice come in on him." Cooper headed for his desk.

"There hasn't been time for one. He ran before we could arrest him. He's been running since."

The second marshal cleared his throat. "We had a sighting just east of here from the sheriff over at Sandy. I was hoping you could help us. We lost his trail up in the mountains."

Cooper rubbed his head. "If it wasn't for this gold shipment we're trying to move, I would help. If you need extra hands, I can offer a few of my deputies."

"We'd be mighty appreciative, Sheriff." The deputy handed him a sheet of paper. "He could have passed on north to Canada. But we have to be sure. His name is Dalton Jennings."

"Papa's home!"

"Papa! Papa!"

"Papa, you're finally here." Katie dashed out into the lane, her dress sadly sagging and dirt stained. "We've been waiting forever."

"I've only been at the jailhouse for an hour." Cooper eased down from the wagon. Three girls dashed his way.

"We've been cookin'—"

"Maisie, it's a secret!" Katie interrupted, stomping her foot. "You can't tell."

Cooper chuckled, and his gaze snared Anna's. His entire body tingled just looking at her. How he wanted her touch, her kiss, everything. Need for her shimmered deep inside.

"I'll see to the marshals," Tucker said as he clucked to the horses. "If you don't feel up to riding come morning, you tell me."

"I will, little brother." Cooper watched the wagon bump down the drive, grateful for the ride.

"You're not going tomorrow, are you?" Anna gazed at him with unmasked concern. "The doctor told you to take it easy."

"I'll be all right after a good night's sleep. If I didn't think I was up to it, I would send someone else. Believe me."

The concern in her gaze relented a bit. "I just don't want anything to happen to you. Janet Briggs has ordered a ham for our reception."

"I'd hate a valuable piece of ham to go to waste. I'll be careful. You have my word on it." It felt good, this warm teasing between them. The way she smiled, despite her worry.

It was nice to have someone fuss over him. It was nice to have a bride, after all. A convenient marriage, he'd said. One for his girls, not for him. Wasn't that the agreement?

"I hope you're not too hungry," Anna whispered in his ear. "Katie helped to cook the meal."

"Don't worry. I'm a brave man."

Chapter Eighteen

Her wedding day came far too fast, Anna thought as she approached the church. A marriage of convenience. An amicable match between two single parents for the sake of their children had sounded perfect back home in Ruby Bluff, in a place where old friends often scorned her and little girls were not allowed to play with Mandy.

But here and now, she wanted more. Much more. In less then thirty minutes, she would be Cooper's wife. But would she ever have the love in his heart?

Maisie tore down the front steps and flung herself at Anna's skirts. "You're gonna be my mama today!"

"Yes, I am." She knelt to receive a proper hug.

"Papa and I picked these." She dashed away and returned holding a bouquet of fragrant purple wildflowers.

"These are shooting stars." Anna accepted the sweet-smelling bouquet. "Did you know that whenever you pick a shooting star, you get a wish granted?"

Maisie tilted her head. "Already got my wish."

"Me, too!" Mandy added with a dimpled grin.

Anna squeezed Mandy's hand and knelt to study the

clever braid of flowers crowning Maisie's gold curls.
"Did your Aunt Laura do this?"

"Yep."

"Mandy, I bet we could put flowers in your hair,
too."

"In a star crown, just like Maisie got?"

"Laura can do it! She got lots of flowers." The two
girls ran off, hand in hand, leaving Anna alone.

Cooper leaned against the threshold, unable to take
his eyes off her. She was beyond beautiful. Gold curls
fell around her face and a soft blue dress hugged her
slim body, the ruffled hem fluttering in the summer
breezes.

Then she smiled. Her eyes were bright, and he knew
this marriage would be the right kind. Two mature people, making a vow to raise their children. A commitment about duty, that was something he could agree
to.

"Ready to tie the knot?"

"As long as I don't faint. I can't believe how nervous I am."

"We'll be nervous together. Come." He held out
one hand to his bride.

She laid her palm against his, and he felt it. The
lightning jolt charging from her to him. She smiled,
and his knees wobbled. He wasn't as immune to her
as he'd figured.

A marriage based on duty? Well, he would like the
physical benefits. His blood heated at the prospect of
the wedding night to come.

"Anna." Katie reached out, rare affection in her
voice. She wrapped her arms around Anna's waist and
held tight. "You're going to be my mother now. I
didn't much like the one I had before. She left."

"I know she did." So much sympathy in her voice. "But I'm not going to leave you. Not ever."

"You promise?" Katie's voice lowered. So much need shone in her eyes. "Sometimes people break promises."

"Nothing will make me break this one." Anna laid her hand along the side of Katie's face. "I love you and your sister. I could never leave. I need all three of my girls to make me happy."

Cooper's throat filled. Emotions battered him. That wall around his heart, the one he vowed never to take down, crumbled a bit.

"Anna." Laura held out both hands in welcome. "Look what I did to your little one."

"Mandy." Anna knelt to brush at those silk-soft tendrils and exclaim over the purple-flowered crown Laura had slipped into the child's gold curls.

"We're running out of time." Laura grabbed Anna's hand, his sister as pleased as his daughters over the marriage today. It sparkled in her eyes. "Girls, come help. We've got a bride to prepare."

"I am prepared," Anna argued on a chuckle.

"There's the little matter of the flowers for your hair, for starters. Hurry up. The guests are starting to arrive."

"Hurry, Anna," Maisie spoke up, "cuz the faster you marry my papa, the faster we can go get us a baby."

"Nervous?" Tucker patted him on the back. "Wait, don't answer. Of course you are. No matter how fine the woman, it's a terrifying thing to enter into matrimonial bliss. I personally avoid it at all costs."

"Not a bad philosophy." Cooper ran a finger beneath his collar. The damn thing was too tight.

Cooper saw his girls giggling. Maisie tripped in front of Mandy and the bundle of purple flowers went flying. Both girls had insisted on wearing their play bride veils. Katie walked in front of Anna, solemn as a hanging judge.

Anna looked radiant. The soft blue fabric brought out the depth of her eyes, made her creamy skin luminous. A lustrous smile touched her lips. His heart leaped. Tonight she would be his. And every night after.

Mr. Briggs handed her over to him, tears misting the old man's eyes. Anna's arm felt light in his, although he could feel her nervousness.

"I'm about ready to faint, too," he teased in a low whisper.

She rewarded him with a smile. He could not tear his gaze away from her lips, soft and sculpted. She tilted her head. Her golden curls caught the light, made it gleam like sunlight on clouds, rich and alluring. So much grace, so much gentleness, he felt as if he could drown in her. And that was the problem.

He wanted to keep aloof. It was all right to need her for his girls, to keep his house, to cook his meals, even to make love to in the dark of night. But this way she made him feel, it was something that frightened him.

When he said, "I do," it was for the girls, for Katie who needed a mother to love her without end, for Maisie who needed a mother to adore her. That's all.

It wasn't because he was falling in love with her.

"I think the ham is a success." Janet swept out from behind the buffet table in the hotel's dining room to wrap Anna in a hug. "You look so happy, dear. I can't tell you how sorry we are to see you leave. Why, you've filled up a loneliness in our lives."

"The same way you've filled up one in mine." Anna returned the hug. "You and Frank are like parents to me."

"I'm so glad to hear that." Janet's eyes filled.

"Look at our bride." Leslie pressed a kiss to Anna's cheek. "Goodness, the wedding couldn't have been more beautiful. The way the girls stood up with you and you were married like a family. I used up three hankies during the ceremony."

"So did I." Laura came up and hugged her hard. "Now it's official. We're sisters."

Anna's throat closed. Her only regret was that her own sister couldn't make the wedding.

"Now that the wedding is over, it's time to talk about gifts," Janet began, eyes sparkling. "So I'm giving you and Cooper my best hotel room for the night."

"Janet, we can't possibly—"

"You have to," she interrupted. "Leslie put together a lovely gift basket. And Laura and Larry have agreed to take the girls for the night."

"You deserve to be alone," Leslie added. "Two young lovebirds. How I remember being a newlywed. I didn't see the light of day for two weeks."

"Oh, yes," Janet sighed, fond of her memories.

"I haven't seen much daylight," Laura confessed. "And I'm not complaining."

"Maybe I should fix you two up a hotel room."

They all burst into laughter.

"What are you beautiful women giggling about?" Tucker towered over them, looking dashing in his white shirt and dark tie. "I get it, womanly things. I

don't want to know. Janet, I came to beg another slice
of that ham from you.''

Janet's hand squeezed hers. ''See? I knew it would
be a success. Coming right up, you handsome deputy.''

''Can I sweet talk you into some more of those
mashed potatoes?'' Tucker handed her his plate, then
laid an arm around Anna's shoulder. ''You're part of
the Braddock family now, for better or worse.''

''I think the worst part is having you for a brother,''
she quipped.

''He's the worst of the bunch,'' Laura agreed.

''Hey, give a man some credit. I have a few good
traits. I bathe often.''

Laughter filled the room, light and sweet and full of
joy.

They were finally alone. Cooper's hand covered
hers, drawing her gaze. He saw the truth in those eyes,
dark as the night and twice as bold. She wanted him.
The same way he wanted her.

''It's a beautiful evening.'' Her voice vibrated across
the sensitive rim of his ear. ''Just right for a romantic
walk. The sun is setting.''

He hadn't been thinking about going on a walk with
her. The room was spacious and beautiful, dominated
by the big four-poster bed. A gift basket sat on the
table. He saw the neck of a wine bottle, caught the
scent of fine cheese. Anna ran her hand over the textured handle of the basket and smiled.

''I think Janet and Leslie are determined to marry
Tucker off next.''

''Did you see how fast he downed that ham? He ran
for home, terrified they would start bringing him
brides.''

"Maisie didn't help when she said if he got married, then he could go get a baby, too." She blushed, although her eyes were laughing.

"I've been waiting a long time for this night."

"You didn't have to wait." She stepped forward.

Somehow, his hand found hers. "Yes, I did." He needed her that night more than he'd ever needed anyone. He didn't want to need. He didn't want to depend on anyone so much. "Let's go on that walk you want."

The town was quiet with twilight shrouding it. Bright bold crimsons and purples painted the sky in wide swaths, clouds twisting with shades of color.

"This is my favorite time of day," Anna breathed as the last bit of twilight faded.

Everywhere he looked, he saw her and nothing else. The moonlight, the breeze, the ruts in the road all centered on her. Light shone silver in her hair, as magical as fairy dust. The wind sent tantalizing whiffs of her flowery perfume, innocent and seductive, to tempt him.

Stars twinkled as far as he could see, scattered across the velvet black of the sky, an enormous dome of glittering light. A thin moon hung low, glinting like an angel over the deep, black water of the small meadow lake.

"My cousin and I used to go for walks like this." She leaned toward him, her shoulder sizzling hot against his arm. "I would climb out the bedroom window, crawl across the roof, and swing down from a big old apple tree."

"Scandalous." Cooper kept walking toward the edge of the lake. Every step, she was right beside him. The rustle of her skirts. The roll of a pebble caught beneath her shoe. Every sound moved through him.

"I was ten." She knelt down along the shore to pick up a small stone, then cradled it in her palm. "Jessie and I would meet at our special tree."

"A special tree?"

"Yes. Sort of like Maisie's outlaw hideout. Except it was a castle."

"You were the princess?"

"No, I was a knight." She ran one finger along the curve of the stone. "Girls can be knights, too."

How she enchanted him. His chest cracked, dangerously vulnerable.

"Jessie and I would sneak along the riverbank just to watch the moon move through the stars." She tossed the rock up and caught it, as if testing its weight, then flicked her wrist. The stone skimmed once, twice, three times along the water's surface. Ripples radiated outward, disturbing the calm of the lake.

That's what she did to his life. Disturbed the surface, and it radiated clean down to his soul. Nothing was the same since she'd breezed into his life. Not one thing.

"We skipped stones and dreamed of the men we would marry one day." Another pebble hopped six times across the mirrored water.

Cooper knelt and found a rock of his own. "What kind of man would a girl knight dream about?"

"A boy knight." She searched for another pebble, then stopped. Her gaze collided with his. "You."

He needed her. Anna could read that in his eyes, sense it snapping in the air between them. In the faint, filtered light she could see the slash of his mouth and the serious slant of his eyes.

Wisps escaped from her braid and batted in the mountain breeze, tangling in front of her eyes. Cooper reached out and brushed them away.

His touch felt searing hot. His palms cupped either side of her face. His fingers cradled her jaw. Such gentle hands. Sweet desire pumped through her veins, so fast she couldn't breathe. Excitement thrummed inside, deep and intoxicating. How she wanted him.

His mouth found hers with a buzzing contact that scattered every ounce of thought. There was only the damp heat of his mouth, and she reached up to seal the kiss.

"I don't believe in love." He spoke featherlight against her lips. "And look what you're making me do. I'm falling in love with you."

Anna laid her other hand against his chest, over his rapidly beating heart. Hope fluttered within her. Nothing had ever felt this powerful.

His kiss was like fire, engulfing all her senses. She gave herself up to the enchanting heat. He nibbled blazing trails along her chin and her jaw, laved his way down her neck. Sensation skidded across her skin, then coiled tight in her stomach.

"Oh, Cooper." She moaned his name when his hands slid over her shoulders, caressed down her arms. Despite her cotton sleeves, she felt naked at his touch.

His mouth sealed hers. His hands anchored her against his chest, wondrous and wide. She laced both hands around his neck and held on. His tongue caressed her bottom lip and she gasped in pleasure. Every part of her ached for his touch.

He guided her to the pebbled shore, and she knelt with him. She could not bear to have him stop touching her. Then he tugged off his jacket and spread it out for her. She only saw his smile, the tenderness of it, as she settled to the ground, arranging her skirts.

Anna waited, her pulse drumming in her ears, as he

laid one hand on her shoulder. That hand brushed downward, grazing her breast. Delicious pleasure spilled through her. She wanted more.

As if he sensed it, Cooper released the buttons at her throat. Faux pearl gave way beneath his strong hands. His mouth caught hers and the slow agony of anticipation pounded through every inch of her body. He laid her back onto his jacket. She pulled him over her, the solid weight of his body felt luxurious—so different and exciting—his arousal hard against her hip.

"What if someone sees us?"

"There's no one around but the deer." His hot breath against her throat tickled.

She laughed. "But I worry—"

"Don't. There's no one here but us." He interrupted with a flick of his tongue. "I need you. All of you."

Desire shone in his eyes, shadowed by the night. At the first brush of his fingers against her breasts, she moaned his name. Gave herself up to his touch.

Exquisite pleasure twisted inside, tight and growing tighter. His lips grazed her nipple, and the sharp-sweet sensation left her breathless. Delicious sensation coiled more tightly inside her. Emotions licked through her, bright as flame. Anna felt lost, unable to hold on. This love she felt for Cooper shimmered deep inside, brighter than the stars in the sky and just as everlasting.

She lay back as he tore off her clothes. She reached up to help him, laughing as he lost a button. A cool breeze lifted off the nearby water and shivered across her bare skin. She felt his warm hands span her ribs. Sweep down her stomach. Her thighs trembled as he slid her drawers down until she lay naked beneath him.

His lips grazed hers. Moonlight touched his face and showed his heart, this shining hero who filled all her dreams. He was everything she wanted, all she could ever need. His hard shaft pressed against her inner thigh, and Anna melted beneath him. How wonderful he felt. Wanting him, she tilted her hips and he filled her, delicious and slow. She moaned at the feeling, at the stretching full sensation, at the thrill of being joined to him.

As if he felt it, too, his eyes met hers. Held. The entire world silenced, even the breezes off the water. He moved inside her once, withdrawing just enough to fill her again.

She closed her eyes and gave herself up to him, to the pleasure, sharp and sweet. She arched up to meet him. He withdrew, only to thrust again. Over and over, he built a sharp, breathless rhythm.

Then it happened. Red-hot sensation spiraled through her. Spikes of unbearable pleasure radiated tight and hard through her stomach. Growing brighter, bigger, until it burst, tearing her into a thousand pieces, putting her back together again. Breathless, she could only cling to him as Cooper's body stiffened. He surged inside her, harder, deeper, sparking more rippling waves of pleasure. He groaned low in his throat. She felt the hot spill of wetness pulsing deep inside her.

She loved him. She would always love him.

"Look at me." His simple request.

It was all she could do to lift her gaze. Love shimmered in his eyes like the brightest star, guiding her to him, leading her home.

She'd stopped believing in fairy tales long ago, of honorable knights who rescued distressed damsels, who saved the knights in return.

But in this wonderful man, her husband, she'd found her happily-ever-after.

Chapter Nineteen

The first light of dawn woke him. Cooper found himself spooned around Anna's sleeping body, one hand cupping her breast, her firm fanny against his groin. Her gold curls tumbled everywhere, tousled from their passion, as luxurious as fine silk. Desire stirred, yet after a night of lovemaking, Anna deserved a little sleep. He slipped from the bed, careful not to wake her.

She stirred as he was tugging on a shirt. She stretched like a cat, a contented smile touching her lips. "Good morning."

"It's nice being alone, isn't it?" He sat down on the bed beside her. She looked warm and luxurious. He could spend all day with her here, loving her as thoroughly as he'd loved her last night.

"It won't last for long. I wonder how long Laura can hold off bringing the girls home." Anna sat up, the sheet draping her breasts, leaving her creamy shoulders bare.

His groin kicked. "As long as we don't leave this room, then everyone will leave us alone."

"Good thinking." Anna caught his hand, began unbuttoning his shirt. "Maybe breakfast can wait."

A door rattled open, jarring the peace in the hotel's dining room. Three little girls dashed across the floor, feet pounding. "Mama! Papa!"

"Girls." Anna watched Cooper hold open his arms to hug both his daughters to him.

Mandy flew into her lap and she cuddled the child. She looked tired. "How I missed you, pumpkin. Did you have fun with Aunt Laura?"

"Uncle Larry done popped us some popcorn." Mandy grinned. "It tasted good, but not as good without my mama."

"Nothing was as fun without you." Anna looked over Mandy's blond curls. Cooper's eyes laughed at her. "Did you girls get breakfast?"

"Nope." Katie beamed. "Laura done starved us."

"Made us sleep on the porch."

"Us an' Larry's dog," Mandy added.

Laura's laughter chimed like bells. "You girls are going to get me into trouble. I treated them terribly."

"It shows." Anna stood, adjusting Mandy's weight on her hip. "Well, it's Sunday morning. I was thinking of taking the family to church. What time is the service?"

Laura's amazement slid from her face. "Nine o'clock."

"Then we're just in time."

"I'll go warn Larry." Laughing, Laura knelt down to give each girl a hug. "Try to behave, Katie."

"Just because I was thrown out for bringing a lizard with me last time. He was my pet."

Anna laid her hand on Katie's shoulder. "Is there

any small animal in your pockets we should know about?''

"Not today." Katie winked.

"That's a first." Cooper planted both fists on his hips. "You've been a good influence on her already."

She laughed, knowing he was teasing. He loved his daughter just the way she was. Just as she loved him. Just looking at him made her breath catch, made her heart stop beating. His black hair tumbled across his forehead. The white shirt he wore stretched across his muscled arms when he opened the door.

Keeping three little girls headed in the right direction was no easy feat. Katie stopped to look at a pony poking its nose out of the livery stable, a For Sale sign hanging from its stall. Maisie cried because her veil fell off and they had to backtrack to find it. Mandy decided she wanted a baby bird, taking a dust bath with its family in an alley.

"This is like herding wild cattle," Cooper commented as Anna consoled Mandy. "One's always going astray. Katie, come back here."

"I wanna check out this pony. Maisie and Mandy gotta have one." Katie frowned, both hands on her hips. "We haven't gone to church in a long time."

"We're going to try to be civilized. Maybe learning hymns will have a calming influence on you," he teased.

Katie kept looking back wistfully at the livery. "Papa, you ain't walking beside Anna."

"That's because I'm walking with you."

"You're supposed to be with her, like you're in love."

"Yeah, in love," Maisie added. "Anna's our mama now. You gotta walk with her."

"An' hold hands like Uncle Larry and Aunt Laura," Mandy added. "But they kiss lots, too."

"A lot," Maisie rolled her eyes. "You gonna kiss Anna that much?"

"It's torture for a man to kiss his own wife." Cooper's eyes twinkled at her as he reached out and took her hand. As their fingers touched, fire rippled across his skin. "But I'm tough. I can handle a little torture."

"You have a rough road ahead of you, Sheriff," Anna teased. "Because I'm going to demand a lot of kisses."

The girls laughed together. Cooper's fingers tightened around hers in a gentle squeeze that let her know that he felt it, too. The happiness, the laughter.

Maybe even the love.

"I think church was a success," Anna decided as they headed back toward the hotel. "Katie only caused an interruption once."

"I swear I didn't remember that there was a snake asleep in my pocket." Katie looked innocent. "I put him there so I could take him to Laura's. But I forgot he was there until he crawled out onto Mrs. Briggs."

"Thank goodness she doesn't mind snakes." Cooper ruffled Katie's head affectionately.

Anna saw the livery stable ahead of them. "How much do you think that pony costs?"

The pretty chestnut stretched her nose over the stall as far as she could.

Cooper coughed. "Too much."

Anna wasn't fooled by his no-nonsense tone. "Now, you're a well-paid sheriff of this town, Cooper. And I have my tip money from working for Janet."

"I got gold nuggets from hunting gold." Katie

pulled a few golden-brown pebbles from her pocket. "I got thirty bucks."

"No pony. The girls are too young." But Cooper was softening a little. Maybe it was the way Anna smiled at him, patiently, beautifully, with those lips that had kissed so much of his body last night.

"I think Mandy and Maisie are old enough to learn to ride." She tilted her head, scattering dozens of blond curls over shoulders so slim and fine. "It can't hurt just to look at the pony."

"Katie's already nearly killed herself on Bob. I suggest a ban on ponies. Until you girls are at least sixteen years old."

Anna laughed. "You're outvoted."

"Yeah, Papa." Katie took Anna's hand. "There's four of us and just one of you."

"Unless Anna gets us a boy baby," Maisie added.

He watched his new wife blush. Apparently someone was going to have to tell Maisie they couldn't go pick out a baby the way they could a pony.

Anna led the way down the aisle.

Eric McGraw stepped out of a stall, pitchfork in hand. "Howdy, Mrs. Braddock. What can I do for you and your family, too? Hello, Coop."

It was the first time he'd heard his last name associated with Anna. A strange sensation curled around his heart. "Tell us about that pony out back."

"Well, she's a sweet thing." Eric led the way down the aisle to the back of the stable where the stalls faced the alley. The chestnut pony nickered when she saw them approach. Apparently she knew the value of belonging to little girls.

"A fellow passing through with his family left her in trade. They needed repairs on their wagon. Going north to homestead. Their girl had outgrown the pony, but she sure was attached to it. My guess is that she's been treated gentle. Look, she's good with the girls.''

Katie held her hand out flat for the pony to scent her. She eagerly bumped her nose against Katie's fingers, begging for a pat. ''She's awful gentle, Papa. Not cantankerous like Bob.''

Maisie and Mandy clattered close, eager to pet the pony.

''I can be grateful about that.'' Cooper fished out his billfold. ''How's her health?''

''Just fine.'' Eric gave a grin, already knowing he'd made a sale. ''I also have a new appaloosa mare. Cute as could be. Would be real nice for the missus.''

Anna's head swung up. ''I have a weakness for appaloosas.''

It was true. He was outnumbered. So he opened his wallet and started counting out bills.

''Go, Daisy!'' Maisie ordered, holding the reins in her hands. She and Mandy were both appropriately dressed in their cowboy hats, holsters and chaps. Mandy, clinging on the pony's back behind her, paled with fear.

Daisy looked at Anna with beseeching eyes. ''It's okay, girl.'' Anna took hold of the bit. ''We're going to walk nice and slow around the yard—''

''Very slow,'' Cooper added, standing protectively beside the girls, ready to catch them if they fell.

''Oh, Papa.'' Katie turned from unbridling Bob. She had just returned from an adventure with Davy. ''That pony ain't gonna buck them off.''

Anna gave the gentle Daisy a little tug on her bit. She started walking slow and gentle. When Maisie shrieked, "Giddy-up" and kicked the mare's side, Daisy didn't even blink.

"Bob!" Katie ran across the yard after her badly behaved pony, who had climbed the back steps and stuck her head through the door. "She did that at Davy's house and Mrs. Muldune screamed and grabbed the broom. She thought it was a charging elk."

"Maybe she smells the cake I brought home from the hotel." Anna flashed a smile at Cooper. His gaze met hers, confident and brash. Twilight deepened; it was almost night. Almost time to go to bed together. As man and wife.

She shivered, aching for more of his touches, for the feel of his weight holding her down on the mattress, for the pulsing excitement of him moving inside her.

"Mama, we don't wanna stop," Mandy informed her.

She hadn't realized she'd stopped walking. Cooper's fingers curled around her elbow. Heat snapped up her arm, bolted through every part of her body. His smile drew her gaze to his mouth and she knew the pleasure waiting there.

"It's bedtime, girls." Cooper lifted Mandy to the ground.

"Papa, outlaws ride their ponies at night."

"Well, I'm the law and I'm bringing you little outlaws in." He set Maisie to the ground next. "You girls run upstairs and get ready for bed. I'll see to the pony."

Anna ached to call him back to her arms. But there were little girls to tend to, hair that needed to be brushed and nighties put on and stories told in the cozy upstairs room. Mandy and Maisie shared a bed for the night. Tomorrow there would be changes. Katie would have her own room down the hall.

"Read to us, Anna." Katie held out her latest dime novel and Mandy and Maisie clapped in agreement.

As she read, the littlest girls slowly drifted off to sleep. When she reached the end of a chapter, Katie took the book from her. "I can do it myself now."

"I'll turn the wick low." She twisted the wick just enough for Katie to read by. "Don't forget to put out the light before you fall asleep."

Katie caught her hand. "Anna?"

"Yes." She felt the need in that touch, a need Katie would never admit to.

"I know you love us, not like my first mama. Cuz you smile all the time."

Anna dared to brush a kiss on Katie's brow. "You enjoy your story."

"I will."

She paused at the door just long enough to see Katie dig into her book, face hidden by the pages, already lost in the wild adventure story.

Anna shut the door. Felt a hand curl around her shoulder. Heat telegraphed through every inch of her. "Our girls are tucked in for the night."

"Would you like me to tuck you in, Anna?"

So seductive that voice. She burned just thinking of the bed in the room down the hall, the bed they would share. "Come tuck me in," she invited.

He led her into the room brushed by moonlight and loved her until the moon passed through the room and left them in darkness.

Cooper walked to work whistling. He hadn't whistled in a long while. Maybe it was because he was content. Katie was working on a quilt with Anna.

Maisie was now outgoing and happy with Mandy imitating her every move.

And he had Anna.

The federal marshals were waiting at the jailhouse.

"You're back." He offered them coffee at the stove. They declined, all business.

"There's no sign our fugitive has traveled north of here. We'd like to do another sweep of the area. We'd appreciate your help."

"Whatever you need, you've got." Cooper grabbed the sugar jar. "I've worked too hard to keep criminals away from this town. I don't want more to start moving in."

"Round up your best trackers," the marshal ordered. "We've got us a mountain to search."

Cooper ached from fatigue and hunger as he rode his stallion through the dark toward the stable at the back of the house. Alone in the night, he listened to the creak of boughs rubbing together in the wind, heard the screech of a hunting owl, a distant call of coyotes, saw the stealthy shadows of grazing deer.

He'd had a tough day combing the mountainside with the marshals. They'd found two-week-old tracks that led nowhere, nothing more, nothing fresh. Cooper hoped the fugitive lawman had headed north, away from his town. He wanted the citizens he protected safe.

He dismounted and tended his horse. The new appaloosa nickered, begging for extra grain. Daisy the pony looked up and down the aisle, perhaps hoping her little girls had come to see her, too. Bob showed her teeth; she didn't like sharing her stable with the new horses.

Limping from being in the saddle too long, he headed toward the house. He saw the lit kitchen window. A woman's silhouette moved across the closed curtains. A woman's naked silhouette. Cooper dropped his cigarette. Mesmerized, he was unable to look away.

She stood between the light and the window, and he could see her movements clearly. He could also see the silhouetted curve of her breasts, the nip of her slender waist and the appealing slope of her hips and thighs. Then she knelt, and he could no longer see her.

But how he ached for her. It beat in his blood, a risky flood of desire and emotion that left him weak, on the edge of control. He retrieved the fallen cigarette and strode toward the house.

He climbed up the steps and onto the small porch. No curtain covered the panes of glass in the door. He could see her clearly. The sheen of lamplight burnished her hair a vivid, liquid gold and brushed inviting glimmers across her silken, creamy skin. His fingers ached for her. Already he knew her by feel, by memory.

Air lodged in his throat when she lifted her arm, a washcloth held in her free hand. He watched breathless as she soaped the curve of her graceful neck, then caressed the sudsy cloth across her slender shoulder and along the full curve of her breast. How he wanted to be that cloth, touching her so intimately.

He turned the knob and opened the door. He was breathing fast. He was already hard, already wanting her.

"Cooper." She smiled at him, rinsing off in the steaming water.

The scent of roses tickled his nose. Made desire thrum in his veins. He shouldn't want her so much. He shouldn't let her dominate his thoughts, his days, have such a swift affect on his body.

But it was too late. He tried to fight it, he really did. He wanted to hold back his heart, he wanted to keep distance between them. A safe barrier to hide behind, to make himself less vulnerable to her and to the power of her love.

Anna stood. Water sluiced down her silken skin, winking like diamonds in the lamplight. Caressing the fullness of her breasts and the curve of her hips, knowing the sweetness of her inner thighs that he wanted to taste.

It was too late. He'd fallen in love with her. He trusted her with his children, his love and his future. And why shouldn't he? She'd proven herself honorable, shown her love again and again. She was more than his wife, she was his love, all of his heart.

Cooper crossed the room and took Anna in his arms. Her mouth met his, her fingers tugged at his buttons. It was so late, all the girls were upstairs asleep and they were alone in the lamplight, alone with their love.

Dalton Jennings watched the sun rise over the town of Flint Creek. Clean streets, clean shops, it looked like a real friendly place. Too bad the marshals on his tail had nearly found him yesterday. And it was all thanks to that sheriff. He was a good tracker. If it hadn't been for the creek, they might have found his hideout, an old prospector's shanty he'd stumbled across one night.

Those lawmen would be searching harder today. And they might discover him. He had to make his move today. He would wait until the good sheriff and the marshals were tracking up in the high country.

Then he would take Anna when she was alone. And unsuspecting.

Anna was the only living witness who could identify him as the bank robber and murderer. She hadn't spoken up yet, but she could. And he would silence her. His freedom—his very life—depended on it.

"Katie, you aren't dressed." Anna set the fresh apple pie, in the best pie plate, on the kitchen table. "You can't wear trousers to Mrs. Muldune's house."

"But Davy and me were gonna go ridin'. We got more gold dust to hunt for." Katie tugged on the end of her ribboned braid.

"Then why don't you ride Bob over with us?" Anna grabbed the small tin she was using as a sewing box. "I could use some help."

Katie obliged, carefully balancing the tin in both hands. "I'll put this in the wagon for you."

"Under the seat, please." Anna rushed upstairs to tend to the little girls.

Excited by the prospect of another dress-up party hosted by Davy's young sister, both Maisie and Mandy had raided the attic. One wore a too-large plumed hat, the other had donned a bonnet sporting two large pink ribbon lilies. Faux pearls in long ropes reached down to both their knees.

"We're ready, Mama," Mandy announced, tripping.

"My flower's fallin' off," Maisie complained.

Laughing, Anna set the girls to rights and hurried them down to the wagon. Katie, atop a saddled Bob, waited. Both the pie and the tin were beneath the seat, just as she'd asked.

The ride was a short one. Clouds gathered against the mountains. The air smelled like rain. The wind was so blustery Mandy lost her hat and Katie and Bob had to chase it down Maple Street.

The Muldune's front yard bustled with activity. Little girls ran screaming around the front yard, for the tea party had been raided by whooping little boys. Davy galloped out on his pony, and Katie joined him.

"Anna is here," Leslie called from the front porch, hands out to take the dessert. "Oh, that pie looks wonderful. And look at you. Married life suits you."

"So far so good." Anna set the brake and handed down the fragrant pie.

"Anna. There you are." Laura hurried down the porch to wrap her in a hug. "I've saved you a place on the sofa next to me. Oh, and I picked up the nicest thimble at Leslie's store. I got one for you. You'll have to come try it."

"As soon as I take care of the horse." Laura really did feel like a sister. They were all becoming a family, day by day. Anna lifted down Maisie, then Mandy, and laughed as the girls hurried off to join in the fray, still wearing their outrageous hats.

She unhitched the wagon, then unharnessed the patient appaloosa. She led the mare into the Muldune's stable and into an empty stall. A barn cat came to beg a few pats.

She could hear the distant shouts of the children, then the squeak of the back door opening. Katie and Davy had ridden their ponies this way. "Katie?"

"No, Anna." Straw crackled beneath a heavy boot.

Chills skidded down her spine. Hair prickled on the back of her neck. He'd found her. Despite Meg's lie and the considerable distance between Flint Creek and Ruby Bluff, he'd tracked her down.

"Your sister was very helpful," he spoke in her ear, his voice silken smooth and confident. "Don't worry, I didn't hurt her. She refused to cooperate so I had the postmistress watch her mail. A letter finally came. You had to go and tell her about the wedding, didn't you?"

Anna had hoped Meg could come. "I haven't told anyone about you, Dalton, even though it would be the right thing to do. I have a child to raise."

"I have federal marshals tracking me, Anna. Somebody talked." A cold revolver nosed her in the temple. "Not one word or you won't be the only one to die this morning."

Fear shot through her. But anger, too. Her friends were in that house, her children in that yard. Anna bit her lip and refused to say another word.

"Who's that man with your new ma?" Davy reined in his pony on the crest of the hill.

"It ain't Papa." Katie stood up in her stirrups, trying to figure out who it was. "Ain't Tucker, either."

Something reflected the waning sunlight. Clouds were gathering overhead. Katie looked harder. When she squinted, she could make out the revolver held in the strange man's hand.

"They're ridin' outta town." Davy sounded scared.

She was scared, too. "Some man is takin' my new mother." She knew Anna would never leave. Anna said so. She'd made a promise right there in the church to love them, to stay with them forever.

But her real mother had left. Her real mother had a man who came to the house sometimes. A stranger she didn't know. Old fears jumbled around in her chest.

But Anna was different. Anna truly loved her. Anna had answered her advertisement. Anna had answered her letters. Anna had come all the way to Flint Creek just because she'd asked her to.

Anna wouldn't leave.

"C'mon, Davy." Katie kicked Bob into a full gallop and headed straight into the wind.

"We can't go after that man, Katie," Davy argued. "We don't gotta gun."

"But my papa does. We just gotta find him."

Chapter Twenty

"Coop!" Tucker rode breakneck up the trail, despite the driving rain and the crack of lightning.

Cooper spun his palomino around, shouting over the explosion of thunder. "You better tell me some good news. We're having a bad day up here."

"Katie came barreling into the jailhouse. Said some man rode away with Anna." Tucker drew his mount to a halt, the mare's flanks heaving, white lather flecking her dark coat. "He had a gun on her."

"What man?" Cooper demanded. His chest turned to stone.

"We don't know. The kids saw them heading north, maybe toward the old Flint Creek trail. There were strange bootprints in the stable yard. Someone could have taken her from the Muldune's barn."

Cooper swore. Cold rain sluiced down the back of his neck, driven by bone-chilling wind. "I took the guards off her and the girls. I thought with Corinthos dead and his gang in prison—"

"This isn't your fault, big brother. Someone waited until she was alone. Someone with dark hair, about the same height as the fugitive these marshals are looking for.''

"Think it's the same man?" Cooper kicked his stallion into a gallop. "With this weather, we'll lose their tracks."

"I sent Barstow to cast for signs. He's following them the best he can."

"Let's ride, men," he called.

He led the deputies and marshals on a fast, hard trip. Maneuvering the steep mountainsides and crossing the rain drenched, dangerous ravines and unmarked paths took concentration. But Cooper couldn't stop thinking of Anna. Of how she'd changed him. Of how she transformed their ordinary lives with her happiness, her sparkling love and first-star-of-the-night wishes.

And yet, as the storm drew darkness across the lay of the rugged land, his hopes broke apart along with the sky. Lightning spiked. Thunder crashed. Rain turned to sleet, and then a fast-moving north wind drove the sleet to ice, then to snow.

He had to find Anna alive. He just had to. And when he got his hands on the man who dared to take her at gunpoint, Cooper would make that outlaw sorry.

"The fastest route to catch the old Flint Creek trail is to follow the river west from here." Tucker sidled his mount closer. "No one's used the trail I know of in a while, and with this weather we'll have a hard time leading the men."

"We'll do the best we can." Cooper swiped at the white flakes weighing down his hat brim.

Like fog, the clouds hugged the rise and fall of the mountain peaks. The wet snow made the steep trails dangerous and the riding uncomfortable. He shrugged on a rain slicker he unrolled from his pack, but unlike the bighorn sheep huddling on a sheltered crag of the mountain, he shivered. Cold seeped its way through his clothes, to his skin and deeper.

As they climbed down in elevation, the snow changed to rain.

"I found tracks. Two horses, one with a light rider, newly shoed. Looks like Eric's work down at the livery." Baxter, their tracker, spun his mare around. "These are fresh. Maybe ten minutes old."

"Eric said the appaloosa was just shoed." Cooper knew it in his guts. Anna. He had to save her. He had to reach her.

Five armed men were waiting at the crest of the old trail. Anna recognized a few of them from her hometown, grown unkempt on their desperate run from the law.

"We spotted riders down below. About a mile and closing," Kurt Baines urged his mount toward Dalton.

"The marshals?"

"Maybe. I think it's the local lawman, the one she's married to. I saw a palomino. The sheriff rides one."

Cooper. Anna's stomach twisted. He had no way of knowing six armed men would meet him on the trail. He'd ride straight into gunfire.

"Set up an ambush," Dalton barked out. "I don't want one of those lawmen left alive. Baines, I need more bullets."

"Wait." Anna caught Dalton's sleeve and held tight until he had to spin around and face her.

A cold flat gaze met hers. "I ought to shoot you first. You're the cause of all this. I could be home, denying the charges and counting my money—"

"I can make the law turn around and leave you

alone.'' She had no illusions. Dalton was going to kill her. But she would not let him kill Cooper.

''Let me try, Dalton. The marshals know you're on the run. If you kill lawmen who are after you, they won't let you rest. You have to let me try.''

''Up there.'' Baxter drew to a halt.

Cooper pushed the stallion into a hard gallop, even aware of the animal's exhaustion. Through the gray curtain of sleet, he could see the appaloosa's spotted rump and the slim set of her shoulders, squared and determined.

''Anna!'' He shouted. The driving wind stole his words. She didn't turn. Yet the distance between them lessened as the stallion's labored gallop ate up the length of road separating them. ''Anna!''

She twisted around on the saddle. Rain drenched her. She wore no slicker as protection from the elements. She dripped with rain. Her hair had fallen around her shoulders, loose, tangled and darkened to a brown-gold.

Thank goodness he'd found her in time. Before something horrible happened. His guts twisted hard. Someone was watching them. It wasn't right, Anna here alone in the rain. He expected an armed man. Maybe many armed men.

''Turn the mare around and head home, Anna.'' He kept his voice low, steady. ''Where are they?''

''I'm not going home, Cooper.'' She met his gaze, spoke just as quietly.

Anger and fear bunched up beneath his breastbone. ''What do you mean you aren't going home? I can handle the man, whoever he is.'' He held two revolvers in hand, cocked and ready.

"I mean, I'm leaving you." Her chin lifted.

He scanned the rain-drenched forest. "Katie saw you with an armed man."

Her eyes widened. Those eyes as blue as dreams, as true as the fairy tales she'd made him believe in. "That man is someone I used to know. He courted me."

"Turn around and ride home, Anna. I know what's going on here."

Now what should she do? Cooper rode by her side like an ancient warrior, strong shouldered and fearless, determined to right all wrongs.

But he didn't understand. Dalton would kill him, kill anyone to keep himself safe. She had to protect the man she loved more than anything. She had to send him home before Dalton grew impatient and started killing.

Using the knowledge she had, Anna took a breath. Found the courage to say the words that would hurt him more than anything. Words that would destroy what little faith he had in her.

"Dalton Jennings came for me. I'm leaving to be with him."

"Dalton Jennings? He's a wanted man." Cooper's jaw tightened, his shoulders tensed, ready for a battle.

"We're lovers. I didn't think he wanted me, but he's changed his mind." The lie tasted sour on her tongue. "I'm leaving you, Cooper."

"Stop lying." Deadly and low those words. Hot with denial.

"It's the truth." Anna spun the mare around to face him. "I love Dalton in a way I could never love you. He's asked me to go away with him, and I've accepted. So go back to town."

"Anna, I can't believe—"

"Believe it." She sharpened her voice, belted out the words so the deputies bowing their heads out of embarrassment for their boss would have no doubt. They would all have no doubt. "I only married you for convenience, Cooper. The same way you married me. Now I have the man I want. I guess I'm not any different from Katie's real mother."

The disbelief faded from his dark eyes and changed to a dark, muddy grief. "What about your daughter? I know you aren't going to leave—"

"She's not Dalton's child and he doesn't want her. So now, neither do I." Keep riding, she told herself. Keep moving away before Dalton changes his mind.

"Anna!" Cooper's voice. "I know you love your daughter."

Keep riding. Tears blurred her vision, burned in her throat. Don't turn around. Don't let him see the truth.

"Anna! You wouldn't leave Mandy. I know you wouldn't. Anna! Don't you leave me." Raw hurt shivered in those words.

She halted the mare and bit the inside of her cheek to keep from crying out loud. But then a snap of a branch caught her gaze. There, hidden by a grove of old scrubby pines, she spied Dalton on horseback. His exposed gun was aimed at Cooper. His thumb drew the hammer back. Fear crawled around her heart. Was he getting ready to fire?

She had no choice. Anna snapped the reins and galloped away from the only man she'd ever truly loved.

As Dalton's horse shadowed her, hidden from sight in the woods, she knew no first-star-of-the-night wishes could help her now. Or her fairy-tale prince who did not follow her, who would not wait for her return.

Gathering her courage, Anna rode straight into the storm.

"The deputies are turning back," she overheard Jennings' scout say.

"Well, Anna, good job. The last thing I need is a dead sheriff to rile up those marshals any more than they already are." Dalton's slow grin twisted, not bothering to mask the cold brutality he once hid beneath dashing charm. "Braddock believed you. Looks like you saved his life. Unless he does something stupid and circles back."

Anna shivered, but it wasn't from the cold. She hoped Cooper kept on riding.

Dalton's sinister smile broadened. "Yes, well, I'm not avoiding a fight as much as saving time. Those damn marshals are after me. Falsely, of course."

"Of course." She tried to keep the judgment from her voice. "I'm here. Alone. I met my part of the bargain. I want your word you will leave my family alone. Especially Cooper."

"I've kept my word so far." Dalton reached into his breast pocket and withdrew a cigar. He lit a match, using both hands to shield the meager flame.

He leaned close. His breath puffed along her ear. The sensation crawled across her skin like a dozen spiders. "I have missed you, Anna."

Like hell he did.

"You left Ruby Bluff in a hurry. Didn't even say goodbye. Imagine that. And we've been friends most of our lives." He laid his black-gloved hand along the back of her neck and curled his fingers around her vertebrae. "Count the minutes, Anna, because that's all the livin' you have left."

She felt afraid, but not as much as the sorrow she felt in her heart. She was leaving her precious Mandy, and the two little girls she'd come to love just as much. And Cooper—

She closed her eyes and hoped he would find some way to forgive her one day. The thought of him hating her was more than she could bear.

Cold rain dripped off his hat brim and ran down the back of his neck. He kept his stallion headed toward town. His chest felt as cold as the rain.

"Coop." Tucker rode up beside him and kept pace as they headed out, their goal clear. "Anna loves you. She wouldn't have left you—"

"No more," he snapped. "I don't want to think. I just want to work. It will be better that way."

"What do you mean? You love her. She's your wife."

"Right now, she's a civilian, nothing more. Baxter, I want you to scout for us. Even in this storm, they can't get far. We'll stop them."

He needed concentration to do the job ahead of him, not his heart.

Chapter Twenty-One

Anna heard the pop of gunfire and saw the old man riding ahead of her slip from his saddle. His body hit the snowy wet earth with a lifeless thud. The mare she rode sidestepped, spooked. The cheek strap slid out of Dalton's grip.

Free, Anna kicked her mount into a swift lope and didn't look back. She ducked low, hearing the escalating sounds of a gunfight—horses' whinnies, men's shouts, the clatter of firing guns.

She didn't know who was fighting whom. It wasn't Cooper, she knew, he wouldn't come for her. Not after how she'd hurt him. But it might be those marshals, for the fight was a serious one. No one had even noticed her escape.

Then she heard the drum of hooves behind her, gaining ground. She urged the mare faster, despite the wet snow making the trail dangerous. Blood pounding, she leaned forward, pressing the horse faster yet.

"Anna." Dalton's voice. Dalton's black-gloved fingers closing around her wrist.

"Get away." She fought him.

His grip tightened. She kicked him hard when he

struggled for the reins. A bullet whizzed into the tree beside her. The mare whinnied in terror and took off in a bolt. Anna screamed as Dalton's grip tore her from the saddle.

She hit the ground with bruising force. Air rushed out of her lungs. Pain snapped through her spine. She leaped to her feet, but Dalton's shoulder hit her in the abdomen and she flew back into the snow.

Icy wetness seeped through her clothes. She struggled to breathe. Panic rose when she couldn't seem to draw air into her chest. Dalton's weight pinned her down. His face, twisted with rage, hovered inches from her own. She looked into eyes dark with demons and saw a man without a conscience, a man who could ride a horse and wear a badge and handle a gun, but who could never be honorable, who could never be a hundredth of the man Cooper was.

She heard bootsteps. The click of a cocking gun. "Get up, Dalton." Tucker's voice.

Before she could blink, Dalton rolled off her, then he took her by the collar and lifted her to her feet, nearly choking her. She tried to fight him, but she couldn't even breathe. Panic rose as he held her tight to his chest like a shield.

"Let her go, Dalton." Broad-shouldered, as tough as his brother, Tucker cocked his second revolver, both aimed over Anna's head, she guessed, directly at Dalton. "There's no way out for you. We've got your men. The marshals are here. You can go easy or not. It's your choice."

The cold nose of a gun jabbed her jaw. "Not so simple. If you value your wife's life, you'll let me go. It's your choice now, Braddock."

Wife? The single word pierced through the fog of

her mind. Air rushed into her chest, and she gasped. Dalton must never have met Cooper face-to-face. He thought Tucker was Cooper. Then where was—

A click of a gun. "Let her go, Dalton. There's no escape. Not for you." Cooper's voice. He had approached Dalton from behind and now held a revolver nosed up against Jennings' spine.

Dalton's grip loosened, and she spun away. Tucker moved, Dalton drew, a shot fired. A man dropped to the ground in front of her. Dalton.

Cooper didn't look at her as he barked out orders to his men. There were outlaws to bind and tie, and riderless horses to catch. Tucker gave her a quick hug, a quick check to make sure she was all right, then strode away to help.

And even though it was over, Anna felt no comfort. Cooper hadn't come to save his wife, she knew. He'd only been doing his job.

The storm had left a thin layer of wet snow in town, which began melting as soon as the clouds parted. The tinkling drip of water from the trees, the rush of tiny trickles creeking in the road, the music of ice tumbling off the roof of the house seemed far too merry for what lay ahead.

Yellow-faced wildflowers poked up through the disappearing snow, undaunted by the brief, momentary loss of summer. Well, she could be just as stalwart, she thought as she dismounted.

Cooper handed the horses over to Tucker and asked him to care for them. Anna stepped into the house alone. Accepting the inevitable was for the best. After what she'd done, the things she'd said, she didn't have to look into the depths of Cooper's eyes to know there would be no forgiveness.

She headed upstairs, chin bowed, unable to see for this one last time the home she'd come to love. She'd already said goodbye. She could not bear to do so twice.

After grabbing a towel from the linen shelf, she closed the bedroom door. Shivering from cold and loss, she began peeling off her clothes. She was wet to the skin. She set out her corset to dry and found a change of drawers and a chemise.

Heavy footsteps sounded outside the room. Cooper's steps; she recognized his gait. Anna jerked a calico work dress over her head and was smoothing it over her hips when the door flew open.

Cooper filled the threshold, dark as night. Jaw set, muscles tensed, fists clenched, his powerful presence shrank the room, made her feel small against his iron solid strength.

Her throat went dry. Her heart, too hopeless to feel anything, skipped a beat. She ought to apologize and try to explain. She wanted more than anything to make him believe—

"Don't you ever do that again." He bit the words out as if they were bitter, with distaste. For her.

And he had every right. She'd hurt him. Intentionally. And now he would ask her to leave. No, judging by the anger tight in his jaw, he would *order* her to leave. Immediately. "Cooper, those things I said—"

"Were necessary, I know." He stepped forward and laid a warm wonderful hand against her face. "You couldn't have meant them."

"I never meant—" She stopped. Blinked. Could it be?

He wasn't ordering her to leave. He understood. Cooper believed her. "How did you know? I tried to hurt you." She laid her hand against his and felt the luxurious male heat of him. "Did you see Dalton in the forest?"

"No." He smiled, slow, tender, sexy. "You couldn't fool me, Anna. I believe in you. I trust you."

"You do?"

"I figured Dalton was nearby. I had to leave, so those men would think you'd succeeded in driving me off. That gave us time for the marshals to circle around and set up an ambush." He brushed a wet curl from her eyes, his gaze intimate, bold. "I will never stop believing in you. Not in my wife and her fairy-tale wishes. Not in a woman of honor."

He saw the tears brim her eyes, happy and filled with promise. Like a rainbow after a storm, like flowers through snow, it gave him hope, too. Made him see their future. There would be more children, more little girls for him to teach to ride and climb trees and play outlaw. And Anna, always Anna, in his bed, in his heart, in his life.

"I married you for convenience, Anna," he confessed. "But I want you to stay for love."

"For love," she agreed. She had his love and all of his heart. She could never want anything more.

He folded her against his chest, and they bound their pledge with a kiss.

* * * * *

This season,

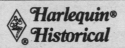

is proud to introduce four very
different Western romances that will
warm your heart....

In October 1999, look for

COOPER'S WIFE #485
by Jillian Hart
and

THE DREAMMAKER #486
by Judith Stacy

In November 1999, look for

JAKE WALKER'S WIFE #489
by Loree Lough
and

HEART AND HOME #490
by Cassandra Austin

Harlequin Historicals
The way the past *should* have been.

Available at your favorite retail outlet.

This season, make your destination Great Britain with four exciting stories from

Harlequin® Historical

In October 1999, look for

LADY SARAH'S SON #483 by **Gayle Wilson**
(England, 1814)

and

THE HIDDEN HEART #484 by **Sharon Schulze**
(Wales, 1213)

In November 1999, look for

ONE CHRISTMAS NIGHT #487
by **Ruth Langan, Jacqueline Navin and Lyn Stone**
(Scottish Highlands 1540, England 1193
and Scotland 1320)

and

A GENTLEMAN OF SUBSTANCE #488 by **Deborah Hale**
(England, 1814)

Harlequin Historicals
Where reading is truly a vacation!

HARLEQUIN®
Makes any time special ™